Drowning Fergus
A Tale of the Fairypocalypse

ADDISON LANE

Drowning Fergus
A Tale of the Fairypocalypse

Copyright © 2013 by Addison Lane

Cover design by Lee Milverton

Addison Lane
www.addisonlane.net

Lee Milverton
www.leemilverton.com

Printed in the United States of America

First Printing: October 2013

ISBN 978-0-9839538-6-9

DEDICATION

To the family, friends, and readers who've
stuck with Fergus through thick and thin.

Special thanks to Mom, Jayce, and David.

Chapter One.

It was a sunny spring afternoon, and the sky over Clohaven was filled with airships, their balloons dotting the clouds with every color imaginable. There were fat red ones with silver brocades, navy blue ones with sails like fish fins, bullet-shaped forest green ones, and deep purple ones decorated with golden flags. There were white ones that gleamed like pearls and yellow ones striped like bees and orange ones studded with brass buttons. On the ground, thousands of people mingled amongst the tradeshow displays and concessions, eating shaved ice and grilled corn. Children ran around with balloons bobbing behind them, pursued by frazzled mothers. In the background, a brass band pumped out merry tunes.

It was hard to imagine a cheerier scene, but Fergus Irvine did not feel particularly buoyant as he slipped through a narrow alley into the square. Looming at three different points amidst the colorful airships were the great black vessels of New Peiling's Air Guard. It seemed at every corner there was a

1

man in the black and silver Air Guard uniform, or police officers in Clohaven's blue-grey jumpsuits. It set his heart capering about in his chest.

At the center of the crowd, there was a large stage. A man stood upon it, waving to a line of blueprints to his right. To his left, surrounded by members of the Guard and the police, sat dignitaries from Clohaven, Lancaster, New Peiling, and even Hampshire. There was the governor of Clohaven, a tall man with a thick black moustache; the mayor of Lancaster, a ferrety looking woman with fading sandy blonde hair; and to her right, the governor of New Peiling, Paige Harriet.

Fergus froze as he spotted her. She was a handsome woman in her early 50s with dark curls and a thin mouth, and she was a menace to every hybrid – every person who shared their soul with a fairy – in New Peiling. It was weird to see her in person; he'd only ever seen pictures in the newspaper. She was shorter than he'd imagined.

He and his friends – Terry, Pip, and Three – had only just returned from their journey to Tír na nÓg under the complaints of a dozen airship malfunctions and foul weather, which would have been easier to deal with if their captain, William Guillory, had not been arrested by Ashton Harriet, the Governor's son and present Captain of the Air Guard. It was Fergus's desperate hope that they'd beaten his fleet back to New Peiling, but there was no way of knowing until they reached the city.

Unfortunately, the *Returner* had breathed its last smoky breath on a farming island just east of Clohaven, and they'd had to take a ferry to the city. They'd arrived just in time for Clohaven's annual airship festival, and the air ferries were running behind schedule. To make matters worse, tickets to New Peiling were sold out for the day, leaving Fergus, Terry, Three, Pip, and the remaining crew stranded.

With nothing better to do, Terry had suggested checking out the festival. Fergus thought he was probably a little too pleased with their bad luck, as Terry was quite the airship enthusiast, but he'd claimed it was because they might be able to find the Count Palatine, the airship tycoon who'd supplied them with the ill-fated *Returner*. If they found the Count, they might secure both a free ride back to the city, as well as an update on recent affairs.

And so they stood, lingering at the edge of the festivities and looking tired and disheveled. Fergus had let Three trim his hair recently, but he was sporting stubble around his jawline and upper lip. Terry had dyed his hair and eyebrows brown. Fergus thought he looked weird without auburn hair. But the dye job was a flimsy disguise at best. If they ran into Captain Harriet, Terry's eyepatch would be a dead giveaway. Still, from a distance, the brown hair might divert unwanted attention.

"What are you waiting for?" Terry asked, nudging him from behind. "If you loiter, you'll make us seem suspicious."

Fergus nodded, taking a deep breath, and moved into the crowd, heading towards the stage. Terry fell into step beside him. He could hear Three and Pip muttering incomprehensibly behind them. Terry slipped an arm around his shoulders, and Fergus glanced at him uncertainly.

"Relax, okay?"

"How can I relax? Paige-Freaking-Harriet is sitting right there, and there's a million Guard members wandering around."

"Who will leave us alone as long as we look like boring, old pedestrians."

Fergus sighed. "I guess so."

"Hey, isn't that Olivier?"

"Olivier?"

"The one who used to work at the penthouse with me. It *is* him. The Count must be around here somewhere," Terry said.

They drew up to the back of the gathering, and Terry withdrew his arm. Three came to stand at his other side, Pip beside her. A young man with long brown hair, a dished nose, and an almost comically generous mouth stepped onto the stage wearing a mimicry of a captain's uniform, though the copious lace, silk, and buckles made it difficult to take seriously. He went to stand by the blueprints.

Fergus stood on his tiptoes, peering over the crowd. "I don't see the Count anywhere."

"Keep looking. It wouldn't surprise me if Olivier was working for the Count and one of his competitors, but it doesn't mean he's not here."

Just then, a woman with short black hair shouldered her way past them. Her face was gaunt, her eyes locked on Paige Harriet.

"Deirdre!" Fergus called.

She turned, dark eyes widening. But just as quickly, they narrowed.

"That's new," she said, eyes flicking from Terry's face to his hair.

Terry touched the eyepatch, smiling ruefully. "I knew I forgot something in Ping City."

She didn't smile.

"Why are you here?" Fergus asked.

Deirdre turned to him and scowled. Something flashed in her right hand, and she quickly shoved both hands into the pockets of her jacket.

He groaned, running his hand over his face. "You can't be serious. You'll be shot down before you can even reach the steps."

"These are my orders. I will see them through."

"Orders from who?" Terry demanded.

Deirdre stared at them flatly, mouth thin and silent. Fergus noticed that Three was subtly moving closer. She caught his eye, smiling uncertainly, but Deirdre seemed unaware of the hurdle now standing to her left.

"Sorry, no suicide today," Fergus said, reaching for her arm.

She snarled and started to jerk the knife free of her pocket, but Three caught her arm before she could take a swipe at Fergus.

"Thanks."

She nodded, but didn't take her eyes of Deirdre.

"You don't know how things are now. This has to be done!" Deirdre whispered furiously.

"You're right. We don't. So why don't you tell us, and we'll think of something better than a one-man, frontal assault," Terry said, stepping closer to her.

Her lips drew back, her cheeks going red. For a moment, Fergus thought she might wrestle free and charge the stage after all, but she deflated under Terry's calm stare.

"You'll regret stopping me," she said, shrugging Three off and turning. "Well, come on."

They followed her through the crowd, past the bandstand. Fergus paused for a minute, wistfully looking up at the players. Sure, it wasn't a rock band. They were playing trumpets and horns and trombones and nothing resembling electric guitars and basses. Still, he felt a pang in his chest. It'd only been a year since he'd returned to his apartment to find Flynn dead, and life had taken him far from those meandering days spent up to his elbows in suds at the Magpie, dreaming of his former band, Everyday Resources, playing at top plate concert halls.

He'd met *real* fairies. He'd learned how to turn himself into a *kelpie*, as well as the truth about his mother and her cohorts, the circle of hedonistic hybrids known as Bandersnatch. He'd even found a gateway to Tír na nÓg. Aside from sporadically jamming with Terry on the *Returner*, it felt like he hadn't given much thought to music for months. But when would he have found the time, he wondered, what with trying to find Tír na nÓg and thwarting organ thieves and escaping evil hybrids out to steal his powers? It was a wonder he was still alive.

Even so, as he caught sight of himself in the shiny curve of a tuba, the longing for strings under his fingers and the heat of stage lights on his face tugged at his heart.

"Fergus, c'mon!"

He started, hurrying after the others.

Deirdre led them to a posh hotel overlooking the square. Fergus felt too tatty to go inside, but Deirdre's impatient glare prompted him to disregard his ragged appearance and hurry across the hollow foyer towards the elevator. They got off on the top floor and went down a marble corridor to the end of the hallway, where she produced a set of keys, letting them inside.

It certainly looked like the sort of room the Count would book. There was an enormous four-poster bed and a picture window facing the square. Deirdre drew the curtains shut, lighting a lamp on the bedside table. Fergus plopped down on the bed next to Terry, while Pip and Three remained standing, lurking in the foyer. Deirdre took a seat by the window, pulling aside the curtain just a little and staring outside intently – most likely straight down at the platform where Governor Harriet was sitting, happily oblivious.

"Is the Count here?" Fergus asked.

"No. He still has some sway in the city, but even he has to be careful about keeping his head down."

"What do you mean?"

"They've been shuffling hybrids off to the colony for the past two months."

Terry sat up straighter. "What?"

Deirdre sighed. "Calling it a colony is a bit of a laugh frankly." She finally looked away, letting the curtain drop. "From what I understand, it has walls on all four sides and guards, just like a prison. Obviously, I haven't been there personally. They're trying to sell it as a desirable housing option – the papers only show pictures of the nicer structures – but word is, it's far worse than the slums, and a lot of people who end up there *somehow* disappear."

"I'm not surprised," Terry said, hooking his arms around his knees and resting his chin on them.

Fergus bit his lip and glanced from Terry to Deirdre. "We ran into Ashton Harriet. Actually, we're on our way to try and intercept him. He said he was gonna exorcise all the hybrids, so that there are no fairy souls left."

7

Deirdre's cheek twitched, and she looked away. "We suspected as much. That's why we have to get rid of *her*."

"But you can't just 'get rid of her,'" Fergus said, shaking his head.

"And why is that?"

"Because it isn't just her. Yeah, she's the leader right now, but there are a lot of people who think like her. If there weren't, she wouldn't have been elected. Are you just gonna go around killing them, too? What about their families? Even if their families agree with us, if you kill them cuz of their ideals, they're gonna hate you, too. They'll just call for more exorcisms, and it'll keep going until there's no one left at all."

She laughed. "Well, you've grown up a bit, haven't you?" She sighed and stood, walking to the nightstand to pour a glass of water. "Everyone realizes that, Fergus. But how do you make those people change their minds? The best we can hope for is to cut off the head of the snake and try to seize power in the ensuing chaos. We might make things better then, if the right people were in charge."

"Who are the 'right people'?" Fergus asked warily.

"Who even knows these days?" She ran a hand through her hair, heaving another sigh. "Everyone is so embittered . . . and with good reason. It would be hard to convince anyone that we shouldn't retaliate *with interest*. This isn't a few Niamh members disappearing in the night. Just wait until you see the lower city. It's a ghost town." She paused. "It's a little ironic."

"How so?"

"The humans have forgotten that it's *our* magic that keeps New Peiling standing. It's our magic that holds the plates together. You can already feel how badly the spells have weakened. It's probably only a matter of time until the whole city goes toppling into the ocean. It'll serve them right."

"Are Ursula and Rosslyn still in New Peiling?"

She nodded. "I don't know where they've gone off to. Ursula has all but abandoned Beathag's, and we only see her and Rosslyn when they want to be seen. I assume they're trying to rally the remaining hybrids to strike back against the Knights of Evalach. As you may guess, the Knights are responsible for rounding us up and sending us off. No doubt, they're also the ones behind the 'disappearances' in the colony." She eyed him over her glass. "You're trying to head Ashton Harriet off? Why?"

Fergus and Terry exchanged looks. "He took Raja, Evelyn, and Guillory."

"Evelyn? You mean that Niamh girl is alive?"

Fergus nodded grimly. "We're hoping they're all still alive, but he arrested Guillory for treason."

"William Guillory would be one of the very few who could possibly stand up to the Harriets, the only one who'd have enough people backing him to make trouble."

"They'll probably execute him and exorcise the others."

"Sounds about right."

"But we can't let that happen. Guillory never did anything wrong, nor did Raja or Evelyn. We have to stop them."

"You'll need to find Rosslyn and Ursula. They're the only ones who can supply you with enough information and people to be of use. The Count's hands are tied. They're tolerating him for now because of his engineering connections, but they're watching him closely."

"Suppose that's put a damper on his aspirations," Terry remarked.

"Which ones?"

"My position to start," he replied, mouth crooking.

"I suppose so," Deirdre said, putting down the glass. "He wanted to be the leader of Bandersnatch, but not long after you left, things fell apart, and now the most he can do is hide the occasional refugee."

Terry shrugged, running a hand through his hair. "It wouldn't have worked out anyway. He was always too exposed to be Badb Catha."

"Well, now you're back. You can take over."

Fergus frowned.

Part of the reason Terry had left New Peiling was to get away from being Badb Catha, Bandersnatch's strongman. He'd never spoken of the role as though he'd enjoyed it. For a moment, Fergus wondered if he'd done something awful by bringing Terry back here. He didn't want Terry to 'take over again' ever again, but though he tried to catch Terry's eye, Terry skillfully eluded his worried gaze.

"He and I have some things to discuss first," Terry said quietly, looking down at his knees.

Deirdre raised an eyebrow, but didn't remark.

Fergus sighed, rubbing his face. "So who sent you on the suicide mission to try and kill one of the most well-protected people on the planet?"

"I volunteered," she replied briskly. "And I suggested it to the Count."

"I'm surprised he agreed," Fergus said.

"It's a sign of how desperate we've become."

"You won't be able to succeed here, though," Terry said. "Unless you can make yourself invisible, you won't get close."

"More importantly," Fergus said, frowning at Terry, "even if you did, you'd just make her a martyr."

"I agree with Fergus," Three said softly from the entryway. "The others will rally around her death and use it as an excuse to wage war on you."

"You think we're not already embroiled in a war?" Deirdre snapped.

"But won't they connect you to the Count? They'll go after him the minute they're finished with you," Fergus pointed out.

She turned away, tucking her hair behind her ear. "We're both prepared for that."

"Look, I get what you're saying. I have no doubt that Paige Harriet and her son *do* intend to get rid of us. They're not the only ones, though, so we have to be smart about this, or we're only gonna make things worse," Fergus said.

"So what are you going to do?"

"First we gotta save Guillory. The humans trust him. He might be able to talk some of them into helping us. After that, I dunno, but we'll find a way."

"Battle is inevitable, Fergus."

"Maybe it is, maybe it isn't. But we gotta do our best to try and make things better."

"Ainslee's son is a pain," she muttered, but he thought he detected a smile.

"Isn't he, though?" Terry said, elbowing his shin.

Fergus rolled his eyes. "Whatever." He walked over to the window, parting the curtain to peer down at the festivities. "Can we trust you not to try again?

Cuz if you do, you're gonna make it a lot harder for us to get back."

"If I see an opportunity, I'm going to take it."

"But no frontal assaults?"

"I suppose not," she replied.

"Good." He turned from the window. "We could use a lift back to the city."

"I came alone on the air ferry," Deirdre replied, crossing her arms. "You'll be lucky if they don't stick the lot of you on a boat straight to the colony."

"And you?"

"I have special privileges, which I doubt the officials will extend to you."

"So what are we supposed to do?"

"I have no idea, but you won't be able to enter by airship."

Fergus gnawed his lower lip, looking up at the ceiling and racking his brain for an answer.

"I need to borrow your shower."

Terry tilted his head, eying Fergus incredulously. "What are you planning?"

"I just thought of someone who might be able to help us."

•   •   •

Fergus was unsurprised by the look of the Crawford residence. Really, he hadn't spent much time wondering what his father's house would look like, but given what he did know about the man, he'd assumed it would be fancy. A wall obscured the yard, but above that he could see ivy creeping along the brown brick façade, winding around large windows and up three storeys to the roof. Two large oaks, knobby and bent, stood between the wall and the house, concealing the windows of the first and second floors to the right. It wasn't sprawling, but it was substantially larger than the Count's penthouse, which was one of the largest houses he'd ever set foot in.

He'd never met his father. He hadn't even seen a photo of him until six months ago. Owen Crawford had run out on a pregnant Ainslee Irvine long before she was due, and her bitterness had never subsided. Fergus had heard mixed descriptions of his father: he was a benefactor and a sympathizer; he was a politician and a liar. He had no firm opinion, save for a measure of his mother's bitterness, hovering like a ghost at the back of his mind. He was all too aware of the fact the man had never once sought him out.

Which meant he probably wouldn't be pleased to find Fergus at his doorstep, but desperate times called for desperate measures, and from what Fergus understood, his father was a politician with considerable influence. If they stood any chance of getting back to New Peiling in one piece, it'd be through Senator Crawford.

Fergus was freshly bathed, shaved, and clothed in garments that were not dirty, fraying, or ripped, but he still felt horribly self-conscious. He sorely wished that he hadn't come alone, because he wasn't sure what he would do, nor what his father would do, and his hands were shaking wildly as he tugged the bell-pull.

He stepped back, holding his breath. Minutes crawled by like decades, and he considered bolting.

And then a brisk female voice crackled over the intercom. "Yes? May I help you?"

Fergus cleared his throat. "I have a message for the Senator."

"From?"

"Professor Miller." He glanced at the notes scribbled on his wrist. "He teaches at the Metaphysical College of New Peiling. My name's Thomas. I'm one of his students."

There was a long pause. "Very well. Wait there."

Fergus hurriedly straightened his hair and shirt. He knew nothing about this Professor Miller. He just needed to get inside, and to that end, he doubted it really mattered what excuse he gave.

The gate opened to reveal a severe woman with a long grey braid hanging over her shoulder. She ushered him inside, and Fergus followed her up the stone path towards the door. A sea of wildflowers filled the front yard. There was a birdbath under one of the trees, inhabited by several bathing sparrows. The space was surprisingly quiet compared to the street outside. He glanced behind him, wondering if there wasn't some kind of magic to it.

The old woman hobbled up the steps to the door, pushing it open and motioning for him to come along. She led him into a small foyer and then into a sunroom off to the side where she told him to wait. Rays of sunlight poured in, making the room hot and stuffy.

The wall across from him was dedicated to family photos. Despite the leaden feeling in his stomach, he went over to have a look. The man from Ursula's photograph – his *father* – popped up now and then, but there was no trace of his mother. It seemed Owen had married a dumpy woman with curly blond hair, and they'd had two equally blonde

14

and squat children. They looked nothing like Fergus, though he realized they were his half-brother and sister. He stared at them in horrified awe, the understanding refusing to sink in.

They were just strangers. There was nothing to connect those round, sunny faces to his own moody reflection. These were Owen Crawford's real children. Fergus was the unwanted changeling baby discarded at the wayside.

For a moment, he wanted to smash everything in the room.

Turning from the wall of strangers, he took in the rest of the space. There were a few watercolor paintings of farms, some cross-stitchings bearing various platitudes, and a bookshelf filled with almanacs and medical guides and histories of the city. At the center of it all was a wicker table decorated with a pot of fresh white daisies. It was nondescript, yet mildly cloying.

He was left to wait for quite some time, though at least the old woman returned to offer him a cup of tea, which he accepted simply because drinking it was something to do. The sunlight left him feeling groggy. He stifled a yawn and rubbed his eyes, wishing he could open a window.

"I'm terribly sorry about the wait."

The man's voice was rich and buoyant. It could easily have been a singer's voice. Fergus snapped awake, suddenly on his feet.

There in the doorway stood Owen Crawford. He had bright blue eyes and dark, unruly hair peppered with strands of silver. He was dressed in a casual periwinkle suit, and he looked as though he hadn't shaved that day. He smiled, and his face showed a dozen lines that hadn't been there in Fergus's photo.

15

Then he met Fergus's eyes, and his cordial expression vanished. He paled, eyes widening, and grabbed the doorframe.

Despite himself, Fergus stepped forward to steady him, but stopped himself halfway. He didn't want to help this man, he reminded himself. He wanted to hit him. And yet he didn't do that either. The tea bubbled acidly at the back of his throat, and he stood there, heart hammering against his ribs.

"Who the devil are you?" Owen croaked.

Chapter Two.

Fergus didn't know what to say. He stood face-to-face with his long lost father, and he knew Owen realized it, too, because his face was a funny shade of grey, but he found he couldn't make his tongue form the word *Fergus*. He just stood there, staring at his father in wordless fascination. He wondered if Owen would throw him out now. Most likely. Still, he didn't answer.

They stared at each other in mutual horror and awe for a long moment before Owen took a stumbling step into the room. Fergus noted that they were about the same height and build, though his father was paunchier and slightly heavier in bone. He seemed somehow very large, and Fergus repressed the desire to move away from him.

"You," Owen whispered. "You're Ainslee's son."

Fergus looked away. "Yeah." He opened his mouth and closed it, and its line formed a sneer.

Owen moved past him, taking a seat at the table, and pulled a carton of cigarettes from one of its drawers. "I'm not supposed to smoke in the house, but one should be fine," he said. "Do you smoke?"

Fergus shook his head mutely.

His father lit the cigarette and leaned back, pointedly looking away from him. He took a long drag, releasing it through his nose.

"How is she? Ainslee?"

The ache of something he'd been ignoring since he learned that his mother hadn't disappeared, but rather drowned herself, welled in his throat. There was so much he wanted to say and do at that moment. Flip the table, punch this oblivious, selfish man, break everything in the room, scream at the top of his lungs – but he just looked away, feeling hot and asphyxiated and stung.

"Is she unwell?" Owen asked. Out of the corner of his eye, Fergus could see the cigarette trembling between his fingers. "I'd be happy to help out with any medical expenses."

"She's been dead for five years," Fergus said, surprising himself with how flat his voice sounded.

Ash dropped from the tip of the cigarette.

"Dead," Owen parroted.

Fergus offered a fraction of a nod. He moved to the doorway, leaning against the wall, and crossed his arms over his chest, fixing his eyes on a point of light refracted in the window overhead.

"Thomas, right?" Owen said, staring at the cigarette as it burned down to the filter.

"Fergus."

He nodded slowly, a ghost of a smile flickering at the corners of his mouth. "My father's name was Fergus. He died when I was a little boy."

"I don't care," Fergus snapped, pushing away from the wall. His father's levity slapped him in the face, made him wild and furious.

You might as well have been dead, he thought, jaw clenched.

He looked up and found himself faced with the wall of cozy family memories and thought this must be the Universe's way of mocking him.

"So you turned out to be a hybrid after all," Owen said, putting out the cigarette and leaning back.

"Stop being so goddamn conversational!"

His father blinked at him. Their eyes were the same shade of blue, and Fergus looked away, forcing himself to breathe.

"I'm sorry. I suppose we both know my efforts to find you, to get involved in your life, to help you – well, they were paltry at best." He sighed, wiping the corner of his mouth with one knuckle, and looked up at Fergus. "I've given you little more than DNA, haven't I?"

Fergus stared at the scuffed up toes of his shoes, swallowing thickly.

"So why are you here?" Owen asked, clasping his hands on the table, his knuckles taut and sallow.

Fergus looked up. He could see his eyes flashing white in the glass of a wedding photo. He closed them, taking a deep breath, and thought of a pond filled with orange and white fish. He thought of rain dripping from round shingles and the smell of pipe smoke. When he opened his eyes, the glass reflected blue again.

"I need to get into New Peiling," he said, doing his best to keep his voice even.

"Why the devil do you want into New Peiling? You know they've already shipped half the hybrids off to that colony," Owen said, brows climbing towards his hairline. "They even shut down the universities. Of course, their city planning rides on the backs of hybrids, so I expect it won't be long before —"

"Yeah, I already know. I still gotta go back. There are things I have to see through, no matter what." He turned to his father, staring at him hard.

Owen lowered his eyes, frowning. "Then this is the first and last time I will ever see you. You look so very much like her."

"Why did you leave her? Why did you leave *us*?" Fergus suddenly demanded, momentarily forgetting that the last thing he wanted was to give Owen the opportunity to spill forth excuses.

"There are always two sides to every story," his father said. "Will you hear mine?"

Fergus didn't want to say "yes," but nodded anyway, sliding into the adjacent chair.

Owen smiled, and the pinched yellow-white of his knuckles eased into a softer pink. "Many years ago, this family held a number of titles. We've always been prominent in politics, but there was a time when our sway was truly impressive. My grandfather ruined that. Scandal followed scandal, and our titles were stripped away one by one. My father sought to regain our former glory, but the most he could do in his lifetime was secure a position as a senator's secretary. My sister and I are twins. We were born on a ship crossing from the continent, and our mother didn't survive the passage. My father died of pneumonia a few years later."

He looked up at Fergus, his brow puckering. "I wish you had not followed in my footsteps."

"It's a little late for that," Fergus said, his voice lower and softer than he thought his father deserved. "Keep going," he added sharply.

"After my father died, we were sent to live with my aunt in New Peiling. Perhaps I had a bit of my grandfather in me. I was rebellious. While my aunt was trying to groom me to restore the family name, I had other ideas. I wanted to study at the magical universities, to discover the pleasures hidden in the slums, to meet hybrids, to maybe even become one. Of course, she wouldn't allow it, and I wasn't clever enough to sneak off on my own.

"When I came of age, I was to be sent straight back to Clohaven to reclaim the family home and enter into a life of politics. I begged and begged, so she let me go alone to the docks. The moment she let me out of her sight, I ran off." He smiled, staring at his hands. "And so I met Ainslee."

"Then you knew she was a hybrid?"

"No. I knew she was poor, I knew she was living on the streets, but I didn't know she was a hybrid. She said she wasn't, and I couldn't conceive of her lying. I was pampered and naïve. I didn't – I couldn't – understand the stigma." He closed his eyes, craning his head back. "I only saw the romance in her life. She didn't seem like she was homeless, she seemed like she was free. I eagerly disappeared into the slums with her. I got away with it a lot longer than you might expect.

"Oh, they were looking for me, but that was part of the fun. We evaded them at every turn, and I started to think I was as clever as she was. I wasn't. The longer I was gone, the more frantic my aunt became and the more effort she put into finding me. And so she did."

"So what, she made you leave?"

He nodded. "I didn't get to say good-bye to Ainslee before I was put on a ferry and sent straight back to Clohaven. What I didn't know at the time – what I didn't know until many years later – was that she was pregnant. Apparently, she tried to go to my aunt, but was turned away. Not a word of it was said to me. I was strictly forbidden to return to New Peiling, and if I did, especially if I met up with Ainslee again, I would be tossed out for good. Well, though I'd had my fun on the streets, I knew I wasn't suited to a lifetime of living hand-to-mouth. Plus, I had recently been introduced to Samantha. There were so many distractions in Clohaven. I moved on."

Fergus stared down at the table, his face feeling overly warm.

"It's not an excuse. It's not meant to be. It's just what happened. My aunt told me about the pregnancy on her deathbed, and by then I suppose I was too ashamed and horrified to return. I couldn't bear to find out what had become of the two of you."

The cards had been laid out on the table, and Fergus didn't feel any better for it. It seemed both of his parents were abject failures. Neither had made any effort to give him a childhood like the one memorialized on the wall to his right, and at that moment, he hated them both in equal measure. But, he thought, he was a bit too old to be clinging to that sentiment. Though he hadn't experienced the luxury of having parents around to complain to, he had more important things to do than air his grievances.

He smothered the sad little voice in his head that screamed and railed.

"We'll need documents for five and transportation to New Peiling," he finally said.

"Fergus . . . "

"Two are foreigners, and me and my best friend are probably the city's most wanted."

Owen opened his mouth and shut it again, blinking.

"There's bad blood between Ashton Harriet and us."

"I wish you'd come for money."

"Don't worry. I have no intention of interrupting your life any further. No one will even know I was ever here," Fergus said, shrugging and looking away.

"That's not what I meant."

"It is deep down." He got to his feet. "Will you help me or not?"

Owen looked up at him, and it seemed to Fergus that he had aged ten years in the space of their conversation. His father pinched the bridge of his nose and closed his eyes, letting out a long sigh.

"I could give you money. There's no reason you should have to return to New Peiling, especially if you're a wanted man. There's no reason for Ashton Harriet to trouble you ever again."

"The only thing I've learned from you and Mom is that I *don't* wanna run away."

Owen pulled out a fresh cigarette. His fingers were shaking again. He swallowed convulsively and looked away from Fergus, staring into the sunlight slanting over the table.

"I'm staying at that big hotel just off the square."

"Which one?"

"The marble one."

His father lifted an eyebrow, but said nothing.

"If you want to help us, you should send someone there by tomorrow. Otherwise, we'll just do what we can," Fergus said, tucking his hands into his jeans and turning to leave.

"Fergus, wait."

He stopped, resisting the urge to look over his shoulder. "What is it?"

But his father remained silent, and so after a moment, he continued on his way.

The housekeeper didn't show him to the door, but it wasn't necessary. Fergus walked out into the daylight. Beyond the front gate, he could hear the sounds of the fair, but the cheerful din was muted. He sighed, pressing his hands deeper into his pockets, and looked up at the blue sky between the trees. Then, with a brief glance over his shoulder, he walked away.

He found Terry lounging against the wall outside.

He frowned. "What are you doing here?"

Terry straightened from his resting place, meandering over to Fergus. He looked up at the house from over the wall and then turned back to Fergus, shrugging.

"Entertaining a whim, I guess."

"'How do you know Owen Crawford?' Is that it?" Fergus asked, glancing at the gate and then starting away from the building.

"Can you blame me?" Terry asked, a wry grin twisting his lips. "I didn't know you were rubbing elbows with the bigwigs."

"I'm not. I just met him," Fergus replied, feeling raw and waspish.

Terry considered him silently.

"Stop making fun of me. It's not like you don't know."

"Not really. I actually have no idea what you're mad about."

Fergus glanced at him, brow lifting incredulously. "Ursula knows something you don't?"

"She must, because I really *don't* know why you'd go to Senator Crawford for help, or why you'd spend over an hour chatting with him. "

Fergus sighed, blowing his bangs out of his face. "Next you're gonna say you've never seen a picture of him."

"Yeah, in newspapers, but it's not like I've got his face memorized."

Fergus stopped at the end of the block, checking to make sure they were well away from the tidy, scrupulous façade of the Crawford residence. Putting aside his reservations, he fished around in his pocket a moment before producing a small stack of photographs. At the very top was a picture of his mother and father around his age. He'd brought it along in case Owen refused to believe him, or didn't recognize him. Fergus shared most of his mother's features, but his eyes and build were unmistakably his father's. He hesitantly offered Terry the photo.

"Oh," Terry said, looking up at Fergus. "Well. That's a bit of a surprise."

"Don't make fun of me."

"I swear I'm not. No one guarded Ainslee's secrets as devoutly as Ursula. She's the only one who even knows the half of it. Ainslee was already working at Beathag's when Ursula's parents died, and she went to live with her Aunt Beatrice. She probably even held you when you were a baby. But I was a toddler when you were born, and I was only peripherally aware you existed until Ainslee died. She wanted to keep you a secret, safely tucked away from the stuff she was meddling in. So no, I didn't know Owen Crawford is your dad. He is your dad, right?"

Fergus put the photos away, nodding.

"And how did it go?"

"Maybe he'll help, maybe he won't. I'm not gonna hold my breath."

The bitterness ballooned in his chest, cramming into all the little bruises still smarting from the meeting with his father. The urge to scream returned, and he took a deep breath, holding it to force the impulse away.

"Hey, I get it," Terry said, slipping an arm over his shoulders. "My parents moved to Lancaster to make sure I wouldn't come knocking again, you know?"

Fergus nodded.

"There're still plenty of people who wouldn't abandon you, who want you around."

"Like you?" Fergus asked, trying not to sound accusatory, but with little success.

Since the day he'd kissed Terry, all efforts to follow up on it or even talk about it had been dismissed out-of-hand. It was frustrating and discouraging and unfair.

"I think by now we've established that you're my best friend, and that's not gonna change," Terry replied, looking stung.

"That's not what I mean, and you know it."

Terry sighed, pulling away. "You were just feeling stir crazy. I mean, months on an airship with a bunch of sailors and Three? Stranger things have happened."

Fergus shook his head. "That's *not* why."

"We'll be back in New Peiling in a few days, and you'll see Ursula again. I bet you'll forget all about it."

"Screw you."

"Fergus," Terry called. "Fergus, wait! You know that's not what I meant." He heard Terry's trainers thudding behind him. A moment later, Terry grabbed the back of his jacket. "Fergus, stop."

"What do you mean, then?"

Terry ran a hand through his hair, sighing. "I'm not saying I'm not interested. I'm saying now isn't the best time. Seriously, I'm not trying to put you off, and I'm sorry if that's not a good enough reason for you, but it is for me."

"So when is a good time? When everyone is equal and Paige Harriet is begging us for forgiveness? When we're not in the middle of running around trying to fix this or find that or stop someone from killing one of us?" He shook his head, walking faster. "Whatever. I'm not asking again."

Terry laughed weakly. "Sometimes, you really are like Ainslee." He sighed, speeding up to cut Fergus off. He put his hands on Fergus's shoulders, regarding him plaintively. "Look, we're here in the middle of a big festival, so how about we just forget about everything and go ride a hot air balloon and eat, I dunno, whatever you want. My treat."

Fergus looked down at his feet to avoid having to see how the afternoon light fell on Terry's cheek and the way his eyes were probably crinkling in that stomach melting way. He didn't feel like entertaining Terry, but he also didn't feel like sulking in Deirdre's hotel room all afternoon, waiting to see if his father would come through.

"You just want someone to drag around to all the stupid airships."

Terry shook his head. "Nope, I wanna drag *you* around to see all the stupid airships. I know it isn't what you want, but . . . But things are probably gonna get heavy the minute we step foot in New Peiling, so for now, can we pretend like we're normal and problem-free?"

"I can eat whatever I want?"

Terry nodded, putting his arm around Fergus once more. "That's right. Whatever you want."

Fergus sighed. "Fine, but food first and *then* airships."

Chapter Three.

Rain picked away at the fog hanging over the water. From where he sat, Fergus could see thunderheads rolling closer. He had a packet of papers open in his lap, which Orson was attempting to help him memorize. Terry, Three, and Pip had learned theirs earlier, and now Pip and Three sat beside him, Three napping on Pip's shoulder, Pip staring into space. Terry had gone above deck. Fergus thought he must have been disappointed that they were returning by sea.

He bit his lip and tried to concentrate on Orson's questions: full name, date and place of birth, parents' names and occupations, business in the city, and so forth. He felt about as focused as the tendrils of mist passing the window.

"No, it's Thomas Andrew Miller. You were born in St. Michael's Hospital in Lancaster on October 3rd. Your father is a spice merchant, who presently lives in Ping City. You're visiting the Count on your father's behalf, as well as to see the city. You grew up in Lancaster." Orson groaned, squeezing the bridge of his nose. "For the love of God, Fergus! If you don't remember at least some of this, you're going to wind up on that colony."

"Sorry. It's hard to concentrate," Fergus mumbled, looking away from the window, though not without a final glance. He could feel the thunder brewing in his bones. They ached as the air pressure continued to drop, twisting his stomach around and around until he was sure that his guts would pop.

He ran his hands over his face. "Maybe I'll just puke on their shoes, and they'll stop asking questions."

"Better not, or they might stick you in quarantine."

Fergus considered this. "I may not be able to help it."

"You have to try. Okay, let's go over it again. Repeat the story to me."

Fergus groaned, pressing his knuckles to his eyes. "Thomas Andrew Miller. Born in Lancaster, October 2nd. Grew up in —"

"October 3rd."

"October 3rd. Grew up in Ping City where my mom lives. My dad's a merchant. I'm here on business. Um, my business is . . .?"

"Spice imports."

"Spices." He paused and looked up. "I don't know anything about spices."

Orson sighed. "Don't worry about that. Just concentrate on not throwing up on anyone and remembering the basics."

Fergus leaned forward, putting his face in his hands. The storm would hit soon. The tension in the air dragged at his muscles, trying to separate veins from flesh, and flesh from bone. He wiped his forehead with the back of his wrist.

"I thought you liked the ocean," Orson said, tentatively patting him on the back.

"Pinch your wrist," Three mumbled sleepily.

Fergus did so. "I do, but I hate storms."

He turned to the window. Through the haze of rain, he could see New Peiling's unwieldy silhouette emerging. It felt like it had been years since he'd seen the city, and despite his queasiness, he got up and went over to the window. He recalled what Deirdre had said about the magic of the hybrids holding it together and wondered what the humans thought would happen once they'd rounded up and exorcised everyone. Even if they left a few around to tend to the magic, surely that wouldn't be enough to keep the towering layers stable.

Maybe it would just fall into the ocean.

It would serve them right, he thought and immediately regretted it. Sighing, he returned to his seat.

"We don't have much time. Okay, quiz me again."

•   •   •

As they stepped off the ferry, the rain began falling in earnest. The docks were all but abandoned, and Fergus had the feeling they hadn't seen people for some time. Some stands looked like they might yet be in use, but most appeared to have fallen into aggravated states of disrepair. There were a few hardy fishermen huddled in makeshift shelters, obscured by colorless rain slickers, but no merchants to be seen. Maybe a storm had come through recently. The docks were always hit the hardest by bad weather. Maybe that was why it looked so deserted.

But he didn't think so.

"Papers," demanded an official in a brown raincoat.

Fergus handed them over.

"Full name?"

"Thomas Andrew Miller."

"Date of birth?"

"October 3rd."

"Place of birth?"

"Lancaster."

Thunder boomed overhead, making the boards under his feet rock and his bones rattle. He missed the next question.

"Hurry it up. No one wants to wait out here."

"What?" Fergus asked, not daring to look away from the sky.

"What are your parents' names?"

"What's taking so long?" Orson demanded from behind. "How long are you going to keep us waiting in this weather?"

Three and Pip also began to grumble and shout, waving their arms angrily.

"Look, there's a protocol I have to follow for the safety of our citizens . . . "

Terry appeared at Fergus's shoulder. "I'm sorry. I was sitting by him the entire time. It's his first time traveling abroad. He's only seasick. Maybe you could just let him go this time?"

Fergus rubbed the rain from his face. He didn't have to pretend to feel nauseated, but he thought he should restrain himself, what with the threat of quarantine hanging over his head. He swallowed and tried to compose himself.

"Seasick?" the official repeated, backing away so that his feet were safely out of Fergus's path. "Are you sure it's nothing else?"

"I had a big breakfast," Fergus said, doing his very best to ignore the first flash of lightning. "A big, *big* breakfast."

The official frowned up at the clouds. "Where will you be staying?"

"Eleven-oh-Five Fountain Circle," Fergus replied.

"Fountain Circle? Why?" the man asked, frowning at Fergus incredulously.

"My father has business with the Count Palatine. He's looking to . . . " Fergus winced as another bolt of lightning illuminated the docks. "He's looking to open up a trade route for spices. He heard the Count—"

"I'm going to keep these. We will return your papers to 1105 Fountain Circle. I hope you will be there."

Fergus scowled, but wasted no time in hurrying towards the city and out of the storm. The slums looked even emptier than the docks. Few of the artificial lights that used to illuminate the lower city were on, and the streets were cast in shadow. A number of shop fronts had been boarded up, many with broken windows, looted and hollowed out. The damage from last year's arson had not been mended, but the shantytown that had cropped up in the ruins was gone, leaving only charred boards and rubble. Even more disconcerting was the lack of glowing fungi, which had once dotted the sides of buildings and filled the cracks in the streets.

The slums were dead.

The others were watching him expectantly, so Fergus started towards the Magpie. If there were people to be found, surely they'd be there. Maybe the pub's owner, Felix, would be around, and he'd know where to find Ursula. But when they arrived, the sign with the merry black-white-blue bird was gone, and the door had been torn from its hinges. He stepped into the darkened tavern.

"Felix?"

Something creaked and fell in the back room. He hurried that way, fumbling for a match, but all he saw was the tail of a mouse disappearing into a crack in the wall. He moved through the tavern, lighting match after match, but the shelves had been emptied of food and drink. The only thing left was the tidy stack of plates by the sink.

The bar had a thick layer of untouched dust coating the counter. He stood before it, pressing a finger into the grime and drawing meaningless shapes. He'd been so sure that if anyone could've avoided the colony, it would've been Felix. The Magpie was a neutral zone. It was the kind of place that even humans visited now and then, and it was the one place where an orphan could find decent work and a free meal. Now it was empty.

He cursed, kicking the bar, and heard a faint tinkle of glass as the tumblers and flutes shuddered in the racks. Swallowing, he turned to the others.

"We need to go to Beathag's. See if Ursula's there," he said, pushing past them through the door.

Beathag's wasn't far from the Magpie. The door was still in place, the glass storefront was in one piece, and it didn't look like it'd been looted, but it was definitely abandoned. There were no lights issuing from within, and the fish tank in the window was covered with green slime. He could see the bodies of the fish floating at the top. He swallowed roughly, pressing his face against the glass. There amongst the nameless angelfish was his little clownfish, Toby, as lifeless as the rest.

Fergus closed his eyes. He'd bought those fish with Flynn, because when he first moved in, Flynn had said he felt lonely when Fergus was at work. They'd only bothered to name Toby, because he was the only one who seemed to have a personality.

Flynn was dead, the apartment he'd grown up in burned to the ground, and now Toby.

He staggered away from the storefront. Turning, he saw that the convenience store across the way – the one Ursula had hated so bitterly – was also closed up, but unlike Beathag's, it'd been ransacked. The sign was partially attached to the awning, flickering and showering the walk with sparks.

Terry put a hand on his shoulder. "She isn't here. I can't smell her or Dom. Looks like there was a fire upstairs."

Fergus followed his gaze to the window of the Labyrinth, the burlesque house that had once stood over Beathag's. He could see black stains on the windowpanes.

"Do you think anyone got stuck inside?"

"Let's just leave it," Terry said, pulling him away. "Ursula isn't here. No doubt, she's found somewhere safer to hole up. She must've, or the city would have come down already. She's managed to keep Beathag's up, hasn't she?"

"She always said Beathag's was more important than I gave it credit for."

"Not Beathag's, but the runes her aunt drew underneath it," Terry replied, continuing to tug his arm. "Come on. We'll go to the penthouse. At least we know *he'll* be there, and he might have a better idea of where to find them."

Fergus nodded and allowed himself to be led towards the lifts. Another man in uniform stood before them. His face was grave, cheekbones hollow, and he glared at them from deeply sunken eyes.

"Papers."

"The man at the ferry took mine."

"What was his name?"

"I'm not sure, sir. It was raining, so we just moved along as quickly as we could."

"Where are you staying?"

"Eleven-oh-Five Fountain Circle."

The man stared at him for longer than Fergus liked, but at last he nodded.

"See to it that you get your papers back, and keep them on you at all times. Get on."

Fergus stepped into the lift, worrying his lower lip and wishing that the official would hurry up and let the others board. Unfortunately, the man also got into the lift with them, and there was no opportunity to confer. He stood towards the back of the car, looking at his reflection in the glass. His blue eyes looked black and dull, lined with worry. Terry nudged him, and he smiled weakly without turning.

They passed into the middle sector, and the lift shuddered to a halt. Terry and Fergus got off without looking back, and so Fergus didn't notice until they neared the end of the block that the rest hadn't followed.

"Where'd they go? Did they get detained?" he asked, starting back towards the lift, but Terry caught him by the elbow.

"Three said she and Pip are going to do a little poking around of their own. They'll be back in a few hours. Orson wouldn't tell me where he was going, but probably to meet up with some of Guillory's supporters."

"Oh," Fergus said, relaxing a little. "So just you and me?"

"It's better this way. I have something to say to *Evan*."

Fergus blinked, tilting his head, but Terry didn't elaborate. He started off across the square, and Fergus had to jog to catch up. There were a few people out and about, strolling with their children by the mermaid fountain and feeding the seagulls that had snuck inside. From the corner where the penthouse stood, Fergus could see down the street to the edge of the city. Lightning struck, momentarily painting the bricks white, and he gasped, grabbing Terry's jacket. Terry turned to him, putting a hand over his.

"It's just rain. It can't hurt you here."

He rang the bell. It was several minutes before they could hear anyone on the other side of the door.

"Deirdre's still in Clohaven," Terry said, sighing irritably. "And he probably doesn't want to answer his own door."

Fergus snorted softly. "Probably not."

At last, the door opened, creaking dolefully. A couple of inches of light appeared, revealing wheat-colored curls in a state of disarray. The Count's angular, pale features were cast in shadow. He looked sullen, and it took him a moment to open the door the rest of the way.

"You're back. Where's my airship?"

"Somewhere outside Brookston last we saw it. The engine was completely shot. So much for the beta edition," Terry replied.

If the Count noticed the sharpness in Terry's tone, he ignored it. He reluctantly ushered them inside. Fergus saw him pause a moment, looking out into the street before shutting the door, and wondered what he'd been looking for.

"My staff is out, so I can't offer you any refreshments," he said, sweeping past them into the sitting room beyond the foyer.

"That won't be necessary," Terry replied, following him into the room, but not sitting down. He loomed over the Count, crossing his arms.

Fergus trailed in after them, glancing over his shoulder. He had the feeling the Count had been looking for someone, but when he glanced out the adjacent window, the square was as peaceful as before. He shook his head and followed them into the sitting room, leaning on the doorframe. In the past, this would have been the point where the Count sent him off to the kitchen, but perhaps Terry's thinly concealed ire had distracted him. He didn't seem to notice Fergus at all, but rather frowned up at Terry, fingers digging into the arms of the chair.

"What are you looking at me like that for?" he asked, drawing one leg up to his chest like a petulant child.

"I would like for you to explain a few things, and when you're finished, I want you to apologize to Fergus. We'll see how things go after that. After all, Deirdre isn't here, is she?"

"I suppose she isn't," the Count said, eyeing Terry warily. "But I have no idea what you want me to explain. If you think I'm responsible for this city's decay . . . Well, *you're* the ones who abandoned ship."

Fergus started to say something, but Terry cut him off.

"Don't play stupid. You tipped the Abels off about Fergus. You told them he could transform, didn't you?"

"I did no such thing. It's not my fault that Ainslee was well-known," the Count replied, shrugging and looking away.

"Not internationally."

"Word gets around. Darya visits New Peiling now and then. She could've heard it from anyone."

Terry kicked the table beside the armchair. A leg broke off as it hit the floor. The Count eyed the broken table, drawing deeper into the chair, before looking back up at Terry.

"Even if I told them, I didn't ask them to touch a single hair on his silly head."

"Keep lying. See what happens."

The Count stared at Terry's knees and then glanced at Fergus out of the corner of his eye. "It's not like you wanted to be Badb Catha, and I thought the Hunt might be right up your alley. Besides, I can't see why you'd have an issue with Declan's views. You've said the same many times before."

Terry inhaled sharply. Fergus glanced at him, but couldn't see his face. The line of his shoulders was very straight. For a moment, he wondered if Terry was going to hurt the Count. Then wondered if he should try to stop him, but instantly felt bad about it and took a step into the room.

"He has a point," he said, ignoring the Count with as much intensity as the Count was ignoring him. "He couldn't make them do all that stuff, even if he should have kept his stupid mouth shut."

Terry turned to him silently. His face was strained and white, and Fergus had to fight the urge to step back.

The Count took courage, climbing out of his chair. "That's right. I can't be responsible for the actions of —"

The crack of Terry's fist connecting with bone was so loud that for a moment Fergus was afraid he'd broken the Count's jaw. The Count went crashing back into the armchair, which skidded across the floor with an angry shriek. Fergus didn't move. Terry's posture was so commanding, his face so livid, all he could do was watch.

The Count gingerly prodded his face and then turned sharply, glaring at Terry. Fergus was sure the look on Terry's face must have been equally furious. Certainly, a lesser man would have a hard time holding his ground under the heat of that glower, but Terry remained standing straight, full of inert energy ready to be released into kinetic rage, and perhaps the Count realized that he was outdone. He sunk back into the chair, looking wounded and surly.

"Don't forget: I'm not as forgiving as he is."

"Fine. All I did was write to them about city gossip, though. I told them a little about him and a little about you – a little about a lot of people – and I mentioned that you'd be an excellent Huntsman."

"Because you wanted me to leave for good."

"*You* wanted to leave for good. I gave them no instructions, nor suggestions. Only information. I don't loathe Ainslee's son that much."

"Yet you knew the only reason I'd come back here is if Fergus did."

40

"Yes, I suppose that's true," the Count said, his pale green eyes bright with malice. He continued to cower in his armchair, drawing further into himself.

"And the apology."

"I don't have anything to . . . "

Terry took a step closer.

"Fine. I'm sorry I caused you trouble, *Fergus.*"

"Um, it's okay," Fergus replied, rubbing the back of his neck and looking away. "We lived, right?"

Terry continued to glower at the Count for a moment before asking, "Have you seen Ursula or Rosslyn lately?"

The Count dropped his hand, looking away, resentment taking the place of spite. "No. They don't drop in much anymore. I couldn't begin to tell you where they are or what they're doing. Maybe they're in the slums. Maybe."

"I'm going to have a look around. Fergus, I'm going to leave you here. I need you to just stay here until I get back. Don't worry about him," he added, thumbing at the Count. "Hopefully, our host has learned his manners."

Fergus nodded uncertainly, looking between Terry and the Count.

"But shouldn't I look, too?"

"No. For now, I just need to know where you are."

"Yeah, but I also . . . " Fergus started.

"I'll be back, and if I haven't found anything, you can search."

Fergus sighed, feeling defeated. "So what, are we supposed to play cards or something?"

"I have things to do," the Count snapped, getting to his feet and poking his face tentatively. "Entertain yourself." He pushed past them both and stomped off towards the stairs leading to the bedrooms.

Fergus sighed. "Be fast, okay?"

Terry nodded, putting a hand on his shoulder. "It'll be a couple of hours at most. If I haven't found anything by then, I'll come straight back."

He watched Terry go, chewing his lip. The door shut with a soft click, and Fergus was left standing in the empty corridor. He let out a long sigh, running a hand through his hair, and headed for the kitchens. If there was nothing else for him to do, he might as well have some lunch.

The cupboards were nearly bare, but he managed to find some bread and jam, and though he found it overly sweet and unsatisfying, made do. He couldn't just stand around eating bread all afternoon, though. Besides, not knowing where the Count had gone worried him.

He roamed the hallways between the Count's massive paintings, depicting vulgar acts between fairies and humans. Every few minutes, he looked over his shoulder, but as he arrived at the painting of the Wild Hunt, he forgot his paranoia. The creatures in the image ran round and round on a never-ending track. Off to the side stood Badb Catha – Terry – naked and glowing in contrast to the murky background.

He frowned at the image, bothered that Terry had sat for the painting in the first place and jealous that the Count had shared that sort of relationship with him when he kept pushing Fergus away.

"Fergus?"

He turned to see the Count skulking about at the end of the hallway. He was still in his robe, though he looked like he'd patched up his face. He smiled at

Fergus, and Fergus frowned, wondering what he wanted.

"Yeah?"

"I'm short on staff these days, and there's quite a bit of rubbish piling up in the kitchen. Would you mind taking it out?"

He raised an eyebrow.

"You'll be paid."

Fergus sighed. "Okay. Fine, I guess."

He started down the hallway, past the baths, and down the stairs into the kitchen, heading over to the cupboard. Several bags, which smelled of long-spoiled cabbage and onions, were stacked in the corner.

"Seriously?" he muttered, wrinkling his nose.

The Count grabbed him by the shoulder, using it for leverage as he forced a cloth into Fergus's face. Before Fergus could protest, his legs gave out from under him, and tumbled into blackness.

Chapter Four.

Fergus sneezed, jerking back to life. His elbow rubbed against cold stone, and his cheek rested on coarse fabric, which he found had been tied over his head. His wrists ached, twisted behind him and bound by prickly rope. He growled and realized he'd also been gagged. Also, swallowing was a very bad idea. His mouth filled with the taste of old sweat and grime, and he retched, asphyxiated by the rag. He panicked, rolling and kicking, but his feet met neither wall nor body. Still, he shouted and struggled until he was too exhausted to move.

He needed to think.

Maybe he could peel the sack off, which would be a start. He sat up, catching the fabric between the thin bones of each knee, and pulled, but it caught under his chin and refused to loosen. He cursed around the gag, stamping the floor. Between contorting and the prickly rope, his wrists had blistered and broken. He shifted, trying to find a position that'd ease the strain, but nothing helped.

Sitting still once more, he returned to examining his circumstances. He could hear muffled dripping from somewhere outside his immediate vicinity. The sack drowned out all other smells. He was dressed in something much thinner than what he'd been wearing, which didn't bode well. Plus, wherever he was, the room was clammy enough to chill him to the bone, which was saying something – he *was* a kelpie after all. He shivered and pressed his knees to his chest.

It was very dark, and not just because of the bag over his head. He thought it might be some sort of potato sack, so if there had been light, it would've shown through the weave. It was pointless to call out, since he was gagged, and whoever had taken him obviously didn't care to hear his complaints.

Who had taken him? Was it the Count? The last thing he recalled was the Count's hand on his shoulder, but he was certain he wasn't in the penthouse. He was also sure the Count wouldn't have been able to move him any distance alone. He must have knocked Fergus out, but then what?

He heard thick-soled boots on stone and went still, heart pounding in his ears. He strained to hear anything more, ears twitching with the effort, but the area was too spacious, and the echo of the boots drowned out anything else. He heard a metal door screech open, and one set of footsteps halted a few feet away. For a moment, nothing happened, and then he felt a hand near his throat, and the sack was yanked free. He was in a gloomy concrete cell, lit by only the slimmest beam of grey light from outside. Three members of the Air Guard stood by the iron bars at the front of the cell.

Ashton Harriet towered over him, looking all too smug. He cast the sack over his shoulder and kicked Fergus in the chest. Fergus fell backwards, cursing furiously, and rolled onto his side, drawing his knees up to block further assault. He glared up at Harriet, wishing he could set him ablaze with his eyes.

Harriet laughed, black curls falling into his face. "You're stupider than you look, coming back to New Peiling of all places."

His skin prickled with inert magic, hot and uncomfortable. He wondered whether he could get away with turning into a kelpie here, or if Harriet's men would panic and shoot him on the spot. He wondered if he could move quickly enough to avoid that, but it was a small space, and he'd learned that small spaces and big fairy horses didn't mix. He continued to silently glower at Harriet's shiny, black boots.

"I'll shoot you myself if you try using your aberrant magic, so just stay quiet." Harriet turned to the others. "Leave us."

Fergus didn't look away from Harriet's toes as the others filed out of the cell, their footfalls meandering down the corridor. He thought they sounded hesitant, which gave him a fleeting sense of gratification. It didn't last. Harriet walked over to the door and pushed it shut with a resounding *clang*. He leaned against it, crossing his arms, and turned his attention to the slat of light sifting down from the window overhead.

A shadow passed over the sky. A gull screeched. The wind whistled through the narrow opening. A tower in the middle of the ocean? Fergus frowned. The answer was not a happy one. He must have been imprisoned at Andrew's Rock: the most

46

infamous and remote prison for hundreds of miles. Trying not to let his worry show, he turned his attention back to Harriet's boots.

"Have you worked out where you are yet?" Harriet asked in an unpleasantly conversational tone. "Don't worry. You'll get to see New Peiling once more."

Fergus remained silent, resting his cheek against the floor and staring at the wall behind Harriet's legs.

The Captain's mouth curved into an ugly smile. "You must realize your situation by now."

So they hadn't beaten the Guard back, but outrunning Ashton Harriet had always been a long shot. After all, the *Returner* barely made it to Brookston, and the Air Guard ships were renowned for their speed. Given Harriet's intense and relentless hatred for him, he expected the only reason Harriet intended to bring him back to New Peiling was to exorcise him. He wondered what the Guard had done with Raja, Evelyn, and Guillory. Harriet couldn't go through with condemning his hero, could he? Then again, he'd arrested Guillory in the first place . . .

"You seem surprisingly resigned, or are you thinking that if you bide your time, you'll find a way out? Need I remind you that Andrew's Rock is quite a distance from the city *and* surrounded by the roughest waves and sharpest rocks?"

Fergus snarled.

"Now the animal comes out." Harriet laughed.

He lashed out, but Harriet deftly blocked and countered with a swift kick to his hip. He grunted in pain, seriously reconsidering the kelpie route, even if it would end in gunfire.

"Don't worry. You've still got a few days. We'll make your stay very pleasant," Harriet said, practically crowing. "And I hear exorcism hardly hurts at all. But perhaps you could extend your life by a few days." He crouched down, taking Fergus by the hair and dragging him closer. "If you tell me where Bridges is, I might be inclined to grant you some leniency."

Fergus growled and tried to wrest himself free, ignoring the sting of hair being ripped free of his scalp.

"Very well. You might change your mind. After all, exorcism is very permanent. You might *want* a few extra days to make your peace," Harriet said, releasing him and going to open the door. "Think on it," he added, stepping through and securing the lock.

Fergus listened to him leave, lying still and silent until the echo of his footsteps had faded entirely. He could hear the surf from far away, punctuating the fact he'd been placed high in the tower. Despite the wretched taste, he chewed on the gag and mulled. Even if Terry and the others did figure out what'd happened to him, it would be far too dangerous to try rescuing him. If he wanted to escape, he had to rely wholly on himself.

He heaved himself onto his feet, going to inspect the front of the cell. Torches lit the hallway, the end of which curved out of sight. It would be dangerous to transform and break out, even if it was the only way he could imagine handling so many guards. But he still felt too disoriented, and he didn't want to be stumbling around with people shooting at him.

He needed to free up his hands.

He began to rub them against the bars, but rather than loosen the binds, it only forced the rope deeper into his skin. He gave up and focused on ridding himself of the gag instead, rubbing the back of his head against the bars. The knot gave a little. He pressed harder until he had pulled it down over his chin. Spitting out the foul taste, he took a deep, shuddering breath of *slightly* fresher air.

"Now what?" he muttered to himself.

A soft groan issued from the cell across the way.

"Hello? Is someone there?"

"Keep it down. Damn head is killing me."

A figure shifted in the shadows of the cell across the way, amorphous at first and then taking the shape of a broad-shouldered man with wild hair. He couldn't make out the shade, but the color was undeniably brown. A sloppy beard obscured the man's face.

"Have you been here long?" Fergus asked, pressing his face to the bars.

"Long enough," the man grumbled, rubbing his forehead with his knuckles.

"Do you know anything about this place, or how to get out?"

"Be quiet. They'll hear you," the man said rather waspishly and then went silent, sinking down next to the door of his cell.

"I have to find a way out of here," Fergus persisted more quietly.

"I know. I heard you. I'm trying to think," the man said, resting his head on his knees. "Then again, *should* I help you? You're a criminal. Maybe you belong—" But the man stopped, looking up at him. Under his lank, bedraggled hair, his eyes were a very unique shade of brown, bordering on yellow. They

49

caught the light just so, and though his appearance was decrepit, Fergus felt for a moment that he was looking into the eyes of a lion.

"Guillory!"

"Fergus!" Guillory started to smile, but immediately faltered. "They caught you?"

"Wait, why are they keeping *you* here?" Fergus asked simultaneously. He paused, biting back a sigh, before adding, "Seems I was sold out. Wish I could say it was unexpected."

"I expect they're keeping me here because they don't want my supporters to try and break me out. Rocks and ocean tend to put a damper on rescue missions." He sighed, trying to push his hair out of his face. "It doesn't bode well that you're here."

"You mean, besides the obvious?" Fergus asked, mouth scrunching to the side.

"Where's Bridges?"

Fergus shook his head. "Hopefully far, far away from here."

"You know, this level of the prison is reserved for political prisoners," Guillory said, looking away. "Political prisoners on the way to the executioner's block."

"I should be so lucky," Fergus grumbled.

"How so?"

"Guess you missed the whole . . . " he trailed off. The word left an unpleasant taste. He swallowed roughly, staring down at the floor between his knees. "Exorcism."

Guillory said nothing.

"So I kinda wanna take a rain check on that."

"It'll be hard to find your way out of here. This place is a maze. Supposedly, even the guards get lost now and then." He looked up, pursing his lips and staring at the opposite wall. "Even if the windows were large enough, you certainly couldn't hope to scale the side. The rocks are also treacherous, though maybe as a fairy, you could navigate them safely."

"Have you been here before?"

Guillory nodded. "But I haven't had the grand tour. There's a lift that runs down the very center of the complex. Considering how tall the structure is, it would be exhausting to go up and down the stairs, and the stairs let out into . . . *weird* places. If you don't have a map, you're likely to exit in the wrong place and wind up lost, wandering until you die."

"Grim."

Guillory nodded. "But there's always hope, if you look hard enough."

Fergus couldn't help it, he rolled his eyes. "Easy to say when you aren't looking to be completely annihilated in like two days."

"Start with this," Guillory said, and Fergus heard something slide across the ground. It struck his foot, and he looked down to find a penknife. "Someone left it in this cell. They loosed me as soon as I was inside, so I didn't need it, but you never know . . . "

"Well, at least it can cut these," Fergus said, maneuvering around to pick up the knife and start sawing at the cords. "So you're saying my only hope is to get on that lift and then get past all the guards at the gate?"

"Essentially, yes."

"Pretty tall order. How many guards do you suspect I'd have to get through?"

"At the front gate? At least a dozen. You know, if you had the right bargaining material, it might not be as hard."

"Bargaining material?"

"A hostage. Of course, first you'd need a key." Guillory pursed his lips, scratching his chin.

"I'm guessing they don't let us stretch our legs much here."

"But they do bring meals, and all of the guards have keys. There are a number of obstacles throughout the building, though. If you stray from the common passages . . . "

"I'm not worried about that. Even if they shoot on sight, that'd still be better than exorcism," Fergus said, feeling the rope finally give. He dropped the knife and yanked his hands apart. The twine snapped, and he rubbed his wrists. "A penknife isn't a very good weapon. Say I managed to grab the right hostage, I don't think anyone's gonna feel too threatened."

"I know. You'll need a real knife, if not one of their pistols, but it can be arranged if we play our cards right."

"How's that?"

"If we work together, we'll manage," Guillory replied, lips quirking.

"So we need a key, a weapon, and a hostage."

"*You* need a key, a weapon, and a hostage, yes."

"What do you mean, 'you'?"

Guillory shrugged. "I have no intention of trying to escape."

"But why? Didn't you say everyone on this level's up for execution?"

"I don't believe Ashton will go through with it. I'm certain that he'll come around and give me a proper trial, and if that's the case, as I've done nothing wrong, I'm sure justice will see me freed."

Fergus stared at him.

Guillory sighed, looking away. "I know it's hard for you to see, but Ashton is a good man. He's no worse than your Bridges. They both have strong ideas of how things should be, and they both have the strength to push their ideas on others – by force when 'necessary.' You think Bridges is right because you share the same background. However, many humans think Ashton is right, and that Bridges is the monster you see Ashton as."

"And what about the colony?"

"I can't excuse that," Guillory said. "Nor can I justify his hatred of you, nor how he is going about seeing it assuaged. I can tell you this: his feelings stem from a very understandable place."

"What's that?"

"His father was—"

But the echo of boots coming down the hallway cut him off. Fergus pushed away from the door, receding into a corner.

"Food," the guard said.

Fergus heard the jangle of keys. He glanced up as the guard bent down to shove a plate through the space under the bars. A second was jammed into Guillory's cell. He saw the key ring hanging off the guard's belt, out of reach. He remained quietly in the corner until the guard returned from whence he came.

"Same man the last two nights," Guillory said quietly, pulling his tray over and inspecting the food. "I wonder if it's poisoned." He speared a limp carrot on his fork and held it towards the torchlight.

"Poisoned?"

"I imagine there are those who might find it less appalling were I to 'commit suicide.' Hanging the city's so-called hero is bound to cause strife, even if Governor Harriet hopes to make a point by it."

"I think she just wants to get rid of you before you can convince anyone that she's a nutcase."

"Well, yes," Guillory replied, sniffing the carrot and putting it back down in favor of a potato. "Still, if she can find a way to apply these false treason charges, she can use me as a lesson to those harboring sympathies towards hybrids. She'll scare everyone into submission. After all, if Governor Harriet has the power and ruthlessness to kill even me . . . " He chuckled and put the potato down.

"Here, have a roll," Fergus said, tossing one through the bars.

Guillory managed to snatch it before it hit the floor. "Thank you."

"But you really think 'justice will prevail' or whatever?"

"I honestly do, or rather, I have to. I have to believe that the good in Ashton will win out, and that logic, honesty, and fairness still have precedence over fear tactics and force."

"I think we're both gonna die," Fergus said. "But I'd rather die trying to get out of here than be exorcised."

"Exorcism is a terrible fate," Guillory agreed. "I can't imagine that any but the most twisted souls deserve such a thing."

"Not them, either," Fergus replied. "No one. No one has the right to decide something like that about anyone else."

"I know," Guillory said, sighing. "I know. Certainly, you of all people . . . " He bit into the roll and sighed again. "We'll have to get you out of here somehow."

Fergus stared down at the burned sliver of meat and soggy looking vegetables on his plate and nodded listlessly. "Ha. I didn't get a fork. 'Animals eat with their hands,' I guess."

"Fergus," Guillory said softly.

"It's okay. You can have the rest," he said, giving the plate a shove and sending it Guillory's way. "I'm just gonna sleep." He retreated back into his corner, lying down with his back against the wall.

For a moment, the other cell remained silent. Then, Guillory pulled the tray closer.

"I'll wake you before breakfast."

•   •   •

He awoke from dreams of being trapped on a small, slimy rock out at sea. Seagulls circled above him, laughing in the Count's voice. At first, he wasn't sure what had woken him, or where he was. He sat up, finding that he'd been curled in the back corner of his cell. Everything smelled dank and sour. He ran a hand over his face.

"Is that him?"

Fergus blinked and peered up at two men who were loitering outside his cell.

"Stand up!" barked the guard.

He did, curious about who the second man was. As he drew closer to the bars, he found the stranger to be tall and overly thin, but there was an air of grace about him. His hair was long and pulled back into a tight ponytail. His eyes were a deep, still black. He stared at Fergus indifferently before shaking his head.

"No." His accent was the same as Pip's.

"Who are you?" Fergus asked.

"You were traveling with boy and girl, yes?"

"Who are you?"

The guard rapped on the bars with his baton. Fergus flinched at the sound, feeling a headache coming on.

"Where are boy and girl now?"

Fergus sneered. "Dunno what you're talking about."

The guard went red, reaching for his keys, but the strange man put a hand on his arm, shaking his head.

"They are here. I will find them."

Fergus swallowed, dread wringing his stomach.

"Excuse me."

The man turned without giving Fergus a second look and started down the corridor. Fergus pressed against the bars, straining to follow their path, but they disappeared around the bend. He slumped against the door, cursing under his breath.

"I think it'll be harder to find those two than you think," Guillory said, sitting up and rubbing his eyes with a yawn. "Do you know who that was?"

Fergus looked down, nodding. "I think it's the guy they've been running from."

Guillory said nothing. He stood and stretched towards the window, but the base was several inches out of reach. He sighed and sat back down. "They'll bring breakfast soon. We should act then."

"What's your plan?"

"Trick the guard into opening the door, do what you can, and run. Otherwise, I have quick fingers."

"Weird hearing that from you."

"It won't be easy either way. As soon as you're free, go."

"But what about you?"

"As I said, I'm not sold on the idea that Ashton can go through with this."

"Hey, Guillory, what happened to Raja and Evelyn?"

Guillory shook his head. "I don't know. They weren't brought here, so I believe they're still alive."

"How do you know?"

"I don't. It's just intuition. But I get the feeling Ashton is up to something."

Fergus nodded, tucking the comment away for later. He slowly got up and began looking for anything he could make use of.

"Guess I could always fake an attack or something. Works in books," he said, eyeing the floor and contemplating whether he could pull it off convincingly.

"You could," Guillory agreed, "but it might draw too much attention."

He chewed his lower lip, still searching the cell. "I wonder if insulting him is gonna be enough to get him to open the door."

"Take off your shirt."

"What?"

"Take it off."

"Um, okay," Fergus said, slowly peeling it off. It was most certainly not the shirt he'd arrived in, but a rough, tan shift. He held it out in front of him and curled his nose, noticing just how sour it smelled. "What am I suppose to do with this?"

"Rip it up."

He raised an eyebrow, but shrugged and began to tear the shirt at the seams.

"You'll need to make it into strips. Hurry now. We don't have long. Tear up enough so that when you tie them together, you can make a rope."

Fergus began to rip more earnestly until half the shirt was a pile of uneven strips. He thought he had an idea of what Guillory wanted from him now, though he felt rather uncomfortable with it, easily picturing Flynn's feet dangling as he hung suspended in their old apartment. He tasted bile at the back of his throat, but swallowed it and quickly tied the pieces together.

"Now, be careful to make it so that it isn't really tied, but looks so. You'll need to be able to get up fast when he opens the door. Probably this is just as likely to rouse unwanted attention as faking an attack, but then again, maybe he'll be alarmed enough to inspect first and shout later," Guillory said, leaning against the bars as he watched Fergus work. "No, don't tie it there. You'll need to lure him into the cell. Yes, that should be far enough. All right, sit with your back against the bars. Very good. No, wait, I can see that it's untied. Hurry now! I think I can hear him."

Fergus hastily hid the end of the makeshift rope, holding it under his chin. He bit his lip.

"Lean forward. You have to make it look like you're being held up by . . . Yes, okay, perfect. Now stay still until he comes inside."

Fergus tried to still his features, closing his eyes, and leaned forward as best he could to make the rope look taut. He held the end under his chin, hoping that the strain in his back and shoulders wasn't obvious. Slowly, from somewhere down the corridor, he could hear the heavy tread of boots on stone. He strained his ears, but could only detect one person's worth of footsteps. He forced himself not to worry his lip, to sigh, or to flinch, as the guard rounded the corner and stopped in front of the cells.

There was a moment of silence before the man dropped a metal plate and shoved it under the bars of Guillory's cell. He turned towards Fergus.

"You needn't bother," Guillory said, and Fergus could hear him pull his tray closer, picking up the utensils.

"What?"

"You needn't bother with that one. I suppose it makes sense. I mean, when your choices are suicide or annihilation . . . "

"What do you mean?" the guard asked, and Fergus hoped he was looking at Guillory, because he was sure his shoulders had tensed.

"When I woke up, he was like that."

Fergus knew without hearing or seeing that the guard had turned to him. He did his best to remain relaxed while still pulling on the rope. The second plate went crashing, and the guard cursed loudly, fumbling for his keys. Fergus held his breath, keeping his eyes mostly closed, and tried not to swallow, but the anticipation was building with every fretful thump of his heart. He heard the key catch in the latch, and the guard threw the door open. It shrieked on rusty hinges before smacking against the wall. It echoed loudly, but Fergus paid it no heed.

One step, two, three, and the guard had reached him. He could see the man's knees bending as he reached out to check Fergus's pulse, and he struck. Even he was surprised by how quickly he moved. The knuckles of his right hand connected with the man's temple. He didn't even make a sound as his eyes rolled into the back of his head, and he fell onto Fergus. Fergus threw aside the rope and pushed the guard away. He leapt to his feet and hurried to the door, trying to yank the keys free of the lock, but they seemed to have jammed. He cursed under his breath, but they refused to come loose.

"Leave them!" Guillory said.

"No, I can get you out of here," Fergus said, bracing one foot against the bars and yanking.

"Go! Just go! Someone's coming!"

"I heard a weird sound. Is everything . . .?"

Fergus looked up to see a second guard rounding the corner. The man looked at him, and he at the man. Before he could move, the guard began shouting.

"Run!" Guillory hissed, face pressed between the bars.

"I'll come back for you!" he whispered, before barreling into the guard, shoving him against the wall.

There was a moment of intense grappling. He felt the man's nails bite into his arms. By pure luck, he came out the victor, catching the guard by the lapels of his jacket and slinging him aside. He turned and began running even before the man hit the floor. Footsteps echoed from the hallway ahead, and he knew he wouldn't be able to use the lift. As he sprinted forward, he caught sight of a little hallway leading off from the corridor and managed to slip down it just as he saw the first shadows coming around the bend. He stopped, holding his breath, and pressed against the wall, listening to the men running past.

Out of the corner of his eye, he saw a set of stairs. He briefly recalled Guillory's warning, but more footsteps were following the first group, and he didn't think he could make it to the lift in one piece. He turned and bolted down them. The stones bruised his feet, but he could already hear the men rerouting, realizing where he'd gone and giving chase.

The stairs coiled round and round, spiraling down to the bottom level. There was an unpleasantly wide gap between each floor and the bannister, and though he didn't have time to take a good look, he could tell by the shadows that it was a free fall, possibly all the way down to the first floor. He tried not to imagine what would happen if he slipped.

Distracted by this worry and the echo of boots growing ever closer, Fergus didn't even realize someone was coming *up* the stairs until he bowled into them. It was Ashton Harriet, and perhaps Fergus was lucky that he had run into him, because he inadvertently knocked the pistol from Harriet's hand. The revolver went flying into the air, end over end, and disappeared.

"You," Harriet snarled.

"Outta the way!" Fergus said, trying to push past him, but Harriet latched onto him like a small, angry dog, and Fergus couldn't force him to let go.

He could hear the other guards just above, and he knew that if he didn't free himself now, he'd be thrown back in the cell, handcuffed, and there wouldn't be a second chance to evade exorcism. He writhed about violently, no longer concerned with the drop off. Harriet's grip gave, and Fergus threw himself backwards. The Captain made a grab for him just as Fergus realized he'd thrown his weight a little too far and there wasn't enough railing to support him. He toppled over the side of the stairs, Harriet still attached.

For a moment, he saw Harriet's eyes widen, and then there was the horrible feeling of gravity dragging him through unsupported space into the shadows.

·

Chapter Five.

Fergus wasn't sure how far they'd fallen. He looked up and saw unremitting blackness. His back, head, and shoulder throbbed. Slowly, he flexed his fingers and toes, making sure they were operational, then ankles and wrists, forearms and shins, thighs and upper arms. Finally, he stretched his back, feeling bruised muscle scream in protest, but respond nonetheless. He carefully sat up, probing his scalp. No blood came away, but he felt woozy. He leaned forward, head between his legs, and coughed softly. The world did not immediately settle.

He needed to ascertain Harriet's whereabouts, figure out where he was, and find the nearest route of escape before Harriet came to, but even with a kelpie's innate capacity to see in the dark, it was hard to pierce the gloom. Very slowly and carefully, he felt around him. His fingers brushed thick woolen cloth. He bit his lip and continued. A cold metal button. A warm body.

Well, that was the Harriet Mystery solved.

He rolled onto his knees and pressed his fingers to Harriet's throat. His pulse twitched rhythmically. Fergus sighed, sitting back. The jackass was alive, at least.

Wobbling and queasy, Fergus pushed himself to his feet. Waiting for his eyes to adjust seemed futile, but he thought he should try anyway. He counted to nearly 200 before he could make out the dim outlines of crates and trunks filling the corridor. Without any doubt, he'd landed on one of those queer, labyrinthine floors Guillory had warned him about.

He cursed under his breath.

For a moment, he considered giving Harriet a kick. His chances of finding his way out seemed morbidly low and the likelihood of starving to death grossly high, though if he did die here, he wouldn't be exorcised. That didn't cheer him up. He bit his lip, racking his brain for a plan.

He could hear the whisper of wind coming from somewhere down the hallway. A crack in the wall might not do him much good, but it might shed some light on his proximity to the first floor. He held out his hand, trying to feel for the exact direction, but the entire area felt drafty. He'd have to go by sound. He limped towards the whistle, but didn't make it three steps before something latched onto his ankle.

"You're not . . . going anywhere," Harriet gritted out.

"Let go!" Fergus shook his leg, but Harriet held tight.

"Never. I'll never let go."

Harriet reached for his other ankle, but Fergus threw himself backwards and broke free. He fell against the wall, grunting as his battered body met the unforgiving stone.

He heard a click.

"I fell next to my gun. How unfortunate for you."

"You won't hit me in the dark."

"I'm willing to try."

Fergus pushed away from the wall, moving as quietly as he could. Being barefoot might have been an advantage, but Harriet was recovering his bearings, too. Either that, or he was very lucky. Fergus could just make out the arm holding the revolver, and it was aimed a little too accurately for his liking. He smelled the discharge before he saw it flash. The bullet struck the wall close to where he'd been standing. Bits of stone shattered, pelting him. He froze. Harriet cursed, and he could hear him pulling back the hammer for another shot.

Harriet fired again, and this time, Fergus felt a lock of hair over his left ear lift as it buzzed by. He gasped, stumbling into a pile of old boxes and knocking them to the floor. A third shot nearly got him in the leg before he could extricate himself from the mess. Harriet stood, though seemed incapable of fully straightening. One hand clutched his side, but the other kept the gun trained steadily in Fergus's direction.

It occurred to Fergus that even if Harriet ran out of bullets, he probably had another round on him. If he didn't want Harriet chasing him around, trying to incapacitate him by shooting him in some unpleasantly nonfatal area, he'd have to get the gun away from him.

He leapt over the fallen boxes, lunging at Harriet, and managed to tackle him around the waist. The gun went off again, deafening him as he and the Captain collapsed in a pile of jerking limbs and flailing fists – both striking the other wherever they could.

Harriet clocked him in the temple, and his eyes filled with stars. He shook his head and seized Harriet's gun hand, slamming it against the floor. Something popped, and Harriet let out a cry of pain, dropping the weapon. Fergus grabbed it and threw it as hard as he could into the darkness.

"Damn you!" Harriet snarled, going straight for his throat with both hands.

Fergus tried to pry Harriet's fingers away, but he only pressed harder. He felt nails breaking his skin as the Captain squeezed with ever increasing ferocity. His face turned hot, and little black dots erupted in his eyes. Panic broke over him, and he punched wildly, managing to hit Harriet in the eye. The Captain hissed and loosened his hold just enough that Fergus was able to tear away, half-falling, half-scrambling backwards. He clutched his throat, panting roughly.

It looked like the Captain was about to go searching for his gun, but Fergus cut him off, grabbing him by the back of his jacket and spinning him around to fling him into the boxes. Harriet disappeared into the downed crates, knocking more free from their stacks.

Fergus paused and prodded his throat, still trying to catch his breath. He wondered if he should just run for it, but he had a feeling Harriet was not going to let him disappear into the maze of corridors so easily, and he didn't fancy being hunted down by the Captain. It seemed he'd have to incapacitate Harriet somehow, but he felt it inhumane to leave him stranded.

The boxes stirred. Fergus wondered if he stood a chance of reasoning with the man. The odds were against him, but it would be better than tying him up and leaving him to his fate. Even if it was Ashton Harriet, he didn't like the idea of abandoning someone to starve to death.

"Stop," Fergus said, watching Harriet prod his head. He could smell blood. His stomach growled. He pushed the hunger aside, starting towards the wall across from Harriet, but keeping his back to it. "Just stop and think."

Harriet cursed, still trying to free himself from the debris.

"Guillory told me this place is like a maze. We landed in some weird place, and I bet you don't know where we are any more than I do."

"And?" Harriet snapped, though for just a moment, he paused in his struggle.

"And he told me it was easy to get lost here and never be found. I dunno about you, but that sounds like a pretty miserable way to die, wandering around in this dungeon, hungry, thirsty, and cold. Rotting in here."

"My men *will* find me."

"Maybe. But if he was right, you've only got a fifty-fifty chance. You and I both know he's right a lot of the time."

The Captain was silent.

"So unless you're thinking of resorting to cannibalism while you wait – *if* they ever find you, that is – it's in your best interest to stop trying to kill me."

"How so?"

"For one thing, if you really wanna play rough, I can turn into a fairy and take you down before you can blink."

"How dare—"

"And for another, I see better in the dark, I've got a better sense of smell, a better sense of hearing . . . There's a chance I could find a way out. You, though, are at the mercy of your men's competence, and given that I got out in the first place . . . "

Harriet didn't reply, but Fergus could just make out his face. He looked thoughtful, if dour. Fergus remained quiet and ready as he waited for the Captain to finish mulling over his argument. He wasn't certain he was right. Sure, as a hybrid, he did have superior senses to a human, and as a kelpie, he had a natural penchant for finding water. Still, this place was known for being impenetrable, and he doubted Guillory would have warned him about getting lost if he didn't think that it might be too much for even Fergus's heightened senses.

It sounded good, though. It sounded like something Terry would say, and Terry was good at being convincing.

"And then what? Will you peacefully return to your cell to await your sentence?"

"No."

Harriet glared. Fergus wondered if he was trying to look him in the face. He was about a foot and a half off.

"Then it seems like it would be in my interests to kill you."

"How so? Weren't you the one saying you wanted to make sure all the hybrids could never come back? If you kill me now, you won't be able to exorcise me."

"Yes, but if you make a break for it, you'll be evading punishment altogether."

"I haven't committed any crimes."

"You are a suspect in the murder of Trevor Fennis *and* the arson in the slums, as well as an accessory to William Guillory's treason."

"He's just 'William Guillory' to you now?"

Harriet looked away.

"Look, I dunno why you hate us so much. I dunno why you hate *me* so much. I dunno why you're calling Guillory a traitor when we both know he's the furthest thing from it. But don't call what you're doing justice. Don't talk about punishment and crimes. Whatever your agenda is, it passed 'justice' by long ago."

"Don't act like you know everything! Hybrids are monsters! Sociopathic demons who murder and eat humans!"

Fergus snorted. "If that's the case, then why didn't all the hybrids in New Peiling just eat the humans years ago? Would've saved them the trouble of being swept up into the colony and exorcised for no reason."

"I am defending the human population. I am protecting *humanity*. The reason this concept eludes you is because you're one of them – another *monster*."

Fergus snarled, taking a step forward. "The only monster *I* see is the one weaseling around under a bunch of garbage. There are a lot of people who think the world would be better off without people like you."

Harriet went very still, but his eyes were defiant. "So you're going to kill me?"

"I'm not like you. I'm *not* a monster."

"Are you joking?"

"Just shut up before I show you scary. The way I see it, you have two choices: you let me go and try to find your own way out, or you come with me, but I'm not gonna just walk right back into that cell and let you exorcise me cuz I'm a hybrid. If I could've been a full human like you, believe me, I would've been. Nearly all of us would've picked your life over what we got."

"I have other choices."

"Your chances of survival are a lot slimmer, though."

"Fine. I'll allow you to travel with me, but only because when we're out of here, I *will* see you back in your cell, awaiting trial."

"You can try," Fergus replied with a shrug.

The Captain gingerly climbed to his feet, favoring his left ankle.

Fergus bit back an, "Are you all right?" Instead, he turned towards the sound of the wind, closing his eyes and trying to feel for it again.

"I think there's a window or something this way," he said, heading into the darkness.

Harriet did not immediately follow, and Fergus wondered if he was trying to find his revolver. For a moment, Fergus considered making a run for it. He could probably put a good distance between them while Harriet was busy limping around in the dark. However, presently, he heard Harriet shuffling along behind him.

Even the echo of his footsteps sounded begrudging. Fergus snorted softly, shaking his head, but he had to admit, he felt relieved that he wasn't going to spend the next however many hours playing cat and mouse with the Captain.

They soon reached a wall with a long, narrow crack climbing up the brick. By pressing his face to the break, Fergus could see the sky and the hint of sea, which meant they were yet on a high floor. He sighed, rubbing the back of his neck, and looked around. The slim grey light did little to illuminate the passage. It simply drew a line over yet another stack of boxes.

Harriet paused to have a hopeful peek through the crack, as Fergus continued ahead. He heard Harriet trip over something and paused just a moment to glance back, but the Captain righted himself before Fergus could see what he'd gotten into. He continued on silently, mostly so he'd hear if Harriet changed tactics and attacked him. All he had to go on was a presumably superior sense of hearing, which he doubted would give him an edge should Ashton opt to jump him from behind. It was hard to concentrate on where he was going for worrying about that.

Besides which, the cold was becoming progressively more uncomfortable. The chill sewed itself into his abused muscles. He shivered, wishing he had something to cover up with.

Then he ran into the wall.

"Ow!" he hissed, clasping both hands over his nose.

It hurt like it was bleeding, but he couldn't see his fingers to properly check. Behind him, Harriet snickered, and he turned to give him his very worst glare, which went unseen in the darkness of the corridor.

"Dead end," Harriet drawled.

Fergus's eye twitched.

"Where to now? I thought you had superior eyesight or something."

Fergus took a deep breath, counting backwards. His skin burned under the surface. He breathed out through gritted teeth and forced himself to smile.

"Maybe you should go first. It'd be one less thing to distract me."

"And give you the chance to launch yourself at me from behind? I think not."

Fergus pursed his mouth, feeling his temper splintering. "Side-by-side, then."

"Like we're friends? Pals? Best mates? No, you're the one who said you could find a way out. You lead the way, and I will follow."

"Like a dog."

"If you will," Harriet replied, shrugging.

"What the hell is your problem? What do you have against me?"

"A lot of things. I have a lot of things against you."

"Name one thing. Spit it out. One thing that gives you the right to be such an enormous jackass."

"My father."

"Your father."

He could just barely make out the shape of Harriet's mouth as it curled back over his teeth.

"That's right, *my father*."

"What about him?"

"You ate him."

"Excuse me?" Fergus said, drawing himself to his full height. "I've never eaten anyone."

"Not you, you idiot. Your kind. The monsters."

Fergus said nothing. He vaguely recalled Rosslyn telling him something about Harriet's father dying, but the details eluded him.

"Broke into our apartment, murdered him, and then . . . "

Harriet was breathing hard, shoulders heaving, his words spilling forth with a fervor that made Fergus's skin crawl.

"Hey, take it easy."

"It was eating him. *Eating* him. Like he was an animal. Like a . . . a rabbit."

Fergus pressed against the wall, searching out of the corner of his eye for an escape route, as Harriet continued, his voice growing more frantic and heated, the words tripping over one another.

"He was too disfigured for an open coffin. Mother didn't want me to see, but I did. I *saw*."

Fergus held his breath. It looked like the corridor might continue to his left, but he couldn't be sure. His eyes flicked back to Harriet, still trapped in the recollection of his father's final disfigurement. Not sure what he should say, he remained silent, hoping Harriet would pull himself together. Part of him wanted to point out that horrible things happened to all kinds of people all the time, but he thought that would only incense the Captain further. He didn't feel that condolences would have much effect either, and though he felt sorry for Harriet, he also felt angry that he was being blamed for something that had probably happened before he was born.

"Well? Why aren't you saying anything?"

"What should I say?" Fergus carefully asked.

"I thought you would have some kind of defense. I want to hear it. Why don't you think hybrids are dangerous? Why do you not acknowledge that all of you have the capability to hurt humans, like my father?"

"The capacity to do something horrible to someone who doesn't deserve it is there in everyone, human or hybrid. Being human doesn't make you any less likely to kill someone; being hybrid any more. Yeah, cannibalism is messed up, but so is rounding up a bunch of innocent people and wiping them off the face of the planet for the crime of one."

"It's not the same!"

"*It is!*" Fergus shouted right back, but then stopped himself. He shook his head, looking away, and took a deep breath. "Me? I've felt weird things. I've dealt with them. I have to live with the fact that they exist in the first place, but I do. You? You gave into your feelings and called it something pretty so that you didn't have to feel bad about it. You have no right to judge me or anyone else until you look at what you've done – what you're doing. You had my best friend killed. For all I know, you were the one who murdered him."

"So why don't you avenge him? You're the one who has *all* the power. Isn't that what you said before? So put his soul to rest. Oh wait, I forgot. *It's gone.*"

Fergus bit his cheeks, nails cutting into his palms.

"No," he said quietly. "His soul is still out there. But even if he was gone, I wouldn't go around assuming all humans are evil and should be murdered before they can get us."

"Then why don't you kill the monster behind it all? The one who *is* out to get you?"

Fergus shook his head. "Do you want to die? If you do, go ahead. Just sit down right here and starve. If I killed you, it'd just make you a martyr and me a monster. There'd be no point, and moreover, it'd go against everything I believe."

"And what *do* you believe?"

"Same as Guillory. That we can get along. That there's no reason for us to hate you, or for you to hate us. That if we're treated as equals, things will get better for everyone."

Harriet looked away. "William Guillory is a naïve, absurd idealist."

"You believed in him once."

"Once," Harriet agreed dully.

"So what changed?"

His head whipped up, dark curls bouncing. "He betrayed the city."

"But *how*?"

"He abandoned it on the cusp of its most volatile election. Do you know how hard it was to maintain any semblance of order when he left? The men under me questioned my orders. The people became unruly."

"Maybe it was because they were looking at a regime that was gonna round them up and start exorcising them."

Harriet shot him a dirty look. "There were riots all over. There were hardly enough of us to suppress them."

"And yet I bet you still had plenty of time to run around with Evalach playing 'Bedevere.'"

"No, I didn't."

"So you just thought you'd incorporate it into the system – take care of two birds with one stone?"

"You're awfully pithy today. No, none of this has been half as easy or simple as you're trying to make it sound."

Fergus shrugged.

At least Harriet had calmed down, so he could safely continue searching for an exit. They needed to find it sooner than later. He hadn't eaten since the day before, and he was starting to really feel the bruises and scrapes from the fall. But they still had a long way to go. How could they possibly find a way down before he succumbed to pain and fatigue?

He chewed his lower lip. Was his stamina good enough to outlast Harriet? If it wasn't, he was likely to wind up back in his cell. He couldn't imagine that there wouldn't be a struggle at the end of this: Harriet trying to force him back behind bars, and Fergus jockeying to take Harriet hostage. The one who possessed the greater stamina would be the victor, and his life depended on it.

"What's with this place?" he suddenly muttered, looking around. "I mean, it's just a big, dumb tower in the middle of nowhere."

"And?"

"So how is it possible to get so lost in it?"

"I thought you had *all* the resources you needed to find a way out."

Fergus glared.

"Magic."

"Magic?"

The Captain nodded briefly. "Yes, magic."

"Okay, well, can you explain that?"

Harriet began to walk forward, brushing past him. "Not right now. Right now, we should keep going before night falls, and things get *interesting*."

Fergus narrowed his eyes, but Harriet had already disappeared around the corner before he could demand an explanation.

Chapter Six.

Drip. Drip. Drip.

Fergus licked his lips, chapped from hours of wandering the maze of hallways. His tongue felt fuzzy. His throat twinged. There was water somewhere ahead, hidden in the gloom. He didn't care that the puddle was probably fetid. If he could just find it, he could purify it, but every time he thought they were close, they hit another wall. He was out of patience, out of stamina, and he was getting dizzier by the minute.

"Tired already?" Harriet drawled.

Fergus *tsked*, realizing he'd allowed himself to lean on the wall a moment too long. "Not really."

"Probably cold, too, aren't you? And sore and hungry, and I thought I saw a bit of blood on the side of your neck. Guessing that must be paired with an awful headache."

"*Not really*," Fergus repeated. He forced his jaw to relax. "I'm surprised you can see so well."

"Human eyes also adapt to the dark given time, and by my reckoning, we've been walking for at least three hours, possibly four."

Fergus strained his ears, trying to locate the source of the water and drown Harriet out, but he just kept talking.

"We still aren't anywhere close to an exit, and I imagine we only have two or three hours before the sun sets."

"You still haven't said what's gonna happen when it does," Fergus said.

Harriet was wearing that superior smirk yet again, but Fergus was too tired to feel annoyed. He just stared, expressionless, from his resting place. The clamminess had already settled deep inside his bones. It was a minor complaint compared to the pounding of his head and the dryness of his mouth. Harriet's arrogance was easily the least of his worries. But what with the ominous remarks about the sunset, Fergus wondered why he was acting so self-satisfied. Whatever was about to happen was going to happen to him, too.

Then it hit him.

"You're scared."

"What?" Harriet halted, dark eyes narrowing.

He looked even more pantherine than usual, the lines of his shoulders tense, his face shadowed. Fergus wondered if he was planning to lunge.

"You're all cagey and fidgety. You're scared."

"I am *not* afraid."

"What happens when it gets dark?" Fergus demanded. "Does it have something to do with the magic you were talking about before? What is this place?"

78

Without warning, his legs failed. Too tired to be surprised, he gave into gravity without protest, sinking against the wall. Sighing, he looked up at Harriet and tried to muster enough energy to look exasperated. Harriet's eyes were angry slits, his mouth a white line. He clearly didn't want to answer, and yet Fergus was pretty sure he would. He couldn't keep whatever he was worrying about a secret much longer.

Harriet cursed softly, kicking the ground. "Of course, it does."

"And?" Fergus asked as gently as he could manage.

"And then the bogeymen will come out."

"If there are 'bogeymen' in here, how come I didn't hear or see them last night?"

"They don't often venture into the populated areas of the prison, but once in a while, we find a mangled prisoner in one of the near-forgotten cells."

"Well, that's just great. So there's some kind of magical monster in here."

"Something like that, yes," Harriet said, nodding.

Fergus didn't know what "something like that" meant, but he got the picture. He sighed, peering into the shadows ahead.

"The halls seem to be dark all the time, so why don't the monsters come out now?"

"I think the magic that draws them out is weaker during the day. I don't know. I'm not a wizard."

"Okay. Well, we obviously aren't going to find our way out before nightfall, so what do we do?"

Harriet fell into a pensive silence. Now that he'd put aside the haughtiness, Fergus could see the lines of worry knitting his mouth and eyes. He looked like an old man, and Fergus felt mildly sorry for the jerk with his phobia of magic and fairies and bogeymen. However, before he could think of something consoling to say, Harriet spoke.

"Barricade ourselves as best we can. We'll take some of these crates and build a wall in one of the dead ends. If we make it small enough, they shouldn't be able to sneak up on us."

"You act like they can walk through walls."

"I have no idea how they travel," Harriet said, and a chill went down Fergus's spine.

He cleared his throat. "Better get to work."

•   •   •

By the time they finished building their makeshift fort, Fergus was so sore and exhausted, he could hardly stand. His mouth felt swollen, too, which made the continuous sound of water all the more galling. If he couldn't have a drink soon, he was going to resort to licking condensation from the walls. Harriet was unsympathetic. Probably he was just as hungry, thirsty, and tired, but he was fastidiously hiding it. Still, Fergus noticed that the Captain wasn't putting in an equal effort with the crates. He was somewhat amazed that Harriet could move around at all after that fall. He was still favoring his right ankle.

Thinking he could deal with "monsters" in the dark better than Harriet, Fergus offered to make one last effort to find the source of the dripping. He wasn't sure how long a human could survive without water, though he was fairly sure it wasn't that long, and he doubted a hybrid would be any better off, so he set out alone.

His head spun with every *plink* of a droplet meeting a larger body of water. He fumbled in the blackness, drawn ever forward by the haunting promise of hydration. He tripped over something that sounded like kindling, but when he glanced down, he saw white. Suppressing a shudder, he continued on until at last he found the source of the dripping.

The pool was hardly two feet in diameter and well below an inch deep. It probably was rank, too, but Fergus didn't care. He cast himself upon the floor, pressing his mouth to the stone. As his lips touched the grimy puddle, the liquid grew clearer, the smell of standing water and decay vanishing. He thought he could easily drink the entire supply, but restrained himself for Harriet's sake.

He sat up, licking his lips. He didn't have anything to carry the remainder in. He frowned, wondering how to get around that, when the sound of something large and unpromising arose nearby.

No time to find a container.

He ripped a scrap from the leg of his thin cotton trousers, soaking it until there was hardly any water left. Then he rushed back to the crate fort, feeling all the while that something was right behind him. Yet despite his paranoia, every time he looked over his shoulder, there was nothing but tranquil, soundless shadow.

He forced the rag into Harriet's hands, not even looking to see if he was surprised or thankful or annoyed, and began pulling the crates closer and tighter. He doubted they would keep anything out. Certainly, if these monsters were, as he suspected, somehow fairy in nature, it would be a very paltry barrier. Still, it made him feel a little better as he collapsed on the floor beside Harriet, panting softly and closing his eyes. He could hear the other man sucking on the cloth, trying to draw out every last droplet of moisture, ignoring the fact it was coated in sweat and grime.

Fergus busied himself with listening for any large and hungry visitors, but all he could hear was the wind slipping into cracks in the walls and faint drips from even further away. At last, it seemed Harriet had coaxed all the water he could from the rag. He cast it aside and leaned back with a sigh, which sounded more like frustration than relief.

Fergus cleared his throat, but the Captain didn't look at him. Frowning, he asked, "So what is this place? What did you mean it's magical? And why are there monsters here?"

Harriet cracked open an eye, regarding Fergus wearily. "Simple. This island? You won't find it on any map dated before the Cataclysm. It's one of those places where the earth below the ocean rose up above the sea. From the moment construction began, there were complaints of strange accidents and deaths. Construction continued anyway, and it was finished 25 years ago." Harriet paused, drawing his cracked lips between his teeth, and sighed. "When they began filling it with prisoners, they found that in certain areas . . . "

"They'd end up dead."

Harriet nodded. "And in truly gruesome ways. So they closed up part of the prison. We're actually only able to make use of a few floors. Partially because no one wants to clean up what's left behind."

"So I'm guessing these bogeymen are some kinda fairies," Fergus said, scrunching his mouth.

"No one has seen a *corporeal* anything on these grounds, but one can only assume that yes, they must be some sort of," he faltered and then spat out the word, "*fairies*."

Fergus sighed softly, looking away. "Thanks."

"I'm only telling you because I'm badly dehydrated and have taken a fall."

"So," Fergus said, lowering his voice, "if this island is haunted by some kind of fairy ghosts or whatever, why didn't they just close it entirely? Didn't the guards protest?"

Harriet shook his head. "A number of them had served with Captain Guillory. While a few did go missing before the middle floors were closed off, the rest were simply too proud to run away."

"And what's with the whole maze thing?"

"No one is sure. That's why I said it was magic. Their magic. *Your* magic."

Fergus snorted. "Our magic is what's keeping New Peiling from caving in."

Harriet ignored him. "It's the only thing I can think of that could explain why the floors seem to change. The layout will probably be entirely different by morning. We'll have to sleep in shifts to make sure we don't lose the wall behind us in the night."

"That's a disturbing—"

Fergus fell silent. A soft whuffling sound came from the other side of the boxes. He swallowed roughly, his breath catching. He couldn't hear Harriet breathing at all. There was a soft snort and then silence. They both waited, hardly daring to breathe, but no further sound came from the other side.

Fergus let out a shaky breath. He'd dealt with fairies before. Real ones. *Hungry* ones. He was pretty sure he could handle them. But he was bruised and hungry and thirsty and lost in a creepy, half-abandoned prison, and he couldn't shake the growing sense of dread.

He drew his knees up to his chest, resting his chin on them, and stared at the crates. There was only about a yard between him and the boxes. It was, he thought, a very false sense of security. It'd be all too easy for whatever was on the other side to knock the wall down on top of them and then drag them out as they struggled with the boxes.

He kept that to himself.

Harriet had a death grip on his trousers. Fergus could see the outline of each knuckle through his skin. He didn't have to look at the man to know he was terrified. The smell poured off him in heady waves. It was a wonder that whatever had been sniffing around hadn't noticed it, too. Though he felt uneasy deviating from his comfortable half-curl, he reached out to put a hand on Harriet's, trying to silently communicate that he should calm himself. Harriet jerked away, and Fergus saw him glaring out of the corner of his eye, but at least he didn't smell quite as temptingly prey-like anymore.

They remained frozen a few minutes longer, and then Harriet snorted softly.

"I'm surprised you're afraid."

"I'm not afraid." Fergus caught Harriet regarding him incredulously and hardened his gaze. "I'm *not*. I've dealt with at least as bad. It's just cuz you're all jumpy."

"You certainly look scared to me."

"Would you just shut up?"

The crate hit Fergus in the forehead so hard, he blacked out for a moment. The next thing he knew, sharp teeth had latched onto his arm, and he was being dragged through the rubble of the fallen crates. He couldn't see or hear Harriet, but hoped he was safely concealed by the boxes. That was all the time he had for worrying about Harriet's situation. The creature dragged him over the broken wall, the splintered pieces of wood jabbing his battered shoulders. A pained grunt escaped him, and he frantically felt for something – anything – to stall the beast. His fingers scraped the stone floor, one nail breaking, but he found no purchase. There was no salvation in rotting wood.

The creature wrenched him free of the wreckage, and Fergus had half a second to take it in. It was generally human-shaped, but the fairy was far taller than a man, with hulking shoulders and a hunchback. Its entire body was covered in coarse black hair. Long fangs jutted from its lower jaw, growing so thick and long that the buggane[1] couldn't fully close its mouth. More disconcerting yet was its back legs, which were disjointed and goat-shaped. Its eyes smoldered in the darkness.

Fergus realized that it wasn't biting him, but had sunk its claws into his arm. He beat at its hand, but this only annoyed it, and it slung him against the adjacent wall. His head met stone, and pricks of light flooded his eyes. The buggane let out a deafening screech and released him. He staggered and sank to the floor, and the creature stepped over him, seizing him by the throat. He wheezed and clawed at its arm, but his nails didn't even break its skin, and with a rush of terror, he realized he couldn't overpower the beast. He scratched, he kicked, he punched, but the creature remained unfazed.

He was blacking out. The sound of each failed inhalation roared in his ears. It felt like every blood vessel in his head was bursting. His arms wouldn't lift. His legs wouldn't kick. Panic ebbed, spilling away with the strength of his limbs.

At least he'd managed to get Terry back to the city. Maybe Terry had already found Ursula and Rosslyn. Maybe the three of them were already making plans to rescue all the hybrids in the colony and stop New Peiling from falling – to keep Guillory from being executed, to win the humans over. But then, it was Ursula, Rosslyn, and Terry: Ursula, who hated humans; Rosslyn, who simply wanted to be left alone; and Terry, who solved far too many problems with force, and Ursula would support Terry. Probably Rosslyn would, too.

If Fergus died here, it would make both Terry and Ursula very angry. It was easy to envision what would happen next. The Count would say Fergus had stepped out for a minute and never returned. Terry and Ursula would search for him. Maybe they'd hear he was taken to the prison. If Harriet managed to survive and escape – if Fergus was enough to sate the fairy's hunger – he'd say justice had been served by fate's hand itself, and Terry would go ballistic.

He wasn't sure what Ursula would do upon hearing that he was dead a year after they'd parted and not on the happiest of terms. At the very least, she'd be furious that she hadn't been able to keep her promise to his mother. That'd be sufficient reason for her to attack. The Count would back them, hoping to use their anger towards Harriet to deflect blame. He'd make sure to stand behind them and keep his hands clean. If they were strong enough to get rid of Paige Harriet, strong enough to rally the hybrids and take back New Peiling, then he'd get exactly what he wanted. If not, Fergus was sure he'd find a way to make himself look innocent, while Terry and Ursula took the fall.

He deserved to be punched. He deserved be punched by Fergus himself.

His thoughts came back around to Terry. Terry had made so much progress. He was moving away from being Badb Catha, from resolving injustices with violence. He couldn't let Terry fall back on his old ways. He had to survive somehow.

Half-conscious as he was, he was only vaguely aware that he had begun to shift. Bone stretched, muscle regrouped, anatomy rearranged, and he grew. He opened his eyes, turning his head to find himself at least as tall as the buggane. It had lost its grip on his throat during the change, though its claws were still embedded in the side of his neck. With a roar, he reared and thrust it away from him.

Down the alcove, the boxes shifted, and a very befuddled Ashton Harriet emerged. He stared at the buggane in shock. The fairy monster stared right back, and then it rolled onto its hands and knees, scuttling towards him. Harriet had nearly climbed free of the broken crates, but he would never be able to escape before the fairy was on him. He realized it, too. His eyes widened, mouth parting in horror, and he retreated further into the alcove, but he was trapped. Groaning in frustration and terror, he began throwing pieces of wood and the rotting contents of the crates at the buggane, but all his projectiles bounced off its thick skin.

Fergus sprang forward and latched onto its shoulder. His teeth sank into the leathery hide, and the creature howled in pain, clawing at Fergus's face. He jerked his head, tossing it aside. The fairy rolled head over heels, but righted itself on the last spin. It pounced, and Fergus couldn't turn quickly enough in the narrow hall. The buggane clawed its way onto his back, sinking its teeth into his neck, but his mane protected him. He let out an enraged scream, but bucking, rearing, and slamming into the wall was fruitless, and there wasn't enough space to roll.

If he went down, he'd be stuck. If he tried to turn back into a human, he'd be killed in a second.

He was out of options.

Then something struck the fairy in its eye, and it fell to the ground, howling in agony. It rolled around, clutching the shard of wood jutting from its face. Fergus didn't waste a second, but began pummeling the creature until it was a messy lump under his hooves. Then he lifted it by the throat and shook it, just to make sure. The electric tingle of fairy blood poured over his gums and tongue.

Dead. It was definitely dead. Completely, entirely dead.

He stumbled backwards, the sheer relief sending him back into human form. He swayed in place, blood dripping down his face and neck, and stared at the black pool spreading around his feet. He pressed a hand to the gouges in his neck and turned to stare at Harriet.

The Captain stood with another crate at ready, looking pale and bewildered.

"Thanks," Fergus said and abruptly passed out.

Chapter Seven.

There were times when his bedroom was cold and dank no matter how many covers he piled on, how many layers he was wearing, or even if his mother put hot water bottles between the sheets. It was as if the whole lower city was soaking wet, and there was no escape from the chill. The only advantage was that the cold slowed the pace of the mold creeping across the ceiling and up the corners of the apartment.

The building was quiet. Mr. Farrier was not drunkenly blundering around next door. The girls in the flat overhead weren't giggling or playing music. He couldn't even feel the steady thrum of bass from the strip joint. There was only the sound of dripping.

Slow, dismal dripping. Booming, incessant dripping.

The lights of the strip club across the way blinked in rhythmic succession, and his head pounded in time with each flash of red. He groaned and rolled over. Someone touched the side of his face. He blinked up at Flynn, his cheek painted carmine by the inconsistent light, his curls an unruly silhouette on top of his head.

Flynn smiled at him, replacing his hand with a cold, wet cloth. He dabbed at the side of Fergus's neck. Fergus couldn't think of why Flynn would be washing him, but it was Flynn, so he didn't protest. His eyes didn't want to stay open, but he felt afraid that if he closed them, Flynn would disappear, and with a surge of alarm, he found his voice.

"Hi."

"Hi," Flynn replied, wringing out the rag and wetting it anew.

"Found Tír na nÓg."

Flynn made a noncommittal sound, resuming his task.

"Didn't go in."

"I figured."

Flynn's eyes twinkled, and Fergus felt something in his stomach knot.

"Would you have?" he asked.

"Maybe," Flynn replied, scrubbing more vigorously.

Fergus hissed in pain, but made no move to stop him. "Hey, Flynn?"

"Yes?"

"Don't leave, okay?"

"Give me one good reason I should stay."

Fergus blinked and found himself somewhere dark and unfamiliar. His lips and tongue tingled. He swallowed roughly, tasting fairy blood, and turned his gaze to Harriet, who was dabbing at his wounds with a dirty cloth.

"Where's Flynn?" he mumbled.

"I don't know who that is," Harriet muttered, wringing out the cloth before reapplying it.

He closed his eyes. The cold bled into his skin, teasing his wounds. The discomfort would've kept him awake normally, but he couldn't find it in himself to care presently.

"Flynn," he mumbled, sinking back into sleep.

He stood on a forest path, surrounded by trees with white bark. The forest floor was carpeted in red leaves, though the branches looked full. There was something vulgar about the richness of the leaves.

It was very cold, though no wind rustled the branches. Fergus shivered, wrapping his arms around himself. He turned in a circle, searching for anything he could take shelter in. Amidst the trees, he saw a single wooden bench. Breaking from the path, he hurried towards it and found that just before the bench was a pond. Steam rose from the surface of the murky water.

Forgetting about the bench, he knelt by the water's edge, holding out his hands. Even that fragment of heat was something, and he thought his hands did feel marginally warmer. He didn't even notice when the surface began to bubble.

A black shape rose from the water, and he looked up at the horse towering over him. Water poured down its sleek coat. Vapor rose from its back. It turned one white marble eye on him and drew back its lips in an evil grin, revealing broad, bloodstained fangs.

"Hello," he said to the kelpie.

It snorted, the gust of air blowing his hair from his face. He shivered.

"I'm not about to die, am I?" he asked, recalling that the last time he'd seen the kelpie, he'd been on the verge of having his powers stolen in a forbidden ceremony.

The kelpie just stared at him. He noticed that with each exhalation, its body seemed to shimmer, becoming momentarily skeletal and grotesque, before it breathed in, becoming a splendid black horse once more. He cleared his throat, wondering if he should be worried or not.

"Don't recall it being more than a scratch, so I think we're okay. Well, as long as I don't end up with pneumonia," he added, subtly shifting away from the fairy. But the kelpie just continued to silently regard him. He frowned up at it, brows pinching in annoyance. "You're kinda pissing me off, you know that?"

It tossed its head. Its snort almost sounded like a chuckle.

Fergus glowered. "What?"

The kelpie began to slowly back away, its back legs disappearing into the muddy water.

"Wait," Fergus said, taking a step forward. "Wait! What is it? Why are you here?"

But the fairy ignored him, continuing to sink into the pond.

"Wait!"

The kelpie slid off the bank. Only its head remained above the steaming surface.

"Tell me what you want from me!" Fergus skittered to the edge of the bank and looked down at it. "What is it?"

It ignored his questions and slid under the water. He could swear it was giving him a disappointed look.

"Wait!" he shouted once more, but the kelpie was gone. He punched the surface of the pond in frustration.

"You'll go together."

He whirled around to find Terry standing behind him, dressed in black. His face looked as pale as the bark of the surrounding trees. His hair had a brown tint, like drying blood.

Fergus swallowed thickly, biting his lower lip. "Terry?"

"You'll go together," Terry repeated, closing the gap between them. He reached out and shoved Fergus into the water.

Fergus screamed, water filling his mouth. It was cold. So very cold. He screamed again.

"Be quiet!"

Harriet was holding his hand over Fergus's mouth. It smelled of dirt and mildew. Something was moving close by. Fergus swallowed, letting his eyes adjust to the darkness, and looked up at Harriet. The Captain held his breath, staring straight ahead. A box shifted, followed by a snort, and then Fergus heard whatever it was shambling away. Harriet released him, sinking against the wall and running both hands over his face. He uttered a soft sigh of relief, and Fergus realized he was trembling.

And he wasn't wearing his jacket.

To his great astonishment, Fergus realized that it was draped over him like a blanket. He looked up from the red jacket to its shivering owner and felt utterly nonplussed.

Harriet didn't take his hands away from his face. "A wound like that, conditions like this . . . a normal man would have died."

"Fairy blood," Fergus muttered hoarsely. He could still feel it stinging his tongue. "How long?"

"It's almost dawn, I think."

Harriet suddenly stiffened. Fergus turned to the wall of crates, but all he could hear was the whistling of the wind through the splintered stone walls.

"They'll be gone soon," he whispered.

Harriet nodded, pressing his hands harder against his face. "If we don't find a way out in the next 12 hours . . . "

"Yeah," Fergus said, trying to keep his eyes open. "I might have an idea, but you aren't gonna like it."

Harriet didn't reply.

"You slept?"

He shook his head.

"You should try."

Harriet shook his head again.

Fergus sighed and closed his eyes. "Why'd you help me?"

"Because . . . you rescued me. You could have let it drag me off. I'm sure things would have been easier for you if you did."

Fergus lapsed into silence. His lip disappeared between his teeth. He gnawed at the dead skin, thinking. Finally, very carefully, he spoke.

"You could have left me here. I bet if I had died, it would've been easier for you. You know, they could've followed the smell of my blood and found you." He hesitated. "But you didn't leave me."

"I didn't."

"I won't come quietly. I'm not gonna let you murder me."

Harriet raised his eyes to the ceiling. "A guard will be poisoning Captain Guillory's dinner."

"What?!"

"*Shh!*"

"Why?" Fergus asked, leaning closer.

"I never . . . I didn't want to arrest the Captain. He's like a father to me. Yet he chose you and left me here to deal with this mess. He knows what happened to my father, and he still sympathizes with you." He looked down at his hands, clasped between his legs.

Fergus waited for him to continue, drawing the jacket closer.

"It bothers me, knowing how much he disapproves of practically everything I've ever believed."

"So why don't you try thinking a little differently?"

Harriet shook his head. "I won't let anyone else go through what happened to my father. Mother is right. Captain Guillory is living in a fantasy. I've always known that. I wanted to believe in his vision, but it's not the reality. This is the reality."

"You or us?"

"In so many words. I didn't give the order to poison him, but I did overhear the talk. I didn't stop it – didn't even make my presence known – because I felt it would be better than a public hanging. Better politically and less painful."

"But kinda cowardly," Fergus said.

Harriet looked up, brow furrowing. "What do you know?"

"I know that if my friend was gonna die cuz of me, I'd want to at least look him in the eye when it happened."

"I don't want him to die," Harriet said, burrowing his face in his knees. He looked very young, and Fergus, though he knew better, pitied him enough to crawl over and sit beside him.

"Are you telling me because you want me to stop it?" Fergus asked, tugging his lower lip.

Silence.

"But he's way up there on that top floor."

"He'll be brought down. Nicer accommodations preceding the execution. That's the standard."

"How thoughtful."

"Frankly, I loathe you. I helped you, because you did a favor by me, and I need your help to rescue the Captain, so I'd like to declare a proper truce until he's safe. But believe me when I say this: once that is done, I will put an end to you and all those like you. It's the only way to protect my people."

Fergus blinked. "Well. That was blunt."

"You might consider it a chance to save yourself, if you're smart enough to get away, but this is not a threat. I promise that I will hunt you down someday."

"Don't blame me if you get hurt playing extremist," Fergus said, looking away. "Cuz you better believe I'm not just gonna roll over and die because you want me to."

"Have we reached an understanding?"

Fergus nodded. "Yeah." He sighed, rubbing his hands together. "Well, if you're not gonna sleep, I will."

Harriet nodded. "Until first light, and then I'll listen to this plan of yours."

•　　•　　•

A year ago, Fergus had found himself lost in an enchanted forest. As a human, finding his way out had been a hopeless task. However, as a kelpie, he'd managed it. He wasn't sure he wanted to relive that experience, but here he was. Walking down the hallway, with Harriet holding his mane (perhaps out of fear of more bogeymen, perhaps out of fear of Fergus), he could easily see the walls and doorways moving.

He wondered how the humans could have thought it'd be a good idea to build anything here. Moreover, he wondered why they decided to continue building after the accidents started. He would've thought that after the first few instances, they'd shut down construction and go elsewhere.

But they were so afraid of the intangible, they decided to pretend it wasn't there in the first place. It was the same mentality that had formed the culture of New Peiling. Down in the slums, the hybrids were out of sight, out of mind, and the humans could live their lives without having to give them a second thought.

He supposed hybrids weren't that much better. Declan and Darya Abel, the ringleaders of the Huntsmen – the ones Terry had exiled to Tír na nÓg as punishment for trying to murder Fergus – had steadfastly believed they could overthrow the humans by sacrificing other hybrids and enhancing their powers. In the end, whatever power they'd gleaned from murdering their own still paled in comparison to Terry and Pip's magic.

The Count, too, was just as fearful, just as illogical. How much longer did he think the humans would tolerate him? How was it that he didn't see that Harriet and his ilk weren't the kind who would care about his usefulness in the end? Sure, they might make use of him now, but once they'd finished with the hybrids in the colony, they'd get rid of him, too, and find a full human to replace his engineering know-how. They *weren't* really all that different.

Though full humans did smell much more delicious. He tried to ignore that, as well as the uncomfortable way Harriet was pulling on his mane.

They were close to the exit now. He could smell fresh sweat and grime-caked bodies. They'd been steadily descending for the last few hours, and Fergus thought they must be near the bottom of the tower. Turning the corner, they met a curious wall. Lamplight leaked out along a thin fissure – a trapdoor. Harriet bolted, but though he grunted and threw his entire weight against the wall, it wouldn't budge. Fergus walked up behind him, feeling annoyed, like he ought to bite the human for the attempted betrayal, for the insolence.

However, Fergus controlled his inner fairy and head-butted Harriet aside, so that he could press against the wall. It didn't yield easily, but he did feel the minutest give. He pushed even harder, digging in with his back legs, and heard a low grinding noise. Bits of rock and dust came loose as the wall slowly turned, emptying out into a deserted cell replete with human bones. This must have been one of the "unsafe" floors, Fergus thought, snorting at a grimy old femur.

The iron bars of the cell were rusted, and it took little effort to knock the door from its hinges. It banged loudly on the floor, and Fergus listened for the sound of rushing guards. His ears flicked back and forth, but he could hear no cries of alarm, so he turned and snorted at Harriet. The narrow cell window revealed the red-orange glow of sunset, and he tossed his head, turning and stamping the ground impatiently. Now came the part of the plan that was going to be unpleasant for both of them.

The Captain cautiously approached him, brow furrowed and eyes narrowed. He was wasting time. Fergus came over to him and head-butted him in the chest, nearly knocking him over. He wished that he could speak. For a moment, he tried to. However, all that came out was a growling sound. Harriet got the message. Scowling, he took a handful of mane, put his other hand on Fergus's hip, and climbed onto his back.

It felt unnatural to have his worst enemy perched on top of him, but soon the guards would be bringing Guillory his evening meal, and it would all be over. He tossed his head, which meant, "Which way?"

"Left," Harriet said, giving Fergus a little kick.

Fergus resisted the urge to buck him off and plunged down the hallway. His hooves thundered in the empty passageway, and he was sure the guards would come running at any minute. They reached a stairwell. He tried to go as quickly as he could manage, but his body wasn't meant for narrow steps. He leapt free of them the moment the landing was in sight, hitting the floor hard enough that his knees ached. Harriet slipped from his back. Now he could hear the ocean crashing against the rocks outside. He smelled brine and fresh sea air. Moreover, he could hear and smell humans. Shouting came from around the bend.

"Quickly," Harriet said, scrambling to his feet. "Just ahead you'll find a long hallway that splits in four directions. Go to the furthest door. You'll have to break it down – it's almost constantly locked. Captain Guillory will be in one of those cells. There's a long bridge that connects the prison to the ferry. You're on your own from here." He smacked Fergus hard on the rump.

Fergus cow-kicked, glancing Harriet's leg, and snorted angrily.

"*Go!*"

He didn't need to be told again. Fergus launched into a gallop, turning the corner just as two guards appeared, rifles ready. He barreled right through them, trying not to step on them. The wooden door gave much faster than the iron bars, and he heard a man shout in surprise and pain as it ripped from its hinges, pinning him to the wall. Fergus didn't look back. He ran as fast as he could.

At the end of the hallway, he saw the cell with Guillory inside. Guillory sat by the window, staring out at the ocean, but he turned at the sound of pounding hooves. His mouth parted in surprise, and he got up. Fergus managed to pull up just in time to avoid ramming into the bars. This cell was different. The metal was newer. There was nothing unsound in the bars or stone. He snorted, searching for a spot where the integrity was poor enough that he could smash through.

"Fergus, watch out!"

He turned to see a nearby guard raising his pistol. Fergus reared, lunging at the man. He caught him by the shoulder and felt bones give under his teeth. The guard screamed, and something metallic fell from his pocket, skating across the floor into the cell. The gun dropped from the guard's hand, and Fergus released him to stamp on it, crushing the barrel. The man groaned, hunching down against the bars, and gripped his hair with his uninjured hand.

Fergus turned his attention back to Guillory, tossing his head to try to convey the urgency. The former Captain had the keys in hand, but he didn't move towards the door.

"Fergus, you know I can't."

Fergus snorted, blowing Guillory's hair back from his face, and stamped impatiently.

"I believe in Ashton. I believe that he will recall his sense of justice."

More shouting was echoing from the corridor. Reinforcements had arrived, and Fergus could smell gunpowder. He half-reared and struck the bars with his hooves. They dented, but didn't bend.

"I can't!"

" . . . poi . . . son . . . "

Guillory looked up, eyes widening. "Did you just . . . ?"

Fergus shook his head and, focusing all his will-power on the word, repeated, "Poi . . . son."

He backed away from the cell, glancing behind him restlessly.

"Even so . . . "

Closing his eyes tightly, Fergus gritted out, " . . . kill us . . . both . . . "

As if to punctuate his point, the bar next to him flared to life, sparks jumping free as a bullet shattered against it. Bits of metal struck him, and Fergus let out a grunt of pain. At the end of the corridor, the guard was already reloading.

" . . . won't . . . without you . . . "

"Fergus, I believe in him!"

" . . . sent me . . . get you . . . *please*."

Guillory looked down at the key in his hand, his lips drawn back over his teeth, his brow furrowed. Fergus just barely managed to avoid being shot in the leg. He turned to face the guards, trying not to trample the cowering one in the process, and let out a roar, bearing his fangs.

He heard the creak of stubborn iron, and then Guillory's hands were on his haunches. He didn't dare take his eyes from the guards. There was a painful tug of his mane, and then Guillory settled onto his back. Fergus waited only so long as to make sure he had a good grip before bolting. Bullets whizzed past as he dashed down the corridor. The guard who'd been shooting dropped his weapon and turned to run. The other leaned down to pick it up, but was knocked aside as Fergus rushed by. He could see daylight ahead. He lowered his head and sped up.

For just a moment, as they passed the stairwell, he caught a glimpse of Harriet being fussed over by two of his men. The Captain looked up at him, and Fergus thought he might have smiled.

Just ahead, the guards were fooling around with a panel. Fergus realized that they must be trying to lower the gate, but it seemed to be jammed. Feeling more thankful than he'd felt over anything in his entire life, Fergus threw himself into a final sprint, slamming through the last wooden door and galloping down the long stone bridge towards the dock.

Bullets ricocheted off the stone, brushing his legs, but never making their mark. At the end of the bridge, he saw a small airship hovering by the dock. He didn't have time to worry about it. All he could do was hope it wasn't filled with more guards, because there was only one way off of this island, and it wasn't going to be a short swim.

Fergus tried to mentally prepare himself for the dive as they drew closer and closer to the dock.

"Fergus!"

"Hurry!"

It was Three and Orson.

He felt a jolt of relief as he skidded to a halt, nearly throwing Guillory. Orson was there in a second, catching the former captain as he half-slid, half-fell from Fergus's back. Three waved enthusiastically, then squealed in alarm as Fergus drew up to her, barely avoiding a collision. His body shifted, and he fell into her arms, bloody, bruised, and half-naked, but in one piece.

She wrapped an arm around his back and quickly ushered him to the rope extending from the airship. His body hurt all over, and white dots were bursting in his eyes, but he managed to scramble up to the hatch where Terry dragged him inside.

"You made it," he mumbled, clinging to Terry's shoulder.

Every inch of his skin stung and burned, and he couldn't seem to hold his head up properly. His legs abandoned him, and he fell to his knees.

"You're here."

He smiled at Terry and toppled over.

Chapter Eight.

Fergus awoke to the smell of trampled grass, pungent and humid. He groaned and pressed his palm to his brow. His mouth felt like it was stuffed with cotton. He tentatively cracked open an eye and found himself facing a wall of blue daisies. The wallpaper was peeling, revealing yellowed, moldering plaster beneath. He sat up, and the bedsprings shrieked in complaint.

The room was empty save for a wooden chair with a broken back and the bed. There was a solitary window, taped over with oiled newspaper. The wind had torn a hole in one corner, which flapped as air poured inside. It definitely wasn't the slums, and the room was too still to be inside an airship. Since he wasn't in prison, they must have gotten away. But he wasn't sure where he was.

He peeled back the paper to look outside. All he could see was fog rolling in from the ocean. He pressed the tape back in place. Stretching, he shuffled to the door. Outside, a flickering bulb lit the hallway. Discolored squares dotted the wall where pictures must have hung. The floor began to vibrate. It felt like his stomach was falling independent of the rest of him. He pressed himself to the wall, holding his breath until the tremor subsided.

"What was that?" he muttered, pinching himself, but he seemed to be wide awake.

He hesitantly approached the stairs, which led down into a foyer. There were rows of doors on either side of the space and a set of double doors directly across from the landing. Fergus held his breath, waiting to see if the room was going to start shaking again, and then hurried down them. Like the upper floor, it seemed this room had also been hastily stripped. The walls were dented, as though heavy furniture had been thrust against them, and there were black skid marks on the floor.

He thought he smelled something deliciously salty and laden with grease, but before he could inspect, the front doors burst open. In swept a tall, gangly man, possessing the look of an oversized water bird. Rosslyn's blonde hair was chin length and lank, falling flat against his skull. He was clothed from head to foot in black, including a long jacket that buttoned up to his chin. He looked as sour as Fergus remembered.

Ursula was just a step behind him. Her eyes lit up when she saw Fergus. Her hair had been hacked off, falling around her face in short chunks. She had become thin and worn in his absence, her cheeks hollow, her eyes bruised. Like Rosslyn, she was dressed in black, though there was nothing simple about her jacket or skirt, which were both heavily embroidered. She hurried across the threshold, throwing her arms around his neck.

"I didn't believe it," she said. "I was certain that when you wound up on Andrew's Rock . . . "

Fergus hesitantly put a hand on her back. He'd never seen her *happy* to see him before – not really. He certainly never would've imagined she could smile at him like that. It was like ripping a scab off an old cut only to find that it hadn't healed underneath. He swallowed roughly, trying to smile, but failing.

"Yeah," he said, resisting the desire to crush her against him. It was weird that she smelled the same, felt the same . . .

Ursula stepped back, holding him at arm's length.

"Your eyes are blue. I expected they'd be white. You're handling this better than—"

She shook her head, releasing him, and Fergus frowned down at the floor. Rosslyn came over then, putting a hand on his shoulder very briefly.

"It's good to have you back."

"I, uh, have some of those ingredients you asked for. Well, maybe. They might be at the Count's still, if Terry didn't grab them."

"Don't worry. He brought your things here after he found out what Evan had done."

Fergus wasn't sure what to say. He was furious, but he didn't want to talk about the Count's most recent betrayal. Rosslyn sounded angry and disappointed enough already.

"Yeah," he finally said, clearing his throat.

"We've put him in 'time out,'" Rosslyn said, moving towards the smell of food.

Ursula wordlessly followed him, so Fergus did, too.

"He's delusional. I just . . . I don't know what to say." Rosslyn paused before the door, sighing, before repeating, "Completely delusional."

Ursula slipped around him, going into the kitchen, which was noticeably cleaner and livelier than the rest of the house. Fergus followed her inside, nodding to Rosslyn as he passed through. He would have liked to say something comforting, but he was a little tired of nearly being killed, so it was difficult to muster up sympathy for the Count.

Inside the kitchen, Pip and Three were standing over a stove, muttering to each other as they stirred a large pot. It smelled of brine and vegetables and not meat. He felt a little disappointed. Three looked over her shoulder, smiling.

"Hi, sleepyhead," she said, abandoning the pot to Pip, who offered nothing more than a curt nod.

"How long was I out?" Fergus asked.

"A little under a day," she said, dragging crates around in a circle. "Here, let's sit down!"

Ursula frowned at her, but – lifting her chin imperiously – seated herself upon a crate, Rosslyn beside her. Three plopped down unceremoniously, still grinning.

"Where's Terry?" Fergus asked, lingering near the door.

"He'll be back soon," Ursula said, playing with a string poking from one of her jacket's silver buttons. "He had things to take care of."

Fergus bit back a sigh and took a seat next to Three. "And where are we?"

"Orson's parents' house," Pip mumbled without turning.

"Orson and Guillory are out right now. I'm not sure where they've gone," Three said with a shrug. "His family left when the tremors first started."

"I'm really lost right now," Fergus said, rubbing the bridge of his nose to hide his annoyance.

"The magic is failing," Ursula said, liberating the string and looking up. "Really, did anyone expect otherwise? It's not like that idiot Jane or any of the remaining Niamh parasites are helping. At least now we have Terry, so it isn't quite as bad, but there's still only a few of us trying to keep the whole city from crashing down."

"Who else is helping?" Fergus asked.

"Other members of Bandersnatch. The ones who are left. You wouldn't know most of them."

"The Count?"

Rosslyn snorted. "Evan doesn't have a head for magic. Why do you think he hired me on?"

"Dominique?"

Ursula shook her head, lowering her eyes. "The Labyrinth was raided about a month ago. I expect she and the rest of the girls are either dead or exorcised by now."

"I'm sorry," he said softly.

She shook her head, her hair falling into her eyes, and returned to fiddling with the button.

"So what's the plan? I mean, shouldn't we be doing something about the colony?"

"Like what, Fergus?" Ursula asked, mouth thinning.

"Like getting everyone out."

She let out a derisive laugh.

Rosslyn was also giving him a look, but momentarily shrugged and replied, "*If* we could focus on anything besides trying to keep the city together, we could try to rescue them, but we can't, because the Knights are capturing more of us each day, and we can barely keep up the runes without being caught ourselves. The idiots . . . " He stopped, letting out a shuddering sigh. His cheeks were turning a deep purple-red. "The idiots," he began again, "are now searching for rune circles and ambushing us when we come to check on them. Of course, every single one has been set immutably, so we can't place them anywhere else and expect the plates to hold. We have to keep going back, despite the fact the Knights are bound to be there."

"Luckily, we're smarter than the average human vigilante, so we've been able to stay a step ahead, but not everyone has been so fortunate, and we needed everyone," Ursula added.

"So now what? Abandon the city?"

"It would serve them right if we did," Rosslyn grumbled.

"This is our home, and we have a right to be here," Ursula said over him. "We're the ones taking care of it, so we aren't going anywhere. If anyone is going to leave, it should be the humans. Many already have," she added, haughtily surveying the kitchen. "And good riddance."

Three flinched. Her lips were hidden between her teeth. Her fingers wrestled with the edge of her crate. Fergus tried to offer her a consoling smile, but she didn't look up. Sighing, he ran a hand through his hair.

"So basically, you're going to wait until they're scared off by the tremors and then go rescue whoever is left in the colony."

"Do you have a better idea? Besides, I think it's about time that New Peiling belonged to us."

Fergus closed his eyes, picturing a handsome man with hazel eyes and olive skin standing over Pip with a dagger. He wasn't surprised that Ursula sounded like Declan Abel, but he didn't appreciate it much either. He shook his head.

"What are you gonna do when you bring back all the hybrids, and then the humans decide to return?"

"We'll let them know that New Peiling is a hybrid city."

"Yeah, that'll turn out great. You're gonna have a war."

"We already do!" Ursula spat, leaping to her feet. "Don't act like you know how things have been, Fergus. Where have you been? Gallivanting around the world! We're the ones who've been living with this!"

Rosslyn tugged on the back of her jacket, but she ignored him.

"I know I haven't been here, but I'm back now. And the way I see it, too many people have died already. We can't let this escalate any further."

"Too many of us have been exorcised, you mean."

"The only way to get what you want is to kill every human alive, and there are a lot of them who're on our side. And you know what else? *We're not fairies.* We aren't born fairies. The fairies choose us, but we're born human." He glanced at Three, who smiled faintly, and then at Rosslyn, who hesitantly nodded. "Say you do manage to kill every human on the planet. What if our kids don't wind up hybrids? Are we gonna kill them, too, to make sure they don't turn on us?"

"There's no way to make things work with them," Ursula replied coldly. "They've done too much."

"Some of them. Not all of them. And even the ones who have, I think they can change."

"What? Paige Harriet? Ashton Harriet? You think they can change?"

"Maybe he didn't want to, but Ashton Harriet still went out of his way to save my life back at the prison. He's the reason Guillory and I escaped. And I think William Guillory is a better judge of character than you."

Ursula hissed. For a moment, he thought she might go for him. Her hands curled in the pleats of her skirt, pupils turning to slits.

She took a shaky breath and replied, "This conversation is over. You're talking like you have rocks for brains, like you can't see what's happened out there. You must have hit your head a few times too many, Fergus Irvine."

With that, she swept out of the room, slamming the door behind her.

Fergus groaned, running his hands over his face.

"She really was happy to see you," Rosslyn said.

"I'm sure," he replied, dropping his hands into his lap. "So why aren't you stomping out, too? Would've thought you agree with her."

Rosslyn sighed. "Yes and no. It's ludicrous to think we could kill every human on the planet just because we have a few extra abilities. It's absurd, and even considering it makes us sound like monsters. I'm not a monster. But I don't have answers, either. All I know is this: whatever Ashton Harriet has done to aid you? Forget it, because that was a miracle. If you rely on it ever happening again, you're certain to wind up exorcised."

Fergus nodded, mouth scrunching sideways. "I know. But still, just the fact he helped me at all . . . I think there's a part of him that just . . . I dunno. I feel like I'm not seeing the whole picture. I don't trust him. I mean, he hates me more than anyone. But he saved me despite that. It means *something*."

Rosslyn frowned, shaking his head. "Maybe, but don't count on that whole picture being something that will save you a second time."

"I should go after her," Fergus said, standing.

"The soup's almost ready," Pip interjected, frowning over his shoulder.

"I'll be back."

The door diagonal to the kitchen was open, so Fergus walked towards it. It'd probably been a sitting room once. The walls had shelves built into them, but there were only a few books left. There was no furniture, though the scratch marks on the floor whispered of sofas and tables. Ursula sat on a pile of towels and sheets fashioned into a seat. She had a large book open in her lap, legs stretched out before her. As he entered, she looked up, scowling. He ignored her glare and came over to sit beside her.

"Why'd you cut it? Did Deirdre start a trend or something?"

Her hand went to her hair, and she frowned. "One of them grabbed me by it one night. I barely escaped, so I chopped it off when I got home. I've kept it this way ever since."

"Makes sense."

"Is there something you want?" she asked, mouth pursing.

"It's good to see you haven't changed."

Her frown grew deeper. For a moment, she was silent. Then she replied, "I wish I could say the same."

"And what's that supposed to mean?"

She shook her head, sighing softly. "Nothing. It means nothing, Fergus."

"Are you angry at me?"

"What could I possibly be angry about? The way you went off on some expedition without even telling me what you were leaving to find? Or maybe how I was unsure every day for *months* if you would return?"

"I wasn't sure I was going to," he said, looking away.

They both fell silent.

"What were you looking for?" she finally asked.

"Tír na nÓg," Fergus replied, fiddling with a hole in his jeans.

"And you didn't find it."

"No, we did."

She turned to him, confused. He glanced at her out of the corner of his eye before looking back down.

"You found it, but you're here?"

He nodded. "I decided not to go."

Ursula said nothing, but stared at him expectantly.

Sighing, he said, "The Count set Terry up with these old friends, right? Dunno if you ever met them – Declan and Darya Abel."

"A few times."

"Well, basically, they decided that I didn't deserve my powers." He cleared his throat, lowering his face. "They really liked Terry. Wanted him to become a Huntsman with them. Me, though . . . "

He swallowed, closing his eyes, and tried not to think of dark rooms and disembodied hands holding him down. Shaking his head sharply, he continued, "They tried to steal my soul, but Terry stopped them. I realized that it's both sides. It's both sides that are making things messed up, and it's not something I can turn away from." He sighed, running a hand up his face and pushing his hair back from his eyes. His mouth twitched, the beginnings of a humorless smile.

"This problem is so big, and maybe I can't fix it, but while we were standing there in front of the gate, I realized that both my parents ran away from everything that was hard to face. Whatever happens, I don't wanna be like them. I'm gonna face this, and even if I fail, at least I'll know I never ran away."

Ursula chuckled, putting her hand on his knee. "Only you would decide to fix the un-fixable for such a simple reason."

"I care about humans, Ursula. I care about Guillory and Three and Orson. I care about us, too. I know there's bound to be fighting, but we have to try to change things without resorting to that whenever we can."

"You're right, Fergus. There *is* going to be fighting."

Fergus jumped.

Terry stood framed in the doorway. He smiled, uncrossing his arms, and came over to flop down in front of Fergus and Ursula.

"Terry," Fergus said, feeling an increasingly familiar warmth spread through his chest. He lowered his face, smiling.

Ursula scowled. She didn't look away from Fergus as she asked Terry, "What did you find out?"

"Doesn't look great. There's about ten who are for it, but the rest . . . " he trailed off, shaking his head.

"For what?" Fergus asked, ignoring Ursula's glower.

Terry looked away. "They've sent most of the hybrids to the colony, right? But it seems Harriet knows it's hybrid magic keeping the city together. So they've got a few choice members of our community imprisoned on the upper level."

"Like Raja and Evelyn?"

Terry nodded. "I imagine they're also taking people they suspect will be able to inform them about Niamh and Bandersnatch."

"Does Niamh still exist?" Fergus asked.

Niamh had been a scholarly circle of hybrids dedicated to finding Tír na nÓg. Despite being an academic organization, the vigilante Knights of Evalach had hunted down most of its members and exorcised them. Before they'd even left on their voyage, Niamh's numbers had been abysmal. He couldn't imagine many were left.

"Sort of," Terry said, glancing at Ursula.

She sighed, rubbing the bridge of her nose. "For whatever reason, they haven't taken Jane away. She, Gavin, and Fand are holed up in her penthouse. I imagine if there are any other survivors, they must be there, too."

"Fand?!"

"Yes. Why do you look so shocked?"

Fergus blinked at Terry. "Didn't you tell her?"

Terry shrugged. "There were more important things going on."

"What is it?" Ursula snapped.

"When we got to the gateway, Fand was there. She's a real fairy. *A full fairy.*"

Ursula blinked, mouth parting. "Is she really?"

Fergus nodded. "But why did she return to Jane? I thought she would've been done with her, and with the gate closing . . . "

"I have no idea," Terry sighed. "But it probably isn't good, whatever the reason."

"So," Fergus said, reaching out to nudge Terry's leg with his toe, "how are you planning to get them out of there?"

Terry frowned. "With force. We can't just stroll up and say, 'please.' We'd be taken, too."

Fergus said nothing.

"Their compounds are well-defended." Terry sighed again, running his hands over his face and shaking his head. "They know our magic is the glue, so unless they want this whole thing to topple over tomorrow, they need some of us, but given their platform of eradication . . . Well, they can't let on to that, can they?"

"Surely they must have a plan. I mean, they can't just be sitting up there, keeping a couple of hybrids in the hopes things just work out. What happens when they die?" Fergus asked.

"We have no way of knowing what they're planning to do. Maybe they'll evacuate the city. Maybe they'll continue keeping some of us on hand to hold things together. Maybe they'll start a new religion. Start bringing babies and children from the lower city to be possessed, so that they never run out of hybrids. They're extremists, so probably their plans will be extreme."

Fergus stared down at his hands, brow pinched. "Would they really go that far?"

Terry shrugged. "They shipped most of us off to that colony. They exorcise people for eating breakfast. Crazy is kind of a given at this point, so is it really such a stretch?"

"Not really. So we're gonna bust Raja and the others out?"

Terry grinned and clapped him on the shoulder. "We sure are."

Chapter Nine.

Guillory and Orson seemed to be out every time
Fergus went looking for them. In their place, the
surviving members of Bandersnatch filtered in and
out of the commandeered townhouse. As Ursula and
Terry had said, the remaining group was small.
There were only about eight regulars.

There were two survivors from the raid on the
Labyrinth: a bald girl named Estelle and another
named Tia, who had blue eyes so dark they looked
purple. Then there was a guy who'd survived
membership to both Niamh and Bandersnatch. He
had a large scar running down the side of his neck,
carved there by his own mother when he was eleven.
His name was Laurence. He was friendly enough,
though he brought up Flynn a lot, and Fergus
couldn't help feeling disturbed and jealous of all the
people involved in Flynn's previously secret life.

Besides these three, there were two middle-aged
cousins, who called themselves Leo and Bull. He'd
never seen them before, but both seemed to have
known his mother well. It was awkward. He still

felt raw about her death, so he made efforts to avoid them whenever possible. Deirdre also showed up once. She *almost* looked guilty when their eyes met, and she hadn't given him a chance to approach her.

He wasn't sure about the rest. He knew there was a Corey in there and a Sybil and maybe an Imogen, but he couldn't apply names to the faces. Most recognized Fergus, but they were all strangers to him. More often than not, they left before he had a chance to be introduced, slipping out with whispered orders from Ursula or Terry.

Fergus had been neatly placed on the backburner. Sure, when the time came, they'd include him – he was determined to make sure of that – but he wanted to be a part of the planning. For the last year, everyone had been acting on his decisions. Even Guillory had been willing to defer to him most of the time. He would have thought that'd count for something. But he noticed that whilst Ursula and Terry avoided talking business around him, they didn't seem to notice Pip, who was small, surly, withdrawn, and spoke in his native tongue half the time anyway.

Three, Pip, and Fergus presently sat in his room, the door left slightly ajar to ensure that no one was outside while they talked. Three bounced on the bed, eager to hear the news, and Fergus couldn't blame her. He might not have been bouncing with anticipation, but he was still dying to know what the *real* plan was. Pip frowned, looking at his knees, and fiddled with a loose thread on his jacket.

"Piiiip!" Three groaned, throwing herself onto her back and stamping her feet.

"All right! Fine!" he squeaked, snapping the thread. "The facility is on the second to top level.

It's large. It takes up almost a quarter of the plate. It stretches from the center of the plate to the perimeter, but the outer wall doesn't have windows large enough for us to enter through."

"So that rules out scaling the city," Three said, rubbing her chin.

"Right. And they can't rely on the lifts, because the lifts will be suspended as soon as the first explosion goes off."

"*Explosion*?" Fergus repeated.

"Just wait and let me finish! What they plan to do is blow two holes through the plate under the facility."

"That's insane," Fergus said with a frown.

Pip shrugged. "Breaking into some laboratory-prison thing isn't?"

"Point. Okay, so keep going."

"There are a few access points that don't require making an entrance, but they do necessitate climbing. They're trying to put together a map of every possible escape route, in case any are closed off in the aftermath."

"Yeah, don't wanna get trapped up there."

Pip nodded curtly. "Yes, obviously. They also are trying to decide where to stage the explosions. There are a few things to keep in consideration. The integrity of the plate will be questionable, since the magic holding everything together is weaker now, so it's uncertain what will happen. The entire layer might come down if they aren't careful. The first explosion is a decoy. Some will go up through that hole to distract them. The second group will need to be positioned as closely as possible to where they think the prisoners are being held. While the first group draws attention, the second group goes up, retrieves the prisoners, and escapes back down into the lower city."

"Sounds risky."

"Super risky," Three agreed.

"You can't walk up to the door and ask nicely. You can't even attack the door. So it's either give up, or consider extremes," Pip said, shrugging. "I understand there is a fence around the entire facility and many guards."

"What do you figure is going on up there that they need that much security?" Fergus muttered.

"You probably don't want to think about it, since it is probably happening to your friends."

Fergus sat up. "Oh, there's something else . . . "

"What's that?"

"I think 'that man' might be here. I think he's working with them."

"What?" Three and Pip said simultaneously.

"Sorry, I just thought of it, but back in the prison, this weird guy came and was looking for you. He seemed friendly enough with the guards, so if it's the guy you're looking for, he might be there."

Pip loosed a long string of vehement muttering.

"Good," Three said, her hands dropping into her lap.

"Good? What is *good* about that?" Pip demanded.

"It's good because I want to settle things with him," she replied, staring down at her hands. "If he's in this city, if he's in that facility, and we are, too, it just seems like an opportunity to finish things."

"But last time!"

"I'm stronger now. We both are. Plus, we have Fergus and Terry and the others to help us. I don't want to run from him for the rest of our lives. We're looking for him, right? So if we've found him, good. Let it end here."

Pip made a sharp sound in the back of his throat, turning to Fergus as though expecting him to argue, but Fergus didn't know what to say. Without another word, Pip got to his feet and stamped out, slamming the door behind him.

Three sighed, shoulders slumping. "Do you think I'm being stupid?" she asked, not looking up.

"Not any stupider than breaking into some research facility that's crawling with Evalach cronies."

The corner of her mouth twitched upwards. "I feel like I can do it now. Looking at you, Fergus, I feel like I can do it. You're struggling so hard for something that seems impossible, but you aren't stopping. You aren't running." She licked her lower lip. "I want to be like that, too."

"I dunno about all that."

"No, really! I don't know what it's like to be a hybrid. I don't even know what it's like to be hated because I'm human, because even though I was different from everyone in my village, I was still one of them. I don't know what it was like for Pip and you. For him, being used for his powers and subjugated and . . . For you, being treated like . . . Well, you know." She cleared her throat softly. "But having met you both, I've learned a little. Knowing what you're facing, I'm not really sure how all this can be fixed. But when I look at you, I feel like there has to be a way. Even if you fail, I feel like just knowing you would make others want to try, too."

Fergus was silent. He stared at her, feeling a lump form in his throat. He didn't know what to say. He was pretty sure it was the nicest thing anyone had ever said about him. Lowering his eyes, he turned away and scratched his cheek.

"If I could be more like you," she continued, sliding off the bed, "I think I would like to be. I want to try, at least."

"I like you the way you are," he replied, glancing up.

She smiled and leaned down to pat his head. "I better go find Pip."

"Yeah. I'm gonna try to get Terry to tell me some of this himself."

"Good luck."

•   •   •

He found Terry sitting in his room, which was even more barren than Fergus's. The door was not entirely shut, so as he lurked outside, he could see Terry's shoulders. They were broad, though his body was thin. His shirt clung to his back, exposing his ribs. He was working on something in his lap, but Fergus couldn't see what it was. Fergus watched the muscles shifting under his shirt and wondered what he was up to. After a moment, Terry straightened, putting the item down. He looked over his shoulder, catching Fergus's eye.

"You're not very good at spying."

Fergus came inside, shutting the door behind him. "Yeah, well, I am a big freaking horse monster."

Terry snorted softly and returned to work. Fergus followed the line of his outstretched arm to a pile of pistols. It seemed none were in one piece. The rest of the parts lay around Terry in mounds. He took a gun and began searching through the other piles before picking up a screwdriver and fitting a piece of metal inside.

"Are we supposed to use those?" Fergus asked, tucking his hands into his back pockets.

"Yup."

Fergus was quiet for a beat, leaning against the door. The only times he'd been close to a gun, it'd been pointed at him. He wasn't a fan.

"Just evening out the odds," Terry said before putting the screwdriver in his mouth and searching around for a screw.

"Our powers aren't enough?"

"A lot of them can't turn into fairies, you know," Terry said around the tool. "Plenty can't use magic, either. If we're storming the castle, I wanna lose as few of us as possible. I think we're more crucial to this city's survival than Evalach."

"Shoot to kill, then," Fergus said.

Terry nodded silently.

"Terry?"

"This is the way it has to be. Either we do this, or we just leave 'em to Evalach. I dunno about you, but I think our friends' lives have more weight than a bunch of vigilante kidnapper assholes."

"Yeah, they do, but . . . "

"But what, Fergus? Every Knight we take out is one less person trying to kill us later."

"It just doesn't feel right."

"I know, but this one's on me. You can blame me for it later. I won't mind. I just want to get what needs doing done."

"Standing by and letting something happen is the same as being the one who does it," Fergus replied softly. "At least it is to me."

"And yet you feel sorry for Ashton Harriet."

"I didn't say I felt sorry for him. I *said* Guillory might be right: that there might still be hope for him. If there's hope for him, maybe the rest aren't completely lost, either."

"You are so gullible," Terry said, putting the gun down. It gleamed in the lamplight, the metal barrel ugly and fascinating all at once. "And that's why I didn't want you to know about this, but I know you've had Pip sneaking around, listening in. He's better at it than you are, but you both forget that I can smell you."

Fergus cringed and moved away from the door, coming to stand behind Terry, who resumed assembling the arms. He reached out, putting a hand on Terry's shoulder.

"I'm not changing my mind about this. We can talk diplomacy after we make sure they don't have our friends imprisoned up there."

"I wasn't going to say that."

Terry didn't reply, but sighed, shoulders sagging.

Fergus crouched behind him. "But violence creates violence. If we go in there guns blazing, they'll retaliate."

"They'll be shooting at us either way. The first thing they'll do is open fire. They're terrified of us, Fergus, and there's no one else who'd break into their little laboratory. So they'll shoot first and ask questions later. Having a gun just means that maybe some of us will make it out alive."

"Where'd you get them?" Fergus asked, leaning forward and resting his brow between Terry's shoulders.

Terry stiffened, but didn't rebuke him. "Guillory's friends."

"And they just gave them to you?"

Terry shrugged.

"I'm glad you aren't lying about it, but if I get what you're saying, you had someone masquerade as one of Guillory's people to gather them."

"You're getting better at figuring it out. I remember when I had to spoon-feed you everything. Didn't have to worry about you working out my plans and getting mad back then. Kinda miss that."

"I'm not trying to cause problems."

"You're just trying to be my moral compass."

"No."

"Yeah, you are."

"Maybe."

"Definitely."

Fergus sighed, rubbing his face against the back of Terry's shirt. He smelled like soot and sweat. He didn't smell like Terry. Well, maybe the sweat part did. Still, the scent of gunpowder and oil was foreign. It was a smell he associated with Harriet, not Terry. He squeezed his eyes shut.

"Won't you just trust me this once? After we get through this, I'll hand the reins over to you."

"You won't," Fergus said.

Terry was quiet. Fergus could tell he was frowning.

"What if I promise I will?"

"Then you'll force me to say I believe you and to act like I believe you, but we'll still both know that you won't."

"This is dangerous."

"Really? I never would've guessed. You know how many times I've had a spin with death in the last year?"

"I know all too well, Fergus," Terry said. Fergus felt the shift of muscle as Terry turned to look at him. "That's why."

Fergus didn't reply. He didn't want to have to say that if Terry wouldn't include him, he wasn't going to sit back and wait for Bandersnatch to let him in on their plans. He was already considering taking Three and Pip and joining Orson and Guillory.

It felt like a betrayal, though, and he wasn't sure if he could do it. He didn't want to have his hands tied by Ursula and Terry, but if he sided with them, once again he'd be allowing his loyalties to chip away at his principles. He could still smell Trevor Fennis's blood fresh on his hands as he and Terry threw his remains into the bay. It should have felt like decades ago. So much of what he'd experienced lately did.

Yet it felt like that self-betrayal had happened only yesterday. And he knew he would betray himself again for Terry. Rosslyn had once told him that this was how things were when someone cared about a person who wasn't aligned with their principles. Loving that person would take precedence over integrity.

The thought of it made him feel sick.

He let out a long, shaky sigh and felt the tips of Terry's fingers brush the crown of his head.

"You don't have to come. I wouldn't blame you if you wanted to go do whatever it is Guillory's cooking up. He's more your speed."

"I don't feel like we'll make any headway unless what he's doing and what you're doing come together," Fergus said, getting to his feet.

"Probably not. Can't you just trust me this one time? We do this my way, and then everything else can be your call."

"If you genuinely promise that you'll listen to me later, then okay."

"I sincerely, honestly, and genuinely promise that I will listen to you later."

Fergus paused, fidgeting with his jacket's zipper. "Okay. No take backs." He paused. "Terry, do you hate humans?"

"Kind of."

"Even Three and Orson?"

Terry rubbed the back of his neck, sighing. "No, I guess I don't."

"But all the others?"

He shrugged.

"Why? You kinda grew up like one, right? So, you know . . . "

"I know what, Fergus? That my parents left the city as soon as I ran away to make sure I wouldn't come back home? That people like Ashton and Paige Harriet are keeping people like Raja and Evelyn like zombies up there? You saw Evelyn back at the gateway."

"Yeah."

"Maybe some of us have murdered humans, but not all of us, and we're still the ones being exorcised."

Fergus sighed.

"So when have humans deserved my sympathy?"

"Three saved us at the gateway, and without her and Guillory, we probably would have died back in that cave with the Huntsmen."

"I know," Terry said.

Fergus sighed again, blowing his bangs out of his eyes. "So, how did you learn how to assemble a gun?"

"My dad."

"Was he a member of the Guard?"

Terry shook his head.

"Pilot?"

"Up until I was three. Then there was an accident, and he lost an arm. Had to retire."

"And you love airships."

"Not because of *him*," Terry snapped.

Fergus blinked, stepping back.

Terry lowered his eyes, looking guilty, and turned away. "He had a pretty large collection. He was into firearms of all kinds. He even hunted. Every year, he'd go out to the islands to hunt birds. He took me with him a few times."

Fergus nodded and tentatively sat back down. "So you know about guns and airships. Funny. In another world . . . "

"I could have been friends with Ashton Harriet? Maybe. But I hate the idea of it so much . . . I'll *never* be like him."

Very astutely, Fergus bit his tongue on the remark that Terry was actually a lot like Harriet.

He shrugged, looking away. "Maybe you could show me how they work. Or at least how to put them together."

"Would've thought it'd be a stain on your honor to even hold one."

"Might keep me from accidentally shooting someone in the foot later."

"Come here," Terry said. He turned to Fergus, mouth crooking and holding out a screwdriver.

Fergus sucked down a sigh and forced a smile, nodding and taking the tool.

Chapter Ten.

His fingers shook as he buttoned the jacket. It wasn't cold – in fact, the jacket was making him sweat – but Terry insisted he wear it. Thin sheets of metal had been sewn into the lining, which caused the fabric to drag at his shoulders and neck. Terry had assured Fergus that he and the others would be similarly outfitted. It wasn't a terrible idea, given they were up against Evalach. Didn't make it comfortable, though.

Fergus cursed under his breath, fumbling with the last button, and then gave up for the moment, running his hands over his face. The jacket wasn't the only thing weighing on him. The revolver at his side also felt heavy and alien, like a metal tumor growing out of his hip. He'd already decided he wouldn't use it, but the need to prove something to Terry had provoked him into declaring that he would carry a gun, too.

Worrying his lip, he turned to look at his reflection in the darkened glass of the window, returning to that final button. The coat was dark green and formless, obscuring both gun and inserts. He pulled his hair back from his forehead and put on a black cap. He looked strange, and it was far too warm for so many layers.

There was a knock at the door. He forced himself to stop cataloging all the ways he was uncomfortable and turned to greet his guest.

Rosslyn's mouth twitched, not so much curving up as stretching out towards his ears. He stepped into the room, frowning at the bed before going over to lean on the windowsill. Crossing his arms, he silently regarded Fergus. Fergus stared back, trying not to feel aggravated. The whole silent scrutiny thing was not so cute after the first dozen times.

"What's up?" he asked, returning to fussing with the jacket.

"I have something for you. It's from," Rosslyn paused, reaching into his pocket, "him."

"Him?"

"Evan. The Count."

"What does *he* want to give *me*?" Fergus asked, eyes narrowing.

"I suppose he wants to make peace, so he can get out of the hot water he's in."

Rosslyn pulled out a parcel wrapped in brown paper, tossing it to Fergus. It was surprisingly heavy. Fergus looked up at him.

"What is it?"

But Rosslyn didn't answer, so Fergus sighed and undid the twine, peeling back the paper. Inside was a brass compass on a chain. It looked very expensive. He pulled it out, holding it up by its chain.

"A compass?"

"With a spell on it. An old spell. A powerful one. It was my father's, but I gave it to Evan as a token of affection," Rosslyn said, lowering his eyes.

"That's pretty uncool."

Rosslyn shrugged. "It's his to give now."

"Are you sure? Don't you want it back?"

"No," Rosslyn replied flatly. "Besides, you may need it. We've found a number of escape routes, but this may show you things that weren't on our maps. It was from my father. I brought it with me to Clohaven. My favorite professor put the spell on it. He was perhaps the greatest magician I ever met."

Fergus raised an eyebrow.

Rosslyn pinched the bridge of his nose. "I've never been very good with cities. I grew up in Peygham where it's impossible to get lost. You either walk down to the ocean, or up to the trees, and that's it. When I first got to Clohaven, I was constantly lost. I kept missing his lectures, or turning up late, so he did me a favor and put a spell on it."

"And you didn't need it here in New Peiling?"

"I didn't go out alone much. Besides, it was one of the few things I owned that didn't come from him."

"I guess you're on speaking terms again," Fergus ventured.

"The only person he's seen lately is Deirdre, and if he's alone too often, he becomes more unbalanced than usual. Putting him on 'house arrest' was Terry's decision, and as you know, when Terry punishes, he is severe and unyielding."

"Do you feel sorry for him?"

Rosslyn shrugged. "It's not unexpected. His decisions are based on self-interest. You were almost exorcised because of him, but it's hardly the first time he's ruined someone's life, or nearly done so. It's why Ainslee hated him and why she refused to let him come to our lessons. He was never any good at magic, and he knew it as well as anyone, but he wanted to be included. The fact she wouldn't let him sit in with the rest of us drove him crazy, which is probably why he dislikes you now. Perhaps he would have forgiven her had he been able to add you to his collection, but I imagine Ursula went out of her way to make it hard for him, out of respect to Ainslee."

Fergus snorted.

"So I'm not surprised that he made a deal with Ashton Harriet. I have told him over and over, just as I've told you: *never trust that man*. Harriet does not believe any hybrid is deserving of sympathy or kindness. His 'honor' will only extend so far. Perhaps Evan has bought himself a few more weeks in his penthouse with his luxuries, but that's all. Evan does not possess great foresight. All his little intrigues are for immediate purposes. Otherwise, he would have been a lot more careful about Trevor Fennis, and he never would've considered double-crossing you."

Fergus shook his head. "It still amazes me that someone like you loves someone like him."

"I could say the same for you."

"Were you surprised when he, you know, betrayed you?"

Rosslyn stilled, turning away. He was leaning too closely to the window for Fergus to see his face.

"No. I knew he had it in him. I knew because of his parents."

"His parents?"

Rosslyn nodded. "They died of a 'mysterious' illness while he was a teenager. I always suspected he'd poisoned them."

"What? Really?"

"Yes. The Cavenders were the biggest name in airship design. At least in New Peiling. Though they were not a 'top level' family, they were grossly wealthy and well regarded, so they were always rubbing elbows with people like the Harriets and the Murrays and the Bridges."

"The Murrays?"

"Jane's family. The woman who leads Niamh. The mad one."

"Wait, wait, wait – and the Bridges? Like Terry *Bridges*?"

Rosslyn nodded. "I'm surprised he hasn't told you. His family was very well-to-do. It's probably why when he disappeared, or – as they claimed – succumbed to pneumonia, they suddenly packed up and left. It would have been rather scandalous had he miraculously returned from the dead."

"Does he know?"

"That they had a funeral for him? No. Or if he does, *I* never told him, and I doubt Ursula would have, either. Evan might have out of spite, because theirs is a tumultuous history. After his parents died, Evan took over the family business and promptly came out as a hybrid. Well, the minute he did, the Bridges and the Harriets cut ties with him. Certainly, they still called on him for favors, but they never wanted to be seen in public with him again."

Fergus gaped. *Did* Terry know his parents had not only abandoned him, but also declared him dead? He wanted more than anything to believe that Terry was in the dark, but he knew it couldn't be.

He felt sick.

"But Jane's family didn't turn him away?" he asked, trying to pull himself together.

"No, they didn't," Rosslyn replied, smiling sadly. "I'm sure they suspected Jane was a hybrid, even at that age. I imagine most parents work it out easily enough. They'd had a mind to marry Jane to Evan when she was older. Combine their empires. Jane is nearly a decade younger than Evan, though, and she was still a child when he revealed his nature to the world. Perhaps if he had been quiet about it, they might have gone ahead with the plan, but with that act of rebellion, they quickly took their measure of him. I wouldn't want my child to marry him either, honestly.

"They didn't snub him, but they did begin to drift. He wanted their fortunes and their connections. When he found he couldn't have those, I suspect he arranged for them to catch the same mysterious illness his parents had died of."

Fergus opened his mouth and then closed it. He looked down at his hands, shaking his head.

"Wow," he finally said. "So you think he killed both his and Jane's parents?"

"I think it is very possible."

"Does Jane know?"

"It's hard to say. She's always been a little off. She's very clever and pretty, so most people don't see it at first. However, when you've been around her for any period of time, you start to notice that there's something jarring about her. Something . . . furtive and manic. I don't enjoy her."

"But she used to come to all his parties and stuff. Seemed like they were friends."

Rosslyn shrugged. "In any case, her parents died while she was very young. She obviously needed a nanny, so a woman was hired on. The nanny made it very hard for Evan to get close to her."

"Fand."

"What?"

"The nanny was Fand. She's a real fairy. We met her at the gateway to Tír na nÓg. She raised Jane."

Rosslyn tilted his head, pulling at his lip. "Fand is a real fairy?"

Fergus nodded.

"That explains a lot, including why Jane is almost as bad as Evan about wrecking the lives of others."

"Do you know something?" Fergus asked, straightening. "About Jane and the humans? Fand hinted that there was some kind of relationship . . . "

Rosslyn shook his head. "I told you all those old families were close, didn't I? And of that lot, the Murrays were the most influential. The Murray House is very close to the top layer, closer even than the Harriets' old home. Evan's family wasn't the only one eyeing her. She was a docile, attractive girl from one of the very most influential and richest families in the area. Ashton Harriet was already courting her whilst Evan was away at school. So I imagine she has known him quite intimately from a tender age."

"You're joking."

Rosslyn shook his head. "He's handsome, he comes from an important family, and he didn't arrive at his present position by being an ass to everyone. And while I know you won't want to hear this, you need to: he bears a distinct resemblance to your friend Flynn. Probably, that's her type, and most likely, that's why you want to see some good in him, as well."

Fergus frowned, eyes narrowing. "I think you're wrong about that. Flynn was a great person. He was kind and—"

"Yes, yes, I know," Rosslyn said, holding up a hand. "What I'm trying to impart is that Jane has a soft spot for tall, dark, and handsome. She knew Harriet from a young age, and he became a constant in her life. Whilst her parents may have suspected that she had a fairy hiding inside her, Jane has never come out to society. She's always touted herself as a hybrid rights activist, but she has never admitted to being one herself. I'm sure that's why she turned away from Harriet and took up with your friend. Her parents were sympathetic, a fairy raised her, and she was a hybrid. These were all big influences, but from what I gather, she nevertheless had fallen for Harriet, and she felt that way for some time."

"So basically, he seduced her, but as she grew older, she got scared he'd find out what she was and left him. He must have tried to win her back while she was with Flynn. And then, because it's Jane, and she always thinks about things in the most convoluted way, she told him the truth about herself and Niamh to scare him off. But why didn't he exorcise her, too? Wouldn't he be furious?"

"God only knows," Rosslyn said, shaking his head. "Maybe he loves her. Maybe he's just saving her for last. Don't ask me what that lunatic is thinking."

"That's why Niamh was exposed, but not Bandersnatch. Jane didn't know enough to be a threat."

Rosslyn nodded.

"But surely she told him about how Niamh was just looking for a way out? They were harmless. They were just a bunch of geeky kids chasing fairy tales."

"Ah, but what did Harriet say when he found you at the gateway?"

Fergus bit his lip, brow knitting. "That they were going to destroy it so no more fairies could come out, and then they were gonna systematically exorcise the remaining hybrids."

"Exactly. Ashton Harriet does not care if a hybrid is harmless or not."

"Because his dad was eaten. That's what he told me when we were stuck together in the prison. His father was eaten, and he saw the body or something."

"That would do it. And so he cannot conceive of any hybrid being good at heart. When Jane revealed everything to him, he probably decided that he had to find the gate and destroy it to protect the humans, and before Niamh could open it and risk letting other fairies escape into our world, he decided to wipe them out. It never mattered whether they were dangerous or not. That whole ridiculous spiel about the Knights of Evalach only targeting dangerous hybrids was just to garner the humans' approval."

"And that's why they took Flynn and the others," Fergus said softly, looking down.

"Jane must have realized her mistake too late, but she beat us to the punch even so. She hired men to strip everything of value from your roommate's belongings, but she missed the last, most important thing: the key that led you to the gate."

Fergus nodded.

Rosslyn continued, "Ursula went and took a look herself, but she couldn't find anything. We figured it was either the Knights' or Niamh's handiwork, but if it had been the Knights, they wouldn't have needed to kidnap Audrey or your friend Evelyn. Most likely, Jane found something when she had the room searched and stupidly shared it with the others. She is often painfully simple."

"This is giving me a headache," Fergus groaned. He flopped onto the bed, cringing as a metal plate bit into his shoulder blade. "So let me get this straight. All these old families were super close. Both the Count's parents and Paige Harriet wanted their sons to marry Jane. Then the Count offed his family and came out as a hybrid, so the Bridges and the Harriets cut ties with him, and the Murrays took Jane off the table. The Count out of the way, Harriet swept in and . . . " He idly waved his hand, making a face, before continuing.

"Meanwhile, the Count got angry and removed Jane's parents from the picture, so Fand became her guardian. Even though she didn't come out, Jane was sympathetic towards other hybrids, which caused a rift between her and Harriet. She started university and met Flynn, but then Harriet came back into her life, and she told him everything to put him off. But she miscalculated. Instead, Harriet took what he learned and had Flynn captured . . . "

And tortured to death.

He forced the thought from his mind. "But Jane beat him to Flynn's notes, and so he had to kidnap other members of Niamh to get the rest of information. That's how Evalach found out about Niamh *and* about Tír na nÓg. Where do you think she and Harriet stand now?"

"Who knows?" Rosslyn said with a shrug, pushing away from the window. "Maybe he has a weakness for her, or maybe, as a I said, he's planning to take his revenge on her last. But if he knows she's a hybrid, she won't be able to hide from him forever. Not if she stays here. I imagine she hates him, but perhaps she's harboring a mutual weakness for him. Feelings of love can be very complex, as we both know."

Fergus nodded.

"Never forget, Fergus: these are the people you are dealing with. Don't forget what they have done. Don't forget what they have experienced. You must gauge your sympathies based on this scale, because Evan Cavender, Jane Murray, and Ashton Harriet have ruined the lives of many good people – human and hybrid."

"It's nice to hear someone refer to humans as people."

"I grew up with them, and maybe it's only because they never knew what I was, but the people of Peygham have always been good to me." Rosslyn moved towards the door. "Thank you. This has helped me put a number of things in perspective."

Fergus nodded. "Yeah, me, too. Or, well, hopefully it will all make sense when my head stops spinning."

"You should finish preparing. I imagine Terry means to leave very soon," Rosslyn said, pulling a watch out of his breast pocket. "Keep that compass close. Who knows what will happen up there?"

"Yeah, and tell, uh . . . Tell Evan to stop thinking of me as 'Ainslee's son' already."

Rosslyn snorted. "I'll try. Good luck, Fergus."

Chapter Eleven.

"Is it loaded?" Deirdre asked, checking her pistol one last time before tucking it into the holster at her hip.

"Obviously."

"Let me see." She held out her hand, fingers twitching impatiently.

Fergus sighed and took out the revolver, passing it to her. She looked it over and handed it back.

"Told you so," he muttered and put it away.

The upper levels of New Peiling were looking as deserted as the slums. So many humans had been scared off by the tremors, it wasn't hard to find an empty house with rooftop access.

The tremors were a lot stronger up here, and Fergus stumbled as the building swayed. Maybe the Universe was trying to remind them that blowing holes into an unstable structure was a bad idea.

"Don't daydream!" Deirdre snapped, starting up the ladder.

His fist tightened around the dense, oiled fibers, and he began to climb. Terry was already positioned at the top of the ladder, ready to ignite the second explosive. The rest of the team – Leo, Bull, Pip, Three, and Ursula – trailed behind Fergus. To his left, he could see that the first team had nearly reached the plate. He thought they looked like fireflies, faintly illuminated dots floating in the shadows.

Distracted, one foot went too far through a rung, and he let out an anxious hiss. Deirdre looked down, scowling.

"I know, I know," he muttered, speeding up to get into position.

"Hold on and be prepared to move."

Fergus narrowed the gap between them and stopped, hooking one leg through the rungs. He couldn't see what was going on above, but a moment later, he heard the explosion from the first group. Several harrowing minutes ticked by, and then the second blast rocked the air. The ladder whipped back and forth. He heard Bull cry out and looked down to see Leo grab him. Deirdre glanced down, too, but only for a second before she resumed climbing. Fergus scrambled after her, squinting against the smoke and debris cascading from the plate.

By the time they reached the top, a web of ropes was in place, and Terry was crawling through the hole. Bits of concrete fell, jarring the net, and Fergus's knee slid through the gap. Far below, the tops of the buildings blurred in his vision, and he had an unpleasant image of falling and impaling himself on a lamppost. He shuddered, clutching the netting, and pulled his leg up. Deirdre was already disappearing after Terry. Fergus looked over his shoulder once more to make sure the others were okay and then hurried through the wall of dust into the facility.

Through the smoke, he saw a white room with metal shelves. Most of the floor had fallen away. A woman was screaming over the shouts of the guards, and researchers in white uniforms scrambled through the haze. One ran straight into him, almost knocking them both through the gash in the floor. He shoved the man away and began to dart forward, but Terry grabbed him, stopping him just in time to avoid being shot in the face. The bullet whizzed over his head and struck one of the cabinets.

He put his hands over his head. "Jeez!"

"Keep it together!" Deirdre shouted. "Stick to the plan!"

But thanks to the panic and chaos all around him, Fergus was finding it hard to remember what the plan was.

"Just follow me," Terry said, putting a hand on his back, "and keep that gun close."

He nodded, pulling the gun from its holster, and followed Terry in a crouching jog. They joined the wave of researchers shouldering past the guards, happy for the cloak of smoke and confusion. Outside was a long hallway, and though some dust had strayed from the previous room, it was fairly clear. Fergus ducked as Terry fired off several shots. He saw blood splatter across the wall, and a man in a black uniform went down.

A woman in a lab coat blundered into him, screaming as the guards returned fire and hit her instead. The force knocked them both to the ground. Her frizzy red hair tickled his nose. Terry dragged him out from under the woman and to his feet.

He could smell her blood on his jacket.

Deirdre streaked past them, moving so quickly, Fergus barely blinked before she was on the guards. A blade flashed in her hand, and the first fell without a sound. She spun and struck again, taking out the other. She wrenched the weapon free, turning back to them.

"Come on!" she shouted, pulling out a pouch and throwing it into the adjoining hallway. She disappeared into a cloud of purple smoke.

The cloud was thick, but Fergus found that once he stepped inside, he could easily see. The humans, on the other hand, seemed completely blind. They slipped past the guards and headed up a set of stairs.

Keeping up with Deirdre was hard, though, and they quickly lost sight of her. Boots clamored on the metal landing above, followed by shouts. Fergus took the steps two at a time, coming upon the remains of her handwork: three men flat on their faces. The adjacent door was open. From inside, they heard Deirdre shout in pain.

Terry rushed past, clipping him. He hit the floor with a grunt, but quickly got to his feet and darted inside. He slammed the door shut behind him, casting about for something to bar it with before grabbing a desk and shoving it in place. Behind him, the gunfire was deafening. Just ahead, the corridor was lined with cells. Just outside one such unit, Deirdre gripped the side of her head. Blood trickled down her neck. He turned to Terry in time to see him pulling the trigger on a guard at close range.

"No—"

Blood swept over the white wall, and the guard fell backwards. Fergus stared at the lines of red crisscrossing the floor, connecting the bodies. He looked up at Deirdre and Terry, who were already

145

searching the dead guards for keys. The smell of blood was overpowering. His stomach growled, and little white sparks erupted in the corners of his eyes.

They shouldn't have brought guns. They shouldn't have done this. They didn't need to kill these men to incapacitate them. They were already faster and stronger. They had magic. They didn't need guns. He looked up at Terry and wondered why he had gone along with this plan.

"An unnatural death is a terrible thing."

He turned. For a moment, he didn't recognize the crone. She drew closer to the bars, and he saw the scar contorting her eye.

"Lady Gemini!" he gasped.

She smiled a toothless smile.

"We'll have you out in a minute."

"No need," she replied, patting the bars. "I have not seen anything for a long time. Do you remember when last we met? I gave you a vision."

"Green."

She nodded. "It was one of my last, but I saw one more yesterday evening. This city will fall."

"All the more reason to get you out of here!"

Lady Gemini shook her head. "I saw that I would die before the city collapsed. I saw that when they took me."

"But you don't have to! We can change things. If you know what's going to happen, then just don't do that!"

She tilted her head, looking at him out of her good eye. Then her face contorted, her eye rolling backwards into her head. A gurgle bubbled out of the back of her throat.

"A terrible sacrifice." She twitched, and her eye fell back into place. Clutching her chest, she cackled breathlessly. "Perhaps that was the last."

"A sacrifice? What does that mean?"

But she didn't look at him. She just smiled into space.

"Wait, what—"

"Fergus! I've found them!" Terry shouted, waving him over.

He gave Lady Gemini one last, lingering look before joining Terry, who was fumbling with a heavy set of iron keys. Inside the cell, Raja and Evelyn sat next to one another. Evelyn smiled vacantly. Her eyes were dull, the rest of her face slack, just as she'd been outside the gate to Tír na nÓg, except now her cheeks were even more hollow, her eyes overly large in their sockets. Beside her, Raja wore the same empty expression, his normally electric blue eyes flat.

"I have Dominique!" Deirdre called, a few cells down.

There was a resounding *bang* as something rammed the door from the other side.

"They're coming," Terry said, reloading. "Raja, you in there? You better get up, because Fergus is gonna need help."

"Where are you going?" Fergus demanded.

"To hold them off."

"No way."

Terry ignored him, walking over to Raja and patting his face. "Wake up." He grabbed Raja by the arm and forced him onto his feet, where he stood swaying and smiling at nothing. "At least he can stand." He tried pulling Evelyn up, but she was completely limp. "You'll have to put her over your shoulder and guide him. Would've been nice if Bull and Leo had kept up, but hopefully they're clearing a path for us below." Terry pulled back the hammer on his weapon and headed for the door, pressing against Lady Gemini's cell and watching the desk slowly bounce away from the door with each thrust.

Fergus knelt over Evelyn, hoisting her onto his shoulder. He grabbed Raja by the wrist. "Follow me."

The door burst open, and Terry fired. A man screamed and fell to the ground, causing the guard behind him to trip. Terry leapt over them, throwing himself into the fray beyond.

A small, black cat shot over the downed guards, sprinting towards Fergus. He had to put a hand out to keep Ursula from plowing into him as she skidded to a stop, returning to human form. She recovered quickly, grabbing Raja by the arm.

"I'll take him. You concentrate on her."

"What happened to Leo and Bull?"

She stared at him a moment and then turned to pull Raja towards the door. Out on the landing, Deirdre started downwards, forcing Dominique to stumble along behind her. It seemed Dom was more put together than the others, and the two were already rounding the bend when Ursula called out.

"They've blocked off the entry point! Go to the roof!"

Fergus thought maybe Deirdre had the right of it, though, because getting a heavily sedated person up the stairs was far harder than going down, and he didn't think going to the roof would be conducive to escaping. Deirdre apparently agreed, because she didn't return, but disappeared with her charge. He heard a strangled shout below and thought that if any of them could take care of themselves, it was

Deirdre. He joined Ursula in trying to herd Raja up the steps.

Behind them, Terry crouched next to a concrete partition, leaning around to fire off round after round. It didn't sound like he was making his mark so surely anymore. Just then, a familiar face appeared from over the banister.

"We're clear up here!" Three chirped. "Here, let me help with her," she said, bounding down the steps to Fergus. "Piggy-back should work," she said, putting her back to him and holding out her arms.

"You sure?"

"Trust me!"

He eased Evelyn onto her back and returned to help with Raja.

"Can't you get him moving any faster?" Terry growled, fumbling as he tried to reload. Fergus noticed that his hands were coated in blood. He couldn't tell where it had come from, though he didn't see any tears in Terry's jacket.

"He weighs as much as a small horse," Ursula grunted, slipping around to tug the front of Raja's shirt.

"Three, tell Pip to get down here and help!"

"Pip!" she called from above. "A little help!"

"Fine!"

Pip appeared, scampering down the stairs to Ursula and Fergus, and began to help drive Raja along.

"We can't go any further," Three said as they arrived at the next landing. "It's been blocked off, and—"

She was cut off as a hailstorm of bullets rebounded off the wall beside her. She squealed, jumping back and nearly tripping on the steps.

Fergus barely managed to catch Evelyn as she slid from Three's back.

"Sorry," Three said, clutching her arm.

"Did they get you?"

"Just a scratch. There's a lot of them up there, though. We'll have to go through there," she said, nodding to a metal door across the way.

"Will it open?"

She nodded, taking Evelyn back and kicking it open to reveal an empty storage area. There were a few men on the ground, groaning.

"Um, they'll probably come to soon, so we should hurry," Three said, stepping over a guard and loping towards the door at the other end of the room.

Fergus grabbed Raja by the wrist and forced him into an awkward trot, Pip pulling his other arm. Ursula disappeared from view, shrinking into herself. Back in *cait sìth* form, she sprinted after Three. The sound of gunfire was growing more persistent. Terry flung himself into the room, slamming the door behind him.

"Damnit, let go of him a minute. We gotta block this!"

Fergus saw blood welling between his fingers. "How'd they get past the armor?" he asked, releasing Raja.

Terry shook his head and began dragging one of the unlabeled crates from the wall to the door. Pip and Fergus hurried over to help, as shouting and kicking echoed from the other side.

"They're too heavy!" Pip panted.

"Give me a second," Fergus said, stepping back and closing his eyes.

"We don't have one!"

He ignored Pip, reaching out to the hungry, black thing in the back of his head. The pain of the transformation was sharp and sudden, but his recovery was the fastest it had ever been, and he quickly nudged Pip and Terry out of the way, putting his uncanny strength to work. The crate slid against the door.

"Maybe we should stick Raja on your back," Terry muttered. His face was very white.

Fergus nudged him with his nose, ears flicking.

He shrugged. "It looks worse than it is."

"Move it, move it, move it!" Three shouted from across the room.

"Maybe we *should* put Raja on him," Pip said.

"You up for it, Fergus?"

Fergus stared at him, throwing his head and stamping a foot in protest. Closing his eyes, he struggled to concentrate.

"Fall . . . off . . . " he growled.

"Whoa," said Terry, good eye widening.

"I'll ride with him. Help me, Terry."

It seemed there wasn't a choice. Fergus let them hoist Raja onto his back, and Pip crawled up behind him. He turned, giving Terry a baleful look. Terry just smirked and ran a hand over his cheek. From his present angle, Fergus could see orange light slanting through the door the others had gone through.

Terry pressed his gun into Pip's hand and closed his eye. The air shimmered, distorting around him, and he turned into a great, black dog. His leg was matted with blood, but the *gytrash* ignored it and took off in a lop-sided run towards the doorway. Fergus sped after him, his hoof beats booming on the metal floor.

Fergus smelled the interloper before he saw him. Apparently, Terry did, too, because he slid to a stop, and it was all Fergus could do to avoid trampling him. Looming in the doorway was a tall, wiry man. His hair was pulled back, and his eyes looked like black holes in the gloom. Fergus couldn't immediately place him, but Pip let out a shriek of alarm, clambering from Fergus's back and dropping the gun in his haste.

The man grinned and took out a strange weapon: a sickle attached to the end of a heavy chain. He began to swing the chain over his head, and Fergus saw that there was a lead ball attached to the end.

Pip whipped out a slip of paper, rattling off an incantation. A red light formed around the paper, and he threw it as the man loosed the chain. It zipped through the air, igniting into a ball of flame, but the man gracefully leapt out of the way. Pip grunted as the chain wrapped around his wrist, and he was ripped off his feet.

"It's him – Jun Hyo! *It's him!*" Pip shouted, trying to free his arm as he was hauled across the floor.

Fergus still had Raja on his back, who wasn't even holding onto him, but absently petting his mane. If he fell on the metal floor, he'd probably crack his head open. Pip howled in fear and agony as Jun Hyo reeled him in, and Fergus took a half step forward, but Raja slumped dangerously to the side. He growled in frustration.

The corridor filled with a roaring wind. Fire blazed, and Fergus could just make out Terry's silhouette against the flames. His hands moved in the air like a conductor's, ushering the wave of fire towards their attacker. Jun Hyo dropped his weapon, fleeing into the hallway beyond, and Pip scrambled to free himself. Fergus snorted, trying to get his attention, so that he'd come take Raja. However, Pip ignored him, holding his wrist to his stomach and rummaging for another spell with his good hand.

Jun Hyo darted back into the room, grabbing his sickle. Nimble as a cat, he hopped onto the crates next to the door, swinging his weapon, his eye on Terry. The wall of fire faded, and Terry doubled over, panting and clutching his wound. Pip freed another flaming slip of paper, but again Jun Hyo sidestepped the danger. The chain soared through the air over Terry's head and wrapped around Fergus's neck.

He reared, roaring in anger and surprise. Raja soundlessly toppled from his back, but Fergus didn't have time to feel bad about it. Jun Hyo's speed and strength were unbelievable. He pulled Fergus off his feet, and Fergus barely registered that Pip was there before he fell on him. Pip screamed, and Jun Hyo began to pull on the chain. He gurgled, thrashing as the unforgiving links dug into his windpipe.

"Fergus!" Terry cried, stumbling forward, but his legs went out from under him, and he fell to his knees with a groan.

"Stop!" Pip shouted. "Turn back! *Turn back!*"

The chain squeezed his windpipe, but he knew he'd kill Pip if he didn't return to human form. He closed his eyes, envisioning spotted fish floating in a pond, their colors dappled by the ripples of rain on the surface. He thought of pipe smoke and the drumming of rain on clay tiles. His limbs drew back into themselves, his body rearranged, and he was human once more. Pip dragged himself out from under Fergus, breathing thinly.

Fergus gurgled, the line snapping tighter around his neck. He desperately searched for the end of the chain, knowing his throat was seconds away from being crushed, but his hands were numb, and they shook uncontrollably. He heard a furious yowl, and the tether loosened. He managed to crane his head back in time to see Ursula soar through the air, hit a wall, and go limp. Wheezing, he reached for her, still clawing at the chain with his other hand. White haze filled his eyes.

"*Fergus!*"

Another wave of fire swept towards Jun Hyo. He started to jump out of the way, but as the flame washed over the wooden crates, the air reverberated with a deafening sound. Fergus threw his arms over his face as the explosion rolled over him. The floor shuddered, and fresh air poured into the corridor. Pip crawled over to free him of the chain, and Fergus grasped his throat, blinking back stars.

The chain sparked as it slid across the floor and disappeared into the empty space where the other half of the room had been. The wind whistled through the void, clearing away the smoke to reveal a leaden sky.

Chapter Twelve.

Fergus rolled onto his stomach, swallowing back
bile. His head throbbed, and his chest burned, but he
ignored the discomfort and dragged himself to the
chasm. The wind plastered his hair to his face.
Pushing it from his eyes, he peered into the room
below. It, too, had been damaged by the blast, the
wall fallen away into the ocean. He could see the
plates extending in concentric layers down to the
island. The wreckage obscured most of the next
floor, but Jun Hyo was nowhere to be seen. He
pushed himself into a sitting position and turned to
the others.

Raja sat where he'd fallen, blood dripping from a
gash in his forehead. He blinked vacantly. His
cheeks were tear-streaked and muddy. Pip lay on his
side a few meters away, clutching his torso and
breathing roughly. His face was screwed up in pain.
On the other side of the room, Fergus could make out
Ursula's small, furry shape near the wall.

"Where's Terry?" he asked, searching the rest of the space in case he'd missed something, but Terry was nowhere to be seen. "Pip, where's Terry?"

Pip groaned, pressing his forehead to the floor. "Fergus!"

Three ran towards them, Deirdre close behind. Their footsteps boomed against the steel floor.

"Evelyn?" Fergus asked.

"She's fine," Deirdre said, crouching beside him.

"Pip!" Three gasped, putting her hands on his shoulders.

"I'm fine. Just cracked ribs," Pip managed, his voice a low hiss.

"What happened?"

"*Him*," Pip replied.

"And Terry . . . " Fergus said, staring out at the expanse of ocean and sky as Deirdre lifted his chin to examine his throat. "There was a fire, it hit the crates, and then . . . " He trailed off. "Where is Terry?"

"Fergus . . . " Three said softly, biting her lip.

"Maybe he fell into the room below," he said. He was surprised at how calm he sounded.

He stumbled to his feet. The dust was clearing, and he could see slabs of concrete, exposed beams, and pieces of crate settling on the floor below. A few people in white coats and black jackets were trapped in the wreckage, but no Terry. Fergus stepped back and staggered to the outermost wall, gripping the broken stone. All he could see – hundreds and hundreds of feet down – was sharp rocks and high waves breaking over them.

He shook his head, falling to his knees.

"Fergus, we have to go," Three said, helping Pip up.

"We must," Deirdre agreed, coming over to press Ursula into his arms.

He looked down at the black cat. Her breathing was shallow, her ribs rising and falling sporadically. He could feel hot, sticky blood on his wrist. Deirdre left him to collect Raja. Fergus looked back down at the ocean. It was miles below. His eyes burned. He turned again to Ursula, broken in his arms.

"If he is down there, he'll find a way to meet us," Pip said, jaw clenched tightly. "But she'll die if we don't go now."

Fergus nodded dully. Holding Ursula as gently as he could, he followed the others into the next passageway. Three led them to a chute in the floor. The cover was thrown back, revealing a tunnel leading down.

"It's a garbage chute, I think," she said, stopping before it. "I already secured a line from it to the next plate. The hard part will be getting Raja through. Fergus, you'll have to secure him to your back. Pip, do you think you can climb on your own?"

Pip nodded, though his face was grey.

"I'll go down first. Worst case, you fall on me. After Pip and me, Fergus, you come with Raja, then Deirdre and Ursula. Is that okay? We left the other women in an abandoned house. We'll gather them and try to find the next exit point."

"Do you have the compass?" Deirdre asked, shoving Raja towards him and pulling out a length of cord.

"Yeah," he said, discarding his metal-laden jacket and turning so that she could tie Raja to him. That done, he pulled out the compass, handing it over.

"Good. We can use it to find the fastest way down."

"Everyone ready? Let's go," Three said, slipping into the chute.

Pip followed, letting out a soft murmur of pain as he lowered himself into the shaft.

"It'll be a tight squeeze. Good luck," Deirdre said.

Fergus maneuvered himself and Raja to the chute, trying to adjust Raja's arms so that he wasn't being strangled. He found sliding to be impossible with their combined girth, but he was able to shimmy his way down to the exit. Raja pressed his head to Fergus's cheek, but otherwise did nothing to hinder or aid their progress. As they reached the bottom, he noticed that Three had apparently blown the cover off entirely. The line was attached several feet above the jagged metal. He carefully took hold of it and pushed them over the sharp edges.

Raja remained limp, but Deirdre had done a good job of securing him to Fergus. However, their combined weight was more than he expected, and he lost his grip, skidding downwards. The line ripped into his palms, but he managed to reclaim his hold. They swung wildly for a moment, Fergus gripping the rope for all he was worth, and then, ignoring the sting of his bloody palms, he climbed down the rest of the way.

Three took him by the ankles, guiding him through the window of the house below, and untied Raja. Fergus cast a guilty look over his shoulder at Pip, who was stooped over, breathing through clenched teeth. Evelyn and Dominique were standing in the corner near him. He suspected they hadn't moved since Deirdre and Three had dropped them off. Deirdre appeared a moment later, swinging back and forth on the line until she had enough momentum to come through the window.

"How did you two meet up?" he asked, waiting for her to settle.

"I blew out one of the windows, and the next thing I knew, there she was climbing down with that woman on her shoulder, so I tied Dominique to myself and followed her. No more questions. They'll sweep the level any minute now," Deirdre said, taking out the compass, passing Ursula to Three, and grabbing Dominique by the wrist.

"Let me carry Pip," Fergus said.

Pip regarded him suspiciously, but acquiesced, clambering on piggyback-style. Three put Evelyn on her back and opened up her jacket, using it to cradle Ursula. Fergus took Raja by the wrist and proceeded after the others, trying to move as smoothly as possible.

Deirdre led them out of the building and into the street, down this alley and that, and into another house closer to the center of the plate. There they found someone else's escape route and quickly descended to the next level. Between forgotten maintenance ladders and the trails left by their comrades, they reached the lower city. She brought them to the safe house where the others had reconnoitered. He saw Bull without Leo, Estelle and Tia, but no Terry.

Fergus released Raja and let Pip down, watching as Pip began drawing characters on his empty sheets of paper. He chanted quietly, the papers glowing a pale blue, and then he held them to his chest and stomach. Beads of sweat formed on his brow, but the lines of pain eased from his face. He sat for a moment, catching his breath, before going over to Ursula.

"Will she be okay?" Fergus asked quietly.

"I'll do what I can. Don't distract me."

Fergus nodded and started for the door.

"Where are you going?" Deirdre demanded.

"To look for Terry."

"Forget it. If he's alive, he'll find us. The Knights have increased in size. They aren't the intimate circle you remember. If you go out there, they'll find you, or you'll give away our location. Either way, stay put."

"But Terry —"

"*Stay put.*"

"It's okay, Fergus. Come with me. I have a potion. You should rest, okay?" Three said, taking him by the shoulders and gently ushering him into the room beyond.

A handful of Bandersnatch survivors were already there, nursing wounds, or just staring into space from the makeshift beds. Fergus joined them, taking the potion from Three, and threw it back, letting sleep whisk him away.

• • •

His line bobbed over the surface of the waves. The rod felt heavy in his hands. Nearby, on smaller rocks, Terry and Flynn sat, also holding fishing rods, though theirs had no lines. The sun was rising, creeping over the horizon and sharpening the split between sea and sky. No one said anything. Fergus just watched as the waves rose higher and higher. The tide should be receding at this hour, not coming in, but he didn't remark on it. He felt empty and free of care.

The foam slipped over his rock, soaking his shoes. He looked up to see it slipping over Flynn and Terry's knees before falling away. The next wave came up to his hips. It was high enough that it cut the others off at their chests. And then a final wave poured over them and drew them from their rocks. He could see their hair spreading out under the dark water.

Fergus felt that the emptiness inside of him was no longer a careless vacuum so much as heavy and dismal. A last wave came, dragging him into the ocean. The rod jerked out of his hands, vanishing into the murky depths. Water filled his mouth. He swam towards the surface, struggling to stay afloat. He saw the morning light illuminating Terry's hair just as he sank under the waves. He turned, seeking out Flynn, but he was long gone. He opened his mouth to breathe, to scream, to sob – he couldn't decide which – and found himself thrust against the rocks hard enough that his spine snapped.

The imagined pain woke him. He blinked, staring up at the chipping ceiling of the safe house bedroom. He was alone, save for Pip, who was fast asleep. He sat up, running a hand through his hair and seeking out the phantom pain, but finding it gone with the dream. Deciding he was fine, he got up and joined the others in the next room for supper.

He walked over to Three, who was ladling out a fishy smelling stew. She smiled a little when she saw him, but her eyes were bruised and lined. A moment later, she pressed a warm bowl into his hands. The heat spread from the clay through his fingers, and he felt his throat tighten and his eyes blur. He swallowed the feeling down.

"Terry?"

Her expression fell, and she shook her head.

"Ursula?"

"She'll be fine if she rests for a few days. Her injuries were bad, but Pip knows his stuff."

Fergus nodded.

"He might have made it. He might have just been injured, so he's taking a little longer . . . "

"It's great, isn't it?" Fergus said, interrupting her.

Her eyes widened. "Great?"

"Jun Hyo is dead."

"Oh," she said, looking down. "Somehow, I can't believe it. Maybe because I didn't see it, but Pip says he was right there when the boxes blew up, so he must have been killed either in the explosion or the fall."

They were both silent a moment too long.

"You can finally go home," Fergus said.

She nodded. "We can."

"So?"

Three bit her lip, looking like she couldn't decide whether to smile or frown. "I feel like you still need me. I want to be here for you."

"I'll be fine. This isn't your battle. Maybe it isn't even mine. Maybe . . . Maybe this is the best we can even do."

"What do you mean?"

"I could have prevented this," Fergus said, lowering his voice as he looked over his shoulder. "I knew it was wrong. We could've thought of something better, but we started blowing things up and shooting at them, and of course if the humans feel like they're under attack, they're going to fight back. They're terrified of us, so why would they hold back? I knew that all along, but I wanted Terry to . . . " His voice broke.

She put a hand on his shoulder. "To what, Fergus?"

He shook his head. "I knew it wasn't the right thing to do, but I went along with it anyway. I could have stopped it. If I'd stopped it, then Terry . . . "

His hands clenched the bowl, but it didn't stop their shaking.

Three took the soup, quietly putting it aside. Her arms folded around his neck. Her hand climbed up the nape of his neck, into his hair, guiding his head to her shoulder. But he didn't cry. He just took sharp, unsteady breaths, his fingers tightening in the back of her jacket as she murmured to him about how it would be okay, but he thought it would never be okay again. Flynn was gone. Terry was gone. Ursula was badly injured trying to save him. He couldn't convince himself that it wasn't his fault.

And Terry was gone. Terry, who had lost an eye for him. Terry, who had saved his life time and again. Terry, who loved him best. A sob escaped him. He quickly smothered it, feeling pathetic and ashamed.

"I could have stopped this. I could have. Violence makes for more violence. That's all this was."

"Maybe you could have, maybe you couldn't," Three replied, stroking his hair. "It was an accident. Terry happened to be standing too close. The boxes had something combustible in them. He didn't know that and neither did you. Maybe you could have convinced them to do things differently, but then again, maybe he wouldn't have listened. You aren't responsible for what happened to Terry or Ursula." She drew back, putting his face between her hands. "You aren't."

He looked down at her, feeling hollow again. "I have to get out of here."

"They may still be looking."

"I know, but I grew up here. Plus, it looks like Deirdre returned this to me," he said, pulling the compass out of his pocket. "If you can just distract her, it'll only be a little while."

Three frowned, glancing over her shoulder. "Right now?"

"I'll go through a window in the bedroom."

She sighed. "Come back soon, okay? And be super-duper-extra careful."

He nodded. Picking up the bowl of soup, he returned to the bedroom, sticking it on the floor next to Pip before going to the window and prizing it open. The air outside looked mottled and hazy. He gingerly stuck a finger out and felt a little static, but his hand passed through without incident. For a moment, he waited, listening for sounds of alarm, but none came. A simple glamour. Not much for security, but he couldn't complain. He strained his ears for the sound of anyone outside, but the alley was silent, so he slipped through the window, shutting it behind him.

The slums were vacant, entertaining only shadows and ghosts. He let his sight adjust to the darkness before quietly jogging away from the safe house. He didn't know where he was going. He just knew he couldn't break down in front of all those people. Maybe not at all. He wasn't sure what he felt as he shuffled along. Hopelessness edged into his thoughts, but he carefully repressed it over and over, sucking down rough breaths of the cool night air.

He arrived at the docks. They were unnervingly empty, though he saw someone with a lantern patrolling the boardwalk. He hastily ducked, holding his breath until the light disappeared, and then slipped onto the rocky path skirting the city's perimeter. New Peiling didn't have a coast so much as a collection of sprawling boulders surrounding it. If Terry had fallen past the plates and onto the rocks, he was definitely dead.

Fergus stopped, closing his eyes, and took a deep breath.

What would happen if he found Terry's body? What *would* he do? He didn't know, but he knew he had to look anyway. He forced himself to continue along the narrow, slippery path.

He headed in the direction of the research facility, though it occurred to him that Terry might not have fallen directly below. There was the wind and the force of the blast to consider. He slowed, scanning the water as he walked along, but he saw nothing but foam and seaweed.

He came to the area he thought was below the compound and climbed out onto the rocks. The tide was coming in, rising almost high enough to touch the wall separating the slums from the ocean. The waves soaked through his pants, filling his shoes. His eyes combed every inch of the water, but still nothing. When his fingers and toes were numb and his legs shaking, he relented and returned to the path.

Had the current stolen them away? Were they pinned under rubble? He considered swimming out to check, but he couldn't bear the idea of finding

Terry bloated and discolored under a rock. He shuddered, hugging himself, and sat down. The boulder was cold and damp, and the wetness seeped through the seat of his jeans. Still he stayed there, arms around himself, staring hopelessly out at the water.

He lingered until the sun began to peek over the horizon. It reminded him of his dream, but he was alive, and though very cold, safe. Only Terry and Flynn were gone. He pressed a hand to his mouth, stifling the sound. His fingers tightened in his hair until he felt the sting of strands ripping from his scalp. He wanted to curl inside himself so deeply, he just disappeared.

"Fergus?"

He'd lied to Three about hurrying back. For a moment, he thought she'd come to find him. She was probably really worried, but he couldn't seem to care. However, the voice was male.

"Fergus."

He looked up at Guillory as he lurched and skidded towards Fergus's rock.

"Do you have any idea how hard it was to find you?" Guillory grumbled, glancing over his shoulder.

Fergus looked down, his hair falling over his face. He wanted to wade into the water, to follow Flynn and Terry. Feeling anything else seemed like a pointless effort. It was a strange sensation, the absence of emotion, the coldness in his chest.

"Are you going to drown yourself?" Guillory asked quietly.

Fergus's eyes strayed from the water to the worn out knees of his jeans. He shrugged and pulled them to his chest.

"I found out they were using *my* name to amass those guns. I'll admit, it's put me in a difficult position, since all the people I'd rounded up to help are now second-guessing me. There *are* humans who wanted to help, but you all just attacked. Do you know how many people were killed? You behaved like monsters."

He remained mute, fiddling with his shoestring.

"Are you listening to me?"

"It's my fault," Fergus mumbled. He lowered his face to his knees. "It's my fault."

"It is," Guillory agreed.

Fergus slumped even further, pressing his eyes to his knees until the black space was filled with odd dots and sparks.

"I know they don't always listen to you, but more than anyone, you know that unrestrained violence is wrong. A plan so deeply embroiled in such violence could only cause more problems, more pain. How many times have you said it? That's the reason you came back here instead of going to Tír na nÓg, isn't it?" Guillory's shadow fell over him, but he didn't look up. "You knew it was wrong. I want to know *why* you went along with it anyway."

He shook his head. "Terry said it was the only way."

"But you knew it wasn't. Right now, you're thinking of all the other options, aren't you? But you folded to their warped vision. This is where it's gotten you."

Fergus nodded.

"So what will you do now? Kill yourself? Run away like your mother did? You've lived your entire life in circumstances someone like me can't even imagine. You shouldered them and moved forward more than anyone I've ever met. But looking at you now . . . Well, get on with it."

"Terry is gone."

Guillory didn't reply. He shifted, letting a sliver of sunlight fall on Fergus's shoulder. It felt inappropriately warm.

"My family is gone. Flynn is gone. Ursula is gone. Terry is gone."

"And those are the only people who mean anything to you?"

"No," Fergus said, shaking his head. "No, of course not. But Terry is gone."

"I'm a wanted man. I can't afford to stand around coddling you. I have to try to fix the damage that Terry has done. If you remain here, they're going to find you, and they'll shoot you on sight. I suppose that's only adding to your options, hm? Pull yourself together. This is your fault, so now it's up to you to fix it. Then you can do whatever you want."

With that, Guillory turned on his heel and stormed off. Fergus could hear him cursing as he slipped over the wet rocks.

He lifted his head. The sun had broken past the line of the horizon and was slowly rising into the ether. The sky was golden-pink above the water, fading away into blue. The color seemed thin and cold and distant. Gulls cried overhead. Waves broke on the rocks. But the sound felt muffled by the horrible, growing static inside of him.

He slid off the rock. His limbs felt numb. He imagined himself being covered with snow, disappearing into a world that was empty and painless.

But he needed to return.

Three is worrying.

He started that way, ambling down the familiar streets that led past the now abandoned universities and the garage where Everyday Resources used to practice. He thought he was going the right way, but all the buildings ran together. Maybe the whole city was ensorcelled. Maybe it was all an elaborate glamour.

He stopped at a corner, reaching into his jacket for the compass, when he was snagged by the elbow and steered into the nearest alley.

Gavin looked down at him with his baby face and his big brown eyes, holding a finger to his lips. Fergus hadn't seen him since they'd left for Tír na nÓg. He'd been working at Beathag's then. Once upon a time, he'd been in Niamh, along with Jane, Audrey, Evelyn, Raja, and Flynn. All of them had been searching so desperately. Fergus wondered what Gavin would think if he told him that they *had* found Tír na nÓg, and they'd elected to stay here instead. He wondered how *he* felt about that at present, but quickly crammed the thought back behind the protective numbness.

"You look bad," Gavin noted. His eyes were so deep and warm. It was hard to look into them and not trust him.

Fergus shrugged.

"Will you come with me?"

"Where are you going?"

"To Jane's. We heard you were back. She's been hoping to see you."

Fergus considered whether he wanted to see Jane the morning after Terry died. She'd once been Flynn's girlfriend or lover or something. Certainly, they'd been accomplices. But Jane – the madwoman,

169

the temptress, the martyr – had nonetheless played an integral role in Flynn's murder. Besides which, she'd had the gall to insinuate that Fergus had been responsible.

He wondered if Harriet had told her that he was back. Rosslyn had said they'd been an item. It stood to reason that she was allowed to remain here unmolested because of him. He wished Harriet had kept his stupid mouth shut.

But what did he have to lose?

What *did* he have to lose?

Everything that had happened was his fault: the undoing of Guillory's good work, Terry's death, Ursula's injuries . . . It was because he was a hypocrite and an idiot. And here he was, healthy and whole despite all.

So what did he have to lose?

He imagined what Ursula would say if he went to Jane. Probably she'd yell at him, call him gullible. He then imagined what Terry would have done. Probably he would have asked if Fergus had lost his mind and then skulked around outside her home, listening for the sound of Jane trying to stab him with one of her fancy butter knives. The thought alternatively made him want to laugh and forced him to choke back a sob. He looked away, pulling up his hood.

The loss rendered his vision into a black and white field where there was the world that had Terry and the world that didn't, and in the world without him, Fergus found it hard to care that Jane probably meant to do something horrible to him.

Maybe Ashton Harriet was waiting in her fancy penthouse, ready to jump Fergus and exorcise him the moment he stepped through the door. But if he was, that might be best. The perfect opportunity to get rid of him, even.

"We have to go," Gavin whispered, edging into the shadows. "They'll find us here."

Fergus nodded and, stuffing his hands into his pockets, followed Gavin down the alley.

Chapter Thirteen.

Jane lived in a white penthouse at the edge of the plate. Brick steps adorned with falcons led up to double doors inset with large panes of frosted glass. Fergus paused at the foot of the steps and watched Gavin approach the door. He was fairly sure this was an ambush. He considered telling Gavin that he understood why. He *was* what Ashton Harriet wanted. Turning him over might open up the table for a number of favors or free passes. But he thought that on the off chance it really was Jane and not Harriet inside, he shouldn't say anything to alarm Gavin. So he squared his shoulders and went up the steps.

No click of a hammer, no doors ominously shutting behind him, no triumphant laughter. His entrance was disconcertingly unremarkable. Rather, there was Jane, slipping from a nearby room in a translucent purple dressing gown and matching slippers. Her hair was neatly swept up into a coil at the nape of her neck, and she looked pink and healthy.

172

"It's been too long. Are you hungry, Fergus?" she asked, tilting her head.

Her voice resonated in the bones of his chest, jolting his nerves.

"I guess," he mumbled.

She smiled and turned, shuffling down the hall. Rubbing his sternum, he cautiously followed, keeping his eyes off the line of her body under the robe.

The house had a faintly medicinal scent that made it feel empty and sterile. There were dark rectangles on the walls, the afterimages of paintings. It looked like there'd been rugs on the floor, because the wood wasn't polished, and there was a difference in coloration between the boards at the center and those by the walls. Where had the furniture gone?

He jammed his hands deeper into the pockets of his jeans. He wasn't entirely convinced Harriet wasn't hiding around the corner.

"I've missed you," Jane said, and though the ceilings were high and the hall empty, her voice sounded muffled. Again, he had the impression his bones were vibrating.

"Why?" he asked, not caring that it was rude.

"Why? Why not?" she asked, peeking at him over her shoulder, her voice turning light and effervescent.

"Not like we're best friends," he muttered.

She let out a peal of laughter. It had a distinctly eerie quality, like the croaking of many toads in chorus. Fergus stopped in his tracks, scowling.

"You are growing wiser," Fand said with an unpleasant chuckle, stopping and turning to him. Her finger found a stray red curl, twisting it around and around.

"Why are *you* here?"

"To bring you to Jane, my pony. She hoped to speak to you," she replied, blinking at him dreamily. "Right, Gavin?"

"She just wants to talk. She has no idea what's going on with any of the other hybrids who've managed to remain here."

Fergus jumped, realizing Gavin was standing just behind him.

Gavin smiled consolingly. "Seeing people – hearing a little news – is good for her."

"Is she still . . .?" Fergus trailed off, not really wanting to outright ask if Jane was still out of her mind.

Gavin's smile faltered, and he looked away.

"I see. Okay, fine. I'll play along, but I've got somewhere to be, so I'm not gonna stick around," Fergus said, frowning between them.

"Terry Bridges isn't with you," Fand said, releasing the curl and turning to saunter down the hall again.

Fergus bristled, but bit his tongue.

"The pup is busy engineering secrets, is he?"

"I don't know what you mean," Fergus replied as blandly as he could manage. "Anyway, I thought you weren't interested in the doings of mere mortals."

"I'm simply surprised to see you alone," she said, pulling the robe tighter.

The air around her distorted, and she dropped an inch or two in height, her hair turning a browner shade of red. When she glanced at him over her shoulder, the freckles were gone, her nose was straighter and hooked at the tip, and her mouth was fuller. The face she regarded him from was older than Jane's, but similar enough that it must've been lifted from a family member.

"Who are you pretending to be now?" he asked.

"I'm not pretending to be anyone, but she likes this face."

"And whose is it?"

"You can't guess?"

Fergus looked away. "Must be her mom."

Another unsettling chortle escaped her. "You've always been cleverer than they think. Here we are."

The kitchen had no door. The entryway led straight into a dining room with a long table, its paint fading and chipped, where he assumed the servants must have taken their meals once. At the other end of the table, there was a second entrance from which he could see the stove and some cooking utensils. A row of windows bathed the table in sunlight, and he recalled that the penthouse was actually on the border of the plate.

Jane sat in a ray of light, drinking tea and eating a roll of bread as she read from a moldering old book. She looked like she'd just woken up. Her hair was tangled, but not knotted. Probably Fand had brushed it for her. The sun glowed in the frizzy parts, igniting a golden crown atop her lush red locks. Her face was very gaunt and sallow, but her eyes were bright, perhaps too bright. She turned at the sound of Fand's delicate feet descending the steps and smiled. Her smile was terrible and beautiful. She looked past Fand to Fergus, and it grew. He looked away uncomfortably.

"Fergus," she said, climbing awkwardly from the bench.

Her nightdress got caught on the wood, and he heard a rip, but she paid it no mind as she hurried over to greet him, catching his hands in her own. He didn't return the squeeze, but she didn't seem to care. For a moment, she just looked him up and down, like she wanted to take in every inch of him.

"How good to see you," she said with a sigh, releasing his hands to take him by the wrist and pull him towards the table.

"It's been a while," he said, his voice cautious, the words measured.

She nodded, her eyes momentarily far away as she looked towards the window. She slid back into her seat, folding her hands on the table, and stared into the light. It made her face look waxen. He looked down at his feet. Fand sat down across from her, and so he went to the other side of the table to sit beside the fairy, leaving Jane to Gavin.

"I should offer you food," Jane said, absently staring into the light. "But I'm no good at cooking, nor is Fand." She smiled at the woman wearing her mother's skin.

"I'm good," Fergus said, his stomach starting to knot.

Gavin was watching Jane, who was still staring up into the light, but Fand was staring at Fergus, and he scooted a few inches away.

"I could make something," Gavin offered.

Fergus shook his head. "I'm good," he repeated, a little annoyance slipping into his voice.

Fand smiled at him, her gaze sharp and greedy. He stubbornly stared back at her, but she didn't look away, so feeling disgruntled, he found a whorl on the table to stare at.

"Let's have something to drink. I can manage that," she cackled, getting to her feet.

"I'll help you," Gavin said, catching an unseen cue.

Fergus narrowed his eyes, watching them disappear into the other room. He glanced at Jane, who was gazing at him with a nebulous expression, and returned his gaze to the whorl.

"Fergus," she breathed. She began to tidy her hair, pulling it over her shoulder. "Being around you reminds me of Flynn," she said, absorbed in smoothing the locks. "It's like there's a little piece of him in you. A little piece only I can see. Something just for me."

"Uh huh. Is that what you wanted to talk about, Jane?" he asked, pointedly avoiding her face.

"No, no. I have plans, Fergus. I have so many plans. Niamh is gone." She paused in fiddling with her hair to stare upwards, her face slack. "My Niamh is gone. All the work I did for hybrid rights is gone."

"Because you sold everyone out to Harriet," Fergus replied quietly.

She shook her head forcefully, turning to him with wide eyes. "No, it wasn't like that! He tricked me! He *deceived* me! He's a monster!" Her voice was over-quick, the words coming out spluttered and crammed together.

"Why did you tell him about Niamh?"

"I," she started and then stared down at the table, brow pinching. "I wanted him to leave me alone. I loved Flynn. I wanted to be with Flynn."

"Did you know Flynn had learned how to find Tír na nÓg?"

She was silent for a long moment.

"So you did."

"I thought he had found something, but he never shared."

"And why did you tell Harriet?"

She twisted her hair into a single coil, pursing her lips. "I was angry and drunk. I told him I never wanted to see him again, and that Flynn knew how to get to Tír na nÓg, so we were going to go there together."

"And so he found Flynn and killed him."

Jane stopped playing with her hair. "It wasn't my fault. How could I have known?"

"Because he hates hybrids?"

She lowered her hands to her lap. "If it had only been jealousy, he would have stopped with Flynn, but instead . . . Audrey and Evelyn . . . "

"Evelyn is still alive," Fergus said.

"I know what they do in that place. If she's alive, it's only technically."

Fergus sighed, rubbing his eyes.

"That's why I need to kill Ashton Harriet."

He dropped his hand, blinking in surprise.

Her fingers pressed against the edge of the table, the joints white. "He's left me here out of pride, but his hubris will be the end of him, and I will be the engineer. That's why I need your help." Her fingers relaxed, but she didn't look up. "I know you're Ainslee Irvine's son. I know you can become a kelpie. I need your strength. If we work together, we can get rid of the Harriets and save all the hybrids in the colony."

"So we kill him. Then what? What about the person who steps up to take his place? And the next? This isn't just about two people," he said, shaking his head and wondering how many times he was going to have to say it.

She stared at the table, her eyes flat. "Them, too, then. All of them, if we have to. We'll just weed out all the bad people until it's safe again."

"Do it yourself."

"I can't."

"Even if I helped you, you wouldn't succeed," he said, running his hands over his greasy face.

"What if we just took him prisoner? Held him hostage? We could use him as a bargaining chip. I still have airships. Probably enough to take all the hybrids far away from here, if he would only let us leave." She lifted her face, her eyes dull and sunken. Yet the tragedy that hollowed out her features made her more beautiful still, more fey – ephemeral and strange. "We just have to find a way to force him to listen to us."

"Like brainwashing?"

"Yes, like that. Maybe we could put a spell on him to make him change his mind."

"Won't his mother just say he's unwell and send him away?"

"She might, but it would still weaken their position. A lot of people follow Ashton *because* he's Ashton, not because he hates us."

Fergus frowned. "Are you sure about that?"

She nodded eagerly, leaning over the table. "I've known him and his friends since I was a child. I've talked with them hundreds of times. Some hate us, but there are many others who love him, weak-willed people who rely on his strength, who would change sides if he did."

"And if the spell wears off?"

"It will wear off far away, because I'll take him far away. He'll be my responsibility. If you just help me get my hands on him, I'll take care of the rest."

Fergus sighed, rubbing his eyes. "I'm too tired to think about this right now."

"Then you should sleep on it. We can talk more when you wake."

He looked at her through his fingers, frowning. "There are people who are gonna get worried if I stay here."

"Tell me where they are, and I'll send Gavin."

Fergus shook his head.

"You don't trust me?" she said, lip quivering.

"Not really, no."

"We have to act soon, though. Even if you don't trust me, trust my plan. I promise you, I'll take care of Ashton and make everything right. But I can't risk losing sight of you. What if *they* find you?" She shook her head, leaning against the table, the front of her robe straining against the curve of her breast. "Just stay here and rest, and then you can tell me 'no' if that's how you really feel, but at least give me this chance. *Please*."

He didn't feel like arguing. The idea of a real bed and unconsciousness was so appealing that he just sighed, dropped his hands, and shrugged.

"Fine. Let me sleep, and then we can talk."

She sat up, clapping. The gesture reminded him of a night in a makeshift cottage filled with jars of glowing things and ripped up rags of downed airships, with the smell of honey thick in the air and an old witch cackling in a voice like a toad. Goosebumps ran down his spine.

Jane was already on her feet, hurrying to usher him up and out of the room, and the weight of his grief and exhaustion felt unbearable enough that he let her lead him out of the kitchen and up the stairs to a room with a four-poster bed and a feather mattress with silky blue sheets. He was aware that she was trying to help him pull off his clothes, and then he was fast asleep.

•   •   •

The room was dark when he opened his eyes. He felt groggy and let his mind drift, sinking back into a state of uncomfortable semi-consciousness. But his mind played tricks on him, filling him with the sensation of falling over and over until he gave up on falling back asleep. His head felt leaden, and when he sat up, he saw stars. He winced, closing his eyes, and ducked his head between his knees. Before he could fully banish the vertigo, he felt a tug on the hem of his shirt.

Jane smiled up at him, her skin radiant in the darkness. Her hair spilled over the bed, an inky mass of red waves against the blue linens. She tugged his shirt again.

"Have you been watching me sleep?" he asked quietly, searching for some trace of Fand or Gavin in the shadows.

There was a large window, which stretched from floor to ceiling, across the room from the bed. Heavy velvet curtains blocked out the light, save where it slipped in around the edges. He could hear rain pattering against the glass. Beyond the warmth of the sheets, the room was clammy and cold.

"Maybe," she replied, still gripping his shirt.

He rubbed his face. "That's kinda creepy."

"I used to watch Flynn sleep sometimes."

"I wish you'd stop comparing us."

He could feel his skin puckering in response to the chill. He rubbed his arms and wished she'd go away.

"I like your eyes," she said, wriggling across the silky sheets to wrap her arms around his stomach. She pressed her cheek to his ribcage. "They're so blue. I've never met anyone whose eyes were such a deep blue. It reminds me of swimming deep underwater. When I look into them, I feel so peaceful."

"That's very romantic."

She giggled and released him, moving back to her side of the bed. "You didn't sleep for very long. Why don't you lie back down?" She rolled onto her back, pulling the covers up to her throat. "You talk in your sleep."

"Oh yeah?"

She nodded, glancing at him out of the corner of her eye. "You kept calling for Terry."

"I don't remember."

"Did something happen to Terry?"

He didn't reply.

"I'm sorry," she said, and for once, she sounded sympathetic. "You were close."

He swallowed roughly, pressing his palms to his eyes and nodding.

Her arms encircled his shoulders, hands coming to rest against his chest. Her body was very warm against his back.

"I'm sorry," she said again, pressing her face into his shoulder. "This is all Ashton's fault."

"No," Fergus said, shaking his head. "It's mine. We were trying to save all the people they'd captured: Evelyn and Raja and Dominique. We were trying to do the right thing, but in the wrong way, and Terry used his magic."

"What happened then?" she asked, her breath burning a hot circle into his shoulder blade.

"There was an explosion. He was gone."

She nodded, her grip tightening.

"I searched for his body, but I couldn't find it. He was probably blown out to sea."

She rubbed her forehead against the nape of his neck. "I could help you look. I'm a *selkie*, you know. I can easily search around the rocks."

"I appreciate the sentiment, but you have a human body. I think having a selkie soul won't change that."

"I can transform now," she replied, leaning back. Her fingers dragged through the hair at the nape of his neck, giving him goosebumps.

"You can?" he asked, feeling a curl of apprehension in his stomach.

He felt her nod, her breasts rubbing against his shoulders.

"How?"

"I've been practicing ever since the day Evan and I went to Lady Gemini, and we learned I was a selkie."

"You and the Count went to Lady Gemini?" Fergus asked, trying to look around at her. "How old were you?"

"A girl. After he caused that ruckus by coming out, my family didn't want me to spend much time with him, but I would sneak out. He seemed sophisticated and dangerous. It was like going on an adventure. He said he thought I might be a hybrid, too, so we went to see her, and she said I was a selkie. After that, I decided to take swimming lessons. There's a recreational center in Erstwyre Park. I swam there every day, trying to find something, some mystical presence or magical feeling that I could latch onto.

"I didn't really think things through. If I had transformed back then, can you imagine the scandal it would have caused?" She sighed. "It took so many years. But I finally did it, so I *could* help you. As long as he wasn't pulled out to sea, I could find him for you. That is, if you help me capture Ashton."

Her fingers skirted the hem of his shirt. Her cheek pressed the side of his face. He felt a chill as she slipped her fingers under the cloth. He gently put a hand on her wrist.

"From this angle, your eyes are white, or is it just because of the dark? Flynn's were, too. I guess you know that, since you lived together. A *tarbh uisge* and a kelpie. Your nature should be savage. There's some part of you that wants to hurt Ashton, isn't there, Fergus?"

"I'm thirsty," he said quietly, turning away from her.

"I think we have water and milk. I'll see," she said, sliding off the bed to stand before him, her robes open.

He stared down at his hands. "Either would be fine."

He didn't look up again until he heard the door shut behind her. He went over to the window and pushed back the curtains. The world outside was a marriage of black and grey. Rain pelted the windows, mottling the glass. A bolt of lightning danced across the sky, and he shivered, stepping away from the window and letting the curtain fall back into place.

A moment later, thunder rattled the glass, and then the entire room started shaking. Books bounced off shelves, pictures fell from nails, and his teeth clacked together. It was the strongest tremor he'd felt yet, and he had to grab the curtains to keep from falling.

The pause that followed seemed too still and silent.

He wondered what would happen if Ursula died from her wounds. The only powerful magician left would be Rosslyn, and he remembered hearing that Rosslyn was not as good at magic as potions. Probably the city would collapse in only a few days, maybe a few hours. Even if she pulled through, how much longer did they have?

They needed to focus on breaking the other hybrids out of the colony and getting as far away from New Peiling as possible. But he'd have to go along with Jane's plan to do it. Could they really get away with enchanting Ashton Harriet? Would all those people supposedly loyal to him really turn against his mother and the anti-hybrid supporters?

And he wasn't sure Jane would keep her promise about the airships. He wasn't sure she even had that influence or the resources anymore. But if she did, it would be a godsend, because he definitely didn't want to ask the Count for help.

If they left, where would they go? Maybe they could found a new city. There was a lot of empty space in the world. They could settle practically anywhere they wanted and live unmolested. But if the city was comprised of only hybrids, the children who lived there would grow up separate from and distrustful of humans, just as any nearby humans would fear the inhabitants of the hybrid city. At some point, the segregation would breed conflict.

Maybe they'd just travel the world, dropping people off as they liked, letting them start their new lives wherever they wanted. Most cities required papers for entry, though. Maybe Guillory could find some way to get them all papers, or maybe he knew someone who could forge the documents. Of course, that was assuming Guillory would even talk to him again.

There wasn't a simple solution.

Sighing, he went to lie down, pulling the covers over his shoulders. They'd gone cold in the time he'd spent wandering around the room. He shivered and drew his legs up to his chest. He didn't know if he could make the right decisions, not if it was left entirely up to him. He needed people with experience like Guillory and shrewdness like Terry. He felt very cold and alone.

The door creaked, and he looked up at Jane, who at least had retied her robe. She walked over, holding two steaming mugs, and sat on the edge of the bed beside him.

"I managed to find some cinnamon and chocolate, so I thought I'd make cocoa."

He sat up, taking the drink. The glass burned his palms, but it forced the chill away.

"I can start a fire, too. There's a hearth," she said, putting her mug down and going to the other side of the room to fiddle with the fireplace.

Fergus sipped the hot cocoa, feeling a little better. He watched her out of the corner of his eye, observing the way the silky robe gleamed in the dim light, the way her hair seemed to erupt in color when the kindling caught.

"Is this your room?"

She looked over her shoulder, smiling. "Yes. Or it has been since my parents died. I had a much smaller room as a child. Sometimes, when I feel lonely, I sleep in my little old bed. I know it's impossible, but now and then, I think I can still smell my parents in there. My mother's lavender perfume and my father's lime soap."

He sipped the cocoa, nodding. "I used to think I could smell my mom in our apartment sometimes." He paused. "But it wasn't very comforting."

She rose from the fire, coming to stand before him. He looked up at her in the orange light. Again, he thought she looked very gamine and wild, but her blue eyes were focused, and her hair was tidy. He wondered if she'd stopped to brush it while making the drinks.

Very tentatively, she reached out to take the remains of his cocoa. Then she leaned down and kissed him. She tasted like chocolate and spice.

"Just for now," she murmured.

Chapter Fourteen.

The day had gone from cool to cold, the rain refusing to ebb. They gathered by the hearth in a sitting room made up in forest green and tan. There were a couple of couches and tables covered in crisp white linens on which potted plants rested, dousing the room with the smell of mildew. A picture window punctuated the far end of the room, framed with lacy curtains. Fergus sat beside the marble bust of an annoyed old man. Across from him, Fand and Jane sat on a faded paisley sofa. To his right, back to the window, Gavin had claimed a leather armchair.

Jane had taken a shower and changed into a simple dress and shawl, which made her look more human. Fand still wore her mother's face, though, which was disconcerting. He wished she would at least act a little bothered by it. Fergus had also been permitted a bath, which had been interrupted by another tremor. Even so, he felt like he was properly resituated amongst the living.

"Fergus has agreed to help!" Jane said, smiling brightly at the assembled.

He looked away as Fand and Gavin turned to him, nodding placidly. It irked him that they didn't seem surprised.

"In exchange for helping me free the prisoners in the colony *and* getting them outta here," he added, glowering at no one in particular.

"If Ashton Harriet is under our control, that shouldn't be hard," said Gavin, rubbing his chin.

Fergus nodded shortly.

"Then," Fand said, putting her hand on Jane's knee, "if we free them and take them away, you'll lend us your power?"

Fergus nodded again, wondering why she was repeating what he'd already said. He felt like he'd missed something important, but he couldn't think of what that might be.

"It's a deal." Fand picked up the glass of wine next to her, smiling demurely as she sipped.

He toyed with a loose string protruding from the armrest. "So, how can I help you? I'm guessing you know tons more magic than I do." Which, frankly, was none at all. "Plus, you're already familiar with his hangouts." He worried his lower lip. "Don't think I can take on Evalach single-handedly either."

"We need you to be the bait," Jane said.

"The bait?"

She nodded cheerfully. "There's no one he wants more than you, so all we have to do is tell him we have you and that we'll give you to him all trussed up if he agrees to some of my demands."

"How do you know he won't just barge in here with his lackeys? And why would he believe you?"

"Well, we'll obviously need proof. Maybe a lock of your mane . . . "

189

"But how do you keep him from barging in here with Evalach?" he repeated, eyes narrowed, fingers climbing through his hair.

He'd heard from Flynn that a lock of hair – like a drop of blood, a tooth, or a fingernail – could yield powerful binding magic. He couldn't imagine putting a piece of himself in their hands would end well.

"I'll tell him I'm hiding you until I'm sure he's alone. I know this city as well as Evan or any of your Bandersnatch friends. Besides, we have a history." She tapped her collarbone. "And I know he can't help but think of me as a full-human, despite knowing better."

Fergus bit his tongue, looking away. The indifference in her voice repulsed him. Even after being lovers for years, she had so little regard for Harriet. Would she one day speak of Flynn so carelessly? That callousness was no doubt the reason she'd gone to the Count when Flynn went missing, the reason that Deirdre and Audrey *had* nearly killed him.

Then again, it was Ashton Harriet, who'd done horrible things to a lot of people, and they were only taking him away, not hurting him. Toying with his feelings didn't feel right, but he told himself it was the lesser of two evils. It was better than what Bandersnatch would've done.

"I don't like the idea of giving you my hair," he finally said.

Jane blinked.

"Why does it have to be *my* hair?"

"Because even a human can feel the magic in a lock of kelpie hair."

"Why can't you just dye your hair and give it to him?" he said. "Shouldn't a selkie's be just as good? Or a true fairy's?"

"It's only Ashton. He doesn't have any magical ability. He'll probably just throw it out," she replied.

"But you do," Fergus said, not meeting her eyes. "I promise I wouldn't use it to hurt you."

"Just color your hair and give it to him."

Jane let out an exaggerated sigh. "It's pointless if he doesn't believe we have you."

Fergus didn't reply.

"We can use something else," Fand said. "Do you have anything in your wallet?"

"I lost it when I was arrested."

"Fergus, please. I swear we won't use it against you. I'll stick it straight in an envelope and seal it, so you know we haven't kept a single hair." Her blue eyes were wide and entreating.

He pursed his lips, snapping the thread. "Okay, fine. *Fine.* If you seal it into a letter, if I can watch you do it, then I'll let you have some hair."

"Perfect. So we'll send him the lock of hair with a letter. He'll take the bait, of course. Then when he comes to me, I'll blindfold him and bring him here, where I'll show him how we have you 'captured.' That way, if he doesn't come alone, we'll know very quickly. But I think he will. He isn't afraid of me. I believe he still has some affection for me, even.

"Besides, he won't be able to save face if it turns into another blunder, like how he let you escape from the prison, or how that research facility was broken into. If I know him, he'll want to verify the claim for himself rather than risk further embarrassment. Once we have him convinced you're our helpless captive, I'll invite him for a drink. That's when we put the spell on him."

"What if he decides he's gonna take me? What if he won't compromise?"

"That's what Fand and Gavin are for, silly," Jane replied, shaking her head. "We're not completely useless, you know!" She nudged Fand, who shrugged vaguely, and then turned to Gavin, who smiled fiercely. The look didn't suit him at all.

Fergus nodded reluctantly. "How are you gonna show I'm helpless?"

"Well, it'll require some acting on your part. We wouldn't want you to actually be helpless, would we?" Jane giggled, standing. "If you pretend to be asleep, we can tell him that I've put a spell on you. I'm not a terrible witch, and he knows it. If I tell him I have you ensorcelled, he'll believe it."

"You're really confident."

"Well, I have known him nearly my entire life." Her fingers skimmed the curve of a potted fern beside her. As she reached the end of the frond, she picked up her wineglass, putting it to her lips. "So now we just need you to transform. At your leisure, of course."

The glass in the window began to rattle loudly, the potted plants clattering on the tables. Several books fell from the shelves, and Fergus could feel the sofa shudder beneath him. Jane barely managed to catch her glass before it tipped over. They held their breaths, waiting for the shockwave to pass.

"But perhaps sooner is better," she said, gingerly setting down the glass. "This city doesn't have much longer."

"Not without the hybrids," Fergus said.

"It'd be nice if they could just come back."

He shook his head. "Even if you have Harriet under control, I doubt your plan is permanent enough to guarantee their safety. Besides, I dunno if —" *The magic could be strong enough without Ursula.*

He gazed out the window, keeping his expression vacant and willing himself not to think about the possibility of Ursula going from bad to worse. Part of him wanted to take her, along with Three and Pip, and leave now. Never look back. But he knew he'd regret it if he turned his back on the hybrids in the colony.

It turned out invisible bonds chafed the worst of all.

"Shall we have dinner? And after that, I'll cut off a piece of your mane and seal it up, so we can send it to Ashton. How does that sound?"

"Fine by me," he said.

"You can rest here while we make the preparations," Jane said, getting to her feet and coming over to briefly touch his knee. She smiled, but the smile didn't meet her eyes. "Don't worry about a thing."

•   •   •

He'd fallen asleep. For once, the drone of rain had been soothing. He supposed it made sense, paired as it was with fire and wine and a comfortable sofa. His face felt numb, his eyes gritty. He sat up and realized he'd knocked the remains of his wine over. He frowned, picking up the glass, and placed a pillow over the stain.

The penthouse was quiet. He strained his ears, but all he could hear was the occasional tap of rain on the window. He walked to the door, peering out into the hallway, but it was entirely dark. There wasn't even light creeping out from under the doors lining the corridor.

Pursing his mouth, Fergus cautiously started down the hall towards the kitchen, but that turned out to be empty, too. He headed for the second floor. The aged wood groaned, each step made deafening. Fergus cringed and tried to walk along the edges, but the planks insisted on creaking. As he arrived upon the landing, another shockwave rolled through the plate. The railing swayed dangerously under his hand. He released it and fell straight into the wall.

"Ow," he grumbled, rubbing his nose.

The quaking finally subsided, so he got to his feet, looking around. It was shadowy on the second floor, too, and just as quiet. Goosebumps ran down his spine. This place, with its barren walls and slow decay, was very creepy in the dark. He half-expected to see a ghost. Now hugging himself, he pressed against the wall and peered around the corner towards Jane's room. His breath sounded thunderous in his ears. He closed his eyes and tried to hold it, but the pounding of his heart took its place.

Sighing, he slapped his cheeks, wondering, *Since when am I afraid of the dark?*

He wasn't. He was a kelpie. *He* was the bogeyman. There was no reason to jump at shadows. Straightening, he forced himself to round the corner. Behind the first door, he found another sitting room with a half-finished watercolor sitting on an easel and stacks of books littering the floor. It looked like someone had been here recently, but they were gone now. Scratching his head, he proceeded down the corridor to check the rest of the rooms, but these were also unoccupied.

"Hello?" he ventured, though his voice sounded small and ridiculously timid to his own ears. He cleared his throat, shaking his head sharply, and went back downstairs.

If no one was on the first floor, and no one was on the second floor, then where had they gone? He stood at the foot of the stairs, straining his ears for the slightest sound, and then he heard the barely perceptible sound of scraping coming from below. He quickly got down on hands and knees, pressing his ear to the floorboards.

Sure enough, someone was moving around below him. It sounded like they were pushing furniture. Getting to his feet, he began to search for a set of stairs to the basement. He was pretty sure they hadn't taken a secret passage out of the main sitting room, because he couldn't have slept through that. He walked past the servants' table and down into the kitchen proper, where he found a trap door opening up to a dusty set of stairs.

Tiptoeing, he descended into the cellar. Furniture had been piled along the outsides of the room, which afforded him some cover. He huddled on the steps, peeking over an old piano. Lanterns lit the space where Fand, Gavin, and Jane had assembled. Presently, they were pushing a heavy old table against the far wall. The center of the room was clear.

They'd also stirred up a lot of dust, and he stifled a sneeze, squinting to see what Jane was doing. She had crouched on the floor with a candle in one hand and a piece of chalk in the other. Fand and Gavin finished moving the table, putting it on its side.

Gavin wiped his hands on his trousers and went over to help Jane, but Fand just stood there, silently watching as Jane drew lines on the floor. She'd already drawn a circle, which Gavin began adding symbols to.

Fand looked up at the stairs, and Fergus ducked. He puffed out his cheeks, holding his breath, but if she'd seen him, she didn't say anything. All he could hear was the sound of chalk scraping against the old boards.

He wondered if it would be safe to sneak upstairs, or if he should just announce his presence, but he didn't know what they were up to, and he had a feeling their behavior was anything but innocuous. He wrestled with his anxiety for a few more minutes, listening to the soft sound of the chalk grating on the floor, and then decided he had no reason to hide.

Probably Fand already knew he was there anyway, and it was weird for him to remain huddling like a spooked mouse. What if one of them walked over? There was no way he could flee without being seen. Very quietly, he stood and descended the stairs. Fand watched him mutely, making no motion to alert the others.

The circle was nearly complete. Their chalk arced over the floor, their fingers nearly brushed, and the air crackled with the electricity of magic. The lines on the floor began to glow a faint white-blue.

"Fergus," Jane said, starting as she spotted him standing there just outside the circle.

"Hi," he said, looking down at the runes. "What're you doing?"

She smiled softly, pulling her hair back. "Just a little magic. A trap for Ashton."

"Uh huh," Fergus said. "What's it do?"

"I have a lock of his hair here," she said, procuring a jar. He couldn't see its contents. "I just put it here," she said, setting it at the center of the circle, "and when he steps inside, he won't be able to move."

"Oh. That's a good idea."

She nodded brightly. "It's a little like the magic they're using to support the city. Come here. I'll show you. It's actually very simple."

He eyed the lines skeptically.

Jane laughed. "I swear, the floor isn't going to open up and eat—"

They scarcely had time to turn their heads as the furniture around them began to tremble. A pane of glass fell from a china cabinet, shattering. Then the room really began to sway.

Fergus had the sensation that the floor had just opened up underneath him. It felt as though his stomach had plummeted past his feet. The piano skidded across the floor, threatening to overturn, but Gavin managed to catch it and hold it back. Fand jumped out of the way as a grandfather clock fell over, its glass also breaking across the floor. Jane shrieked in alarm.

A bookshelf tipped forward, knocking Fergus into the circle. Light jumped in spiky, electric lines towards the ceiling. He fell to his knees, staring across the space at Jane. Her red hair was askew, her eyes wide with terror. The white-blue light made them look dull and unnatural.

"Fand," she whimpered.

Fergus tried to sit up, to move his hands from their place on the boards, but he was fixed to the spot.

"What's going on?" he demanded, trying not to sound afraid, but failing.

Fand stood just outside the circle, backed all the way into the table to avoid being caught in the jagged light crisscrossing over their heads. The light hissed, electric arms reaching out and grasping blindly for more bodies to drag inside. Gavin reached for Jane, but Fand held him back, overpowering him as though he was a mere child.

"Jane! *Jane!*" he shouted, reaching for her.

Jane stared at him, her face slack with shock. "This isn't what it's supposed to do."

"Perhaps the tremor damaged the spell," Fand mused.

She allowed herself to be distracted just long enough for Gavin to rip free. He thrust his arm into the light and grabbed Jane by the back of her dress, yanking her out of the circle. She collapsed against him, limp in his arms.

And in her absence, Fergus could clearly see that the broken vial she'd left behind, the one that supposedly contained Harriet's hair, held nothing at all.

Sweat poured down his face, stinging his eyes. It pooled at his chin, fell to the boards between his hands in heavy droplets. He tried to blink it away. Arms of light slipped over his body, stinging his skin. He blinked up at Fand, finding it increasingly difficult to hold his head up. She stood just outside the circle, letting the rogue fingers of light stroke her chest. She watched him blankly, her face cold and distant.

Then she smiled very slowly, cocking her head, bird-like.

Fergus groaned in protest, but the heat had sapped his strength. He had to do something, he had to escape, but his mind was jumbled, his body overheated. It was all he could do to remain upright. Then the orb of light broke, bursting upwards in a single column. It burned through his body. He opened his mouth to scream, but no sound came out. He felt himself lifted by the force of it. It felt like it was going to rip every hair out of his head.

He squeezed his eyes shut. "Terry."

Wherever Terry was, Fergus thought he'd soon be joining him.

And just like that, the spell broke. Gravity brought Fergus's hair back down, pressed his body against the boards, and without the magic gluing him in place, dumped him none too gently onto his side. His fingers and legs jerked out of control. It felt like his heart was beating off-kilter.

He managed to roll onto his stomach. His hair fell over his eyes, clinging to his skin, but he lacked the strength to push it away. He stared at Jane and her accomplices from beyond the screen of sweat and hair. Saliva dripped from the corner of his mouth. His entire face felt deadened.

He closed his eyes and heard Fand shuffle over in her dainty silken slippers. She crouched beside him, stroking his sweaty hair. A toady chuckle escaped her.

He refused to open his eyes.

"Poor pony," she murmured. "You neglected what I taught you, didn't you? If only you had gone through the gate."

He growled. He wanted to knock her hand away. He wanted to bite her.

She leaned over him, and he could feel her cold breath on his ear. "Did you not like my gifts? I gave them to you freely."

"Terry," he said, the word slurring into oblivion.

She stood, moving away.

For a moment, Fergus thought he heard the *click-clack* of nails on wood. Then he fell into the deep, welcoming darkness.

Chapter Fifteen.

The dog wavered, coming in and out of focus. Its tail wagged, a slow-motion smear of ink. It was running, leading him through the streets of the city towards a marble staircase that wound infinitely upwards through the plates. The gytrash barked and began loping up the stairs. Its strides were enormous. Fergus ran and ran, but he could never quite catch up.

A blinding light emitted from the top of the stairwell. He slowed, feeling for steps ahead of him. He could hear the dog's nails scraping on the stone overhead, growing increasingly distant.

"Terry, wait!"

The gytrash paused, still wagging its tail, and then it was off again, disappearing into the light.

The stairwell began to sway precariously. Fergus grabbed for the railing, but it crumbled under his hand, and he toppled over the side. He could just make out Terry's silhouette leaning over the edge, watching as he fell down, down, down . . .

He awoke with a start.

His entire body felt brutalized. Letting out a shaky breath, he tentatively went over his limbs one by one and found that he'd been tied by both wrists, ankles, hips, and his throat. His wrists were blistered, or they had been. They stung terribly when he moved, and he could feel something seeping from the broken skin.

From the smell of dust and old wine, he inferred that he was still in the cellar, though it seemed they had moved the table into the center of the room to lay him on. Out of the corner of his eye, he saw large iron nails embedded in the wood, securing the ropes that bound him.

Not good.

He swallowed dryly and licked his broken lips. He could neither see, smell, nor hear anyone in the room, but he thought there might be feet moving around the kitchen above.

There was a fuzzy kind of dryness in his mouth. His throat twinged. Without thinking, he found himself whispering, "Water."

The stairs creaked, heralding the arrival of one of his captors. He turned his head as much as the rope would allow. Jane's face seemed to glow an uncanny white as she regarded him from the bottom of the steps. She moved, and her body blurred. He squeezed his eyes shut and opened them again. Her skin still seemed to shine, but her features came back into focus.

"Water," he repeated.

She held up a glass, spilling a little over his lips. He choked, but his throat was so parched, he kept drinking until she put the glass aside and leaned over him, resting her hand against his cheek. It was cool enough to soothe, and he sighed, staring dully at the ceiling.

"I'm sorry," she said softly.

"Planning to . . . harvest my soul?"

"I didn't want it to be you. If it could have been Terry or that Ursula woman, I would have been happier."

"I wouldn't," he mumbled, closing his eyes. "Why?"

"I need to kill Ashton, Fergus. For Flynn. To avenge him the way you failed to. But when he's dead, his Knights will come. I don't want to martyr myself. It's not what Flynn would have wanted."

Fergus wanted to laugh at her narcissism, but the effort would have been more painful than it was worth. Instead, he silently regarded her from half-closed eyes. Her fingers threaded through his hair, and she sighed.

"I have to be strong enough to escape. I will do as you asked, though. I'll make sure the rest of the hybrids escape before the city falls. I still have an airship. It can hold some of them, and I'll ask Evan to help, too. So you won't die in vain."

"What right . . . do you have to decide . . . that?" The words faltered across his parched tongue. "To decide . . . what you are doing has a purpose . . . if it takes my life to fulfill it?" He swallowed roughly. "That you are doing what Flynn would want?"

Her eyes hardened, and she stopped stroking his hair. "I knew Flynn. He would want me to be safe."

"Yeah, but he would . . . never want this." Fergus hesitated, licking his lips. "And I knew him better."

She stood, eyes narrowing, mouth thinning.

"I knew . . . you were sick with revenge . . . that night when I found Deirdre at the docks . . . and you wanted me to kill her . . . but I saved her . . . instead." He closed his eyes, momentarily overwhelmed by the pain. "I knew . . . he'd want that more."

"Whatever he wants or doesn't want, he doesn't have to worry about it anymore, does he? Because he's dead. Because they murdered him."

"Because of you . . . and Ashton Harriet."

"But I'm making it right, aren't I? I'm going to kill Ashton for betraying me and murdering Flynn."

Fergus didn't reply. He tried to be as still as possible to keep from further chafing his blistered skin.

"I don't need your permission or your blessing. I can live with killing you. I didn't want to. I liked you. I tried to be good to you. I really *would* have preferred for it to be someone else. Flynn cared about you more than anyone else. But he's gone now, and all that's left is us – our memories and our ghosts. This is what I have to do to chase my ghosts away. I'm going to use your powers to kill Ashton, to escape and start my life over. I deserve that."

"Don't care . . . what you do or don't deserve . . . but you're only helping yourself . . . by killing him. That's what Flynn would hate . . . the most."

"Be quiet, Fergus."

He cracked open an eye. "Or what? You'll kill me?"

For a long moment, she stared at him, her face cold and distant. "We have little time to waste. The city will fall soon. I hope you are prepared." With that, she turned on her heel and retreated up the stairs.

Fergus stared at the glass of water sitting just out of reach and sighed. Maybe if he could knock it over, it might pour onto his hand. He always healed more quickly in cold water. If he could heal one hand, he could snap the rope and free himself. But he'd have to rock the table if he wanted to knock the glass over, and that would require a full body effort . . . or magic, but even though it was water, which was supposed to be his element, he'd never been able to actively use magic.

Eyebrows knitting, he tried to will the water to do anything, but it just rippled a little, and he wasn't sure if that was because of him or the tremors.

"Are the preparations complete?" Fand asked from the top of the stairs.

Fergus stared at the ceiling, wondering what he should do. Fand was blocking the exit, and he knew from personal experience that she was insanely strong. She'd dragged him to his feet while he'd been a kelpie, and he must have weighed close to a ton. It was sheer luck that Gavin had squirmed free of her grasp. Physically speaking, she was easily a match for him. Besides that, she could shift into both people and animals, and so he figured she probably knew other powerful magic, too. He couldn't go through her. He'd have to wait until she was inside the room and out of his escape route.

He chewed his lower lip, trying to stay calm as the three came down the stairs. Gavin walked to the other side of the table – away from the exit – and his heart sank. He'd hoped Fand would've positioned herself there, but she stopped at the head of the table. At least she wasn't directly between him and the stairs, meaning that Jane was all that separated him from freedom. Better than nothing, but not good.

He raised his eyes to Fand. "I thought . . . you liked humans."

She tilted her head. "I did."

"Why'd you change your mind?"

She began tugging at his hair, but unlike Jane's earlier caress, her fingers yanked. He schooled his expression against the discomfort. He didn't think her silence was a non-answer, at least. She seemed to be giving it legitimate thought, and though the furniture began to once again clatter and dance around the room, she remained unconcerned.

"They are like you."

"What?"

She stared into space, unresponsive.

"Spell it out . . . I think I deserve that much," he said, glaring at Gavin and Jane.

Gavin smiled thinly. "Fand offered you two precious gifts: the ability to shift into a fairy's body and an offer to enter Tír na nÓg."

Jane nodded. "You offended her by making light of them."

And one must never turn down the favor of a fairy, Fergus thought, sighing.

"Don't worry. You can see Flynn soon," Jane said, smiling softly.

"No, I can't. He died. I'm gonna be . . . erased."

But she ignored his argument, patting his knee. She didn't look as cold and vicious as before, but he thought it was doubly disturbing that she was slipping into a dreamy mood at a time like this.

"So you wanna punish us all . . . for me not going in?"

"Tell me this, Fergus Irvine: why do humans think they own this world?"

"I dunno. They just . . . always have."

"But we were also a part of it, weren't we? And now you try to lock us away. You destroyed the gate, and there won't be another for many years.

Years here are so much longer than the years there. There, a year feels like no more than a day, and here, a day is like ten years. I don't like that." Her knuckles trailed along his cheek. "It was the humans' fault that our worlds separated, and because they separated, I had to choose. I hate choosing. Why are humans always so insistent on picking one thing or the other? If one must choose, why not pick the option that allows both?"

Fergus flinched as her nails drew a little too close to his eye. "Because our lives are short . . . so we have to make decisions . . . to move forward. Because sometimes . . . you can't have everything."

"But that's so silly, don't you think? So silly and vain, the idea that your lives are so important that it matters what path you take."

He had very little time left. If he could keep them distracted with philosophical arguments, it might give him enough time to transform and escape.

"How do you know . . . the Cataclysm wasn't an act of God . . . or just . . . completely random?"

Fand's hand stopped, and she stared down at him without comprehension.

"You don't . . . do you? You're just so sure . . . because you've gotten good and arrogant," Fergus said, staring up at her and forcing himself not to blink. "Because you've got more power than we do . . . and you live longer . . . but that doesn't give you . . . the right to meddle with us . . . or to judge us."

"I miss the Otherworld," Fand said, ignoring him. "When I saw the rocks blotting out the light, I realized that I want to have both worlds open to me. Not having that option made me feel I had lost something. I never felt like I lost something before, except when *It* happened, and I had to choose to remain here." She smiled, and he noticed that her teeth were needle sharp. "But then I realized I could make this world into my own Tír na nÓg. A place just for me."

"So what, you'd be the fairy queen?" he asked, sneering.

"The fairy queen," she repeated. "Do you think I'd be a good fairy queen?"

Jane giggled. "Can I be a fairy queen, too?"

"You're all . . . so freaking insane," he whispered, closing his eyes tightly. "The Harriets, Evalach, the Huntsmen, Bandersnatch, Niamh . . . You're all so warped."

"That's not very nice," Jane mumbled sullenly.

"Screw you."

"Shall we begin?" Fand asked over him.

His time was up.

"Lucky for you . . . someone left instructions," he muttered, watching Jane take out a silver dagger.

"It *is* very convenient. I've never done this before," she said and began to run the blade over the scars that Declan Abel had cut into him months ago.

Immediately, his chest felt like someone was digging talons into his ribs and pulling. He bit his tongue to keep from screaming, and blood filled his mouth. Bile rose at the back of his throat, and he swallowed it back with a groan. His heart hammered like a frightened rabbit's, and he wondered if he might get lucky and have a heart attack before they could finish, but that seemed like a pretty big gamble when losing meant oblivion.

Help me, he willed the kelpie. *Please, help me.*

The blade dug in deeper, and he let out a hiss of pain, eyes snapping open. Jane stared down at him impassively, continuing to follow the scars that

Declan had left, but cutting more deeply. He panicked, wrenching at his bonds.

"This will only hurt more if you struggle."

The skin around the cuts burned and bubbled. White-hot pain shot across his brain. He screamed, struggling blindly. The ropes around his wrists groaned, and Gavin and Fand latched onto his upper arms, forcing him down.

No! No, not like this! he thought. *Help me!*

This time, the kelpie awoke.

Fand cursed, releasing him. He could hear her starting to mutter a spell, but there was nothing he could do as the transformation began. The ropes snapped, and he rolled onto his side, kicking and grunting. He kneed Gavin, knocking him across the room. Jane dropped the dagger, yelping as she scuttled backwards towards the stairs. The table groaned under his weight and then cracked, falling into two pieces with him in between.

Fergus let out a furious bellow as he struggled to get his feet under him. He knew Fand must be near the end of the spell, and he was still in the middle of the circle. He didn't want to know if he could break out of it in this form. He threw himself at her, leaping free of the circle just as the floor lit up.

On the other side of the room, Gavin staggered to his feet, rubbing his head. He blinked up at Fergus and gasped, pressing against the furniture. Jane still stood at the base of the stairs, looking befuddled. The dagger lay just inside the circle. She straightened and shuffled over, bending down to pick it up.

"Jane, no!" Gavin shouted.

Her fingers passed through the light, and she squealed as the magic danced up her arm, pinning her in place. "Gavin, help me!"

Fergus turned his attention to Fand. Blood ran down his chest, pooling around his hooves. His nostrils flared as he drew his lips back over sharp fangs. Fand eased away from the circle, backing towards the other end of the room, and Fergus forgot his resolution to flee. He heard Gavin shout behind him, joined by Jane, and he thought they must have fallen into the circle entirely. *Good.* One less distraction.

The fairy watched him warily, but not fearfully. Her head was cocked just a little, and she still wore Jane's mother's face.

"Are you going to kill me, Fergus?" she asked, sounding amused.

He sped up, far enough from the circle now that he wasn't worried about stepping into it as he advanced on her.

"I don't feel like dying," she said.

She raised her hands and spoke a fairy word. He recognized it from deep down in his bones. It was magic that didn't have human logic attached. A violent blast of wind struck him. His hooves slipped on the floorboards, and he found himself sliding backwards towards the magic circle. He couldn't let her capture him again. Putting his head down, he surged forward, struggling against the gale. Chairs and bedside tables smashed against the walls, the splinters pelting him. Jane shrieked in pain.

"That's the problem with kelpies," Fand said, frowning as she lowered her hand. "Stubborn. Well, if that won't stop you, let's see if this will."

Her smile made him pause. She lifted her hands to her face. For a moment, her form was bathed in light. Then she lowered them, and Terry looked back at him with his sharp grey eyes and his freckled nose and his generous mouth, which was presently parted imploringly.

"Please don't kill me," she said in Terry's voice.

Alarmed, Fergus took a step backwards, throwing his head.

Fand reached for him. "I won't hurt you, so don't hurt me."

She edged closer, and Fergus shook his head, pinning his ears. He snorted angrily, but surrendered another step. The circle was just behind him. He could feel the magic tickle his ankles. He couldn't afford to back up any further.

"Fergus."

Her tone – Terry's tone – was the same as when they'd been in the enchanted forest and Fergus had killed the shape-shifter and Terry had bravely walked up to him and gotten him to return to human form. The name circled his brain, mesmerizing him.

He mustn't hurt Terry.

"It's okay."

Terry's pale eyes held him, bold and certain. She reached out with Terry's long, calloused fingers.

"Come here, Fergus," she instructed, and he lowered his head, feeling warm, familiar arms slip around him.

But though she looked and sounded exactly like Terry, she smelled like a moldering old spring and magic. Nothing about her was human. Nothing about her was Terry. He lifted his head, feeling a strange calm settle over him, and nuzzled her face.

She chuckled with Terry's voice, a voice he'd never hear again, because Terry was dead. Yet he didn't feel insulted. He felt peaceful and distant as she ran her hands over his face, scratching his forehead. He opened his eyes as she continued to stroke his brow and cheeks and the flat bone of his nasal cavity.

She smiled her froggy, triumphant smile. It looked alien on Terry's features.

"Good boy. Back up."

Fergus started to shift backwards, but even as he did, he turned his head and snapped down on her throat. Thick, effervescent fairy blood filled his mouth.

"Fer . . . gus . . . " she rasped, still wearing Terry's face, still using his voice. He flattened his ears to block out the sound. Terry's eyes stared at him beseechingly. "Why, Fergus?"

He closed his eyes and jerked his head back and forth. Her body snapped from side to side, and she went limp in his jaws. He dropped her, watching her body recede. Long, wavy locks of strawberry blonde hair tumbled across the floor, stained dark with her blood. Her face was childlike, overly perfect in its fine-boned beauty, her skin luminous and golden. It was the first time he'd seen one of the *Sidhe*. She opened her eyes, and they were the most dazzling shade of green he'd ever seen. Her dying beauty was terrible, but though he wanted to look away, he felt lost in her unblinking stare.

Fergus, she mouthed, reaching for him. Dark blood bubbled from the corner of her cherry lips, but he did not bow his head to her.

Her body began to shimmer, the golden hue of her skin becoming more and more pronounced, its

212

radiance painfully bright. And then she burst into a cloud of glittering dust, filling the room.

The granules stung as he breathed them in. He reared, snorting and coughing and trying to expel the powder, but the dust ingrained in his throat, and he fell to the ground, screaming. It poured in through his nose and mouth, infiltrating his brain. He could taste Fand's blood. It dribbled from his chin, rubbing into the open wounds on his chest.

He wasn't sure when he shifted, but he was aware that his body was human again. Pain crashed over him in waves, pulsating down his spine, speeding through his nerve endings. His head was on fire, his nose bleeding. He clawed at the floorboards, several nails snapping. He tore at his hair and face.

But nothing eased his suffering, and the room was turning weird and menacing. The walls loomed closer. The shadows grew dense. Hands formed from the darkness, fingers crawling over the floorboards towards him.

"No, *no!*" he screamed, kicking as they slipped up his legs.

He had to escape. Ignoring the pain, he got to his feet, casting about. The only way out was the stairs. He dove for them, tripping on each step, but the door had been shut and barred. He shouted, pounding with both fists.

Something was forming down there, some horrifying, misshapen thing. It spilled across the basement floor and began to ooze up the steps.

"No! No, no, *no!*" he continued to shout, grabbing the banister and thrusting his shoulder against the door. Something splintered on the other side.

The blight crept closer. Soggy, half-formed hands broke free of the mass, slowly dragging it up the steps after him. He threw himself against the door again, and it cracked, caving. He struggled through the broken wood into the kitchen. The black thing spilled out after him, its fingers curling around his ankle. He kicked ferociously, lurching to the other side of the room, and grabbed everything he could from the walls and counters, pelting the creature.

Still it came pouring up from the cellar. His hands found the sink, and he ripped it from the wall, hurling it at the fiend. Water exploded from the broken pipes, and he threw his arms over his face. The stream diverted, forming an L-shape, and struck the aberration, forcing it back down the stairs. He dropped his arms, blinking once, and then, without hesitating, Fergus turned and fled from the penthouse onto the street.

Chapter Sixteen.

The storm had reached its apex. Windows trembled. The air pulsed. His bones rattled in his skin. Thunder boomed over and over, tattooing its rage on his eardrums, so that he heard it even in the pauses. Lightning flashed in impossible succession, confusing his eyes and sending him running in all the wrong directions. It reflected in broken windows, painted buildings bone white. It revealed unfamiliar streets, illuminated strange landmarks, and told him that he was completely lost.

He'd been running blindly since escaping Jane's house, but every time he stopped, the quagmire caught up to him. It was no longer comprised of black sludge monsters. Now it was made up of garishly colored forms that mutated before his eyes – the colors roiling and mixing and glaring. They fell apart and coalesced again, forming grotesque shapes that reached for him incessantly. He kicked them away, smashed them to bits, but so long as he remained still, they found him again.

An iron fence surrounded the outskirts of the plate. The space between the bars was so narrow, not even a child would have been able to slip through. The bars looked deceptively ornamental, but he found them very sturdy as he bounced off the fence and knocked himself onto his back. He scrambled upright.

How much longer could he keep running? His legs ached, his sides were cramping, and he was dizzy with exhaustion, but he couldn't stand the thought of those things touching him, so he kept moving. If he could make it to the slums, he could find Rosslyn or Pip, and they had to know some sort of magic that could protect him from those horrible things. But he was panicked and the buildings ran together and the street names made no sense.

He was back at the perimeter. He pressed his face against the bars. Rain pelted his skin as he wrapped his hands around them. He sank against them, breathless and aching. For a single, delirious moment, he wondered if he could knock the fence down. Then he could jump. It might not be so horrible. The terrible amorphous things wouldn't be able to get him, and maybe he and Terry's spirits would latch onto new humans at about the same time, so they could meet again.

But he didn't want to die. He wanted to live. What he wanted beyond that, he wasn't sure, but the instinct to survive took precedence, and he turned from the bars, drawing his knees to his chest. Rain trickled down the back of his neck, soaking his shirt. He was too tired to keep running. He watched the polychrome miasma progress from under his bangs.

"Don't touch me."

Distorted hands skittered over the pavement, climbing the hems of his jeans and winding around his legs.

"I said don't touch me!" he snarled, head jerking up, and he shoved at the hands tangling around his legs – now lime green, now a vulgar pink.

"Don't touch me!"

A wall of water materialized around him. Before he could question how or why, it burst, exploding outwards in a wave. The disfigured things were washed away in the unforgiving deluge. As they disappeared from sight, Fergus staggered to his feet.

"What?" he mumbled, hugging himself. His nails dug into his elbows, and he noticed that his skin felt strange under his fingers, misshapen and gelatinous. He poked his wrist, and the skin didn't seem to pop back into place properly. He was struck by an intense fear that if he moved at all, if anything touched him, it would warp his body, and he wouldn't be able to remember what he looked like to set himself straight again.

"Help me," he whispered, but only the rain replied.

Gingerly clutching his arms to his chest, he began to shuffle through the flooded streets. The water leaked into his shoes, soaking his socks. Each footstep squelched unpleasantly.

Go down.

He just had to find the others, and they'd sort him out. Someone had to know what was happening to him. He stumbled upon one of the central express lifts and felt a trill of excitement. If it was working, he could take it straight to the Count's penthouse. However, as he approached, he could see that the glass walls were glazed with dirt, and the metal floor had rusted. He frowned, stepping inside just to see if it might trigger the lift, but it remained silent and still. He couldn't even hear the usual whirr of electricity, pouring life into the cables. Frowning, he stepped outside again, looking around for some kind of on-off switch or lever that might power it up, but he only found a button for emergency shut-offs.

Without electricity, he wouldn't be able to operate it, but the track it ran on was still a direct route to where he needed to go. If he could get to the belts underneath, he could climb down. There was an escape hatch embedded in the floor of the lift, but it had become corroded, and he could neither yank it open by the handle, nor fit his fingers into the cracks to pry it open. He stood and stamped on it. The car rocked, but the metal only dented a little, and he was overcome with the fear that if he kept stamping on it, his leg would become deformed. He backpedaled out of the car, falling onto his bottom.

It took a moment to calm his nerves and convince himself that the shape he was in was exactly the shape he should be. He ran his hands over his face, breathing out a long, jagged sigh, and then got to his feet. He'd ruled out the easiest options, and now he was left with only one possibility. He would have to force the car up enough to climb under it. He searched around and found a trash can to stand on, hoping it wouldn't cave under his weight and the pressure of forcing the lift up.

He put his hands at the top edge of the car and began to push. The metal bit into his skin. The frame was as rusted as the floor. Probably no one had used it since the mass exodus of the human populace, and the spring rains hadn't helped. He briefly wondered where the humans had retreated to, but tucked the thought away. He didn't have time for idle speculation. Those *things* were sure to return any minute.

Grunting, he pushed with all his might and heard the angry squeal of metal. The lift went up a couple of inches. His hands, arms, and back complained. He released the car, hopping from the trashcan, and paused to catch his breath, hands on his knees. It had moved, which meant he just had to push it upwards a little more. He wasn't that big. If he could clear a foot of space, he could squeeze through.

Provided it didn't slide back down and crush him.

Still, his thoughts were muddled, and he couldn't think of a better plan, so he climbed back onto the bin and began pushing. His muscles and joints protested, but the lift slowly gave inch by inch. He jumped off the trashcan again and squatted down. He could see the conveyor belts at the back of the lift. It looked like they were within reach. His hands were still brutalized from escaping the research center, so he ripped the sleeves from his shirt, binding them around his palms.

Swallowing roughly, he eyed the car and then wriggled under it until he could get his hands around the belts. He slowly pulled the rest of his body through the gap. Even with the bandages, the rubber burned his hands as his body swung free, and he nearly let go, but he managed to get his legs around the belt and commenced half-climbing, half-sliding down its length.

•   •   •

He could hear people nearby. He wasn't sure where he was in relation to the penthouse, but there were people, and they smelled like hybrids. The horrible amorphous monsters hadn't followed him, but in their place, weird, undefined things slithered and scuttled just outside his line of sight. When he turned his head, there was nothing there, but it felt like he was being watched, being followed.

His eyes weren't just playing tricks on him. The world as he knew it had merged with something utterly bizarre. He could see tiny droplets of water hanging in the air all around him and orbs of light hovering in the shadows. He wasn't sure what those were, but they had an aura of potent magic, so he diverted his path to put plenty of space between himself and the lights. Colors did not appear as they ought to, and sounds were louder and sharper than they should've been. It was like being a kelpie, except his senses felt simultaneously heightened and disconnected.

Eyes befuddled and hearing muffled, Fergus didn't even notice the man step in front of him until he'd plowed straight into him, knocking him down and sending himself reeling. He collected himself quickly and went over to check on the stranger. He knew he should apologize. He opened his mouth, but the words got stuck at the back of his throat, as he was smacked by a sudden sense of déjà vu.

He stood there blinking owlishly, trying to make sense of this familiarly unfamiliar feeling. The man got to his feet. He was a hairsbreadth shorter than Fergus, the lines of his body fluid and lean, his carriage graceful. His black hair was loose, glued to his cheeks with blood and rainwater, but Fergus thought he saw the remains of a ponytail clinging to his shoulder. His eyes were a lightless, limitless black.

"Who are you?" Fergus asked.

The man studied him, and his coal black eyes abruptly grew bright with recognition. His teeth drew back over bloody teeth, and he reached for a weapon that wasn't there. Fergus didn't move, cocking his head and studying him, trying to work out why he felt so perplexed. Just looking at the man didn't yield answers, though, so Fergus moved closer. He thought he smelled wet dog fur and a sharp, musky tang of magic. His eyes widened.

"Terry . . . You smell like Terry. Where is Terry?" he asked, reaching for the man.

"Fergus!"

He turned. It took him a moment to recognize the tall, dark-eyed woman coming towards him. Her black hair, streaked with blue and green, seemed exceptionally shiny. It swept from side to side as she ran. Its movement was fascinating.

"Fergus, get away from him!" shouted Three, unsheathing her sword.

"He smells like Terry!"

He turned just in time to avoid being stabbed in the stomach. Instead, the blade skirted his ribs. He looked down at the rip in his shirt and the thin line of blood forming underneath. Then he looked back up at the man. The man's eyes seemed enormous, insect-like. He grinned, exposing sharp, yellow teeth. Murky seawater seeped over his swollen lips and poured down his chin and throat. Fergus recoiled.

The man jabbed at him again, and he fell backwards. His assailant lunged, but a wave of fire drove him back as Three jumped between them.

"He smells like Terry," Fergus repeated, tugging on her jacket.

Three ignored him. "Jun Hyo, prepare yourself."

"No, Three, wait! Listen to me! He smells like Terry—"

She darted away from him, sprinting towards the leering Jun Hyo, who abruptly burst into a run. Despite the fact he only had a knife, he met Three's sword head on, fearlessly and effectively. He blocked her, shoving her in the chest and knocking her back. His attacks were relentless, the knife leaving silvery lines in its wake. Three struggled to parry, but Jun Hyo's reach was long, his movements impossibly quick, and Fergus smelled blood.

"Where is Terry?" he demanded, but Jun Hyo was completely focused on Three. "I said, *where is Terry!*" he bellowed, charging, but someone grabbed him from behind. His body jerked, and he felt a painful tension in his shoulder and elbow as he was whipped around to face Pip.

"Stay back, or you'll get her killed!" Pip snapped, pushing past him. The boy's body seemed to undulate as he ran, swaying exaggeratedly.

Fergus groaned and pressed his palms to his eyes. It wasn't any better when he lowered them. Pip was bathed in green light, seeming to float through the air. Three's arms and legs jerked back and forth and up and down, each movement disjointed as the limbs of a puppet. In fact, as he looked up, he thought he could see light reflecting from cords hanging over her, attaching her to Jun Hyo.

Fire formed in Pip's hands, ripped through the air, and thrust Jun Hyo away from her. The strings ripped with a ghastly, organic groan. Fergus covered his ears, moaning and shaking his head.

"Thanks," Three gasped.

Jun Hyo composed himself, studying the duo, and again, Fergus smelled mildew and brine and blood and Terry. If this man was alive, Terry could be, too. The smell was fresh. If nothing else, he had to know where Terry was.

"Wait," he cried. "I need to talk to him!"

But it was like being in a dream, and no matter how much he shouted, no one seemed to hear him. They just kept fighting – sometimes appearing to move faster than his eye could follow, sometimes so slowly that it seemed to take hours for their arms and legs to finish moving. Every time he attempted to approach them, Three or Pip pushed him back. He felt sick with frustration. If they killed this man here, he wouldn't be able to ask where Terry was. If Terry was alive, he had to find him. Even if he was dead, he still had to retrieve the body.

"Stop," he pleaded.

Pip shoved him, this time hard enough to knock him down. He knelt there. Between his fingers, he saw ribbons of color forming in his shadow. The shapeless things had found him. He had to find Terry before the monsters got him.

"Stop," he said more loudly. "Stop, stop, stop!"

But no one listened.

"*Stop!*" he screamed, and just as before, there was suddenly water rushing and roaring around him in an enormous wave.

Three's eyes widened, Pip's jaw dropped, and then all three combatants were caught up in the surge of water. It broke against the buildings across the street. The wave fell away, the water pooling on the concrete. He stared down at it, his hair hanging over his face. He could see tiny droplets forming, rising from the ground to hang in the air around him. Out of the corner of his eye, Fergus saw Pip coughing and sputtering, climbing to his feet. Three and Jun Hyo were still down.

"Fergus," Pip groaned through clenched teeth. Tendrils of pink water snaked over his eye and cheek. Clutching his arm, he glanced back at Jun Hyo and Three and then lurched towards Fergus. "Calm down."

"Stay away from me."

He felt he was on the verge of screaming, but if he started, he thought he might never stop screaming and breaking and ripping and destroying. He wanted to obliterate everything, but it wasn't the kelpie yearning for it. It was the furious, buzzing intrusion searing in his lungs.

"Stay away," he repeated, squeezing his eyes shut.

In his mind's eye, he saw storms and waves and discolored clouds stretching across the sky. He felt the ground trembling beneath him, heard it cracking open. There were high-pitched voices crying out in a language without words. He saw spheres of light dart across the sky, colliding with slabs of earth and toppling into the ocean. Someone was calling his name, except it wasn't his name. It wasn't even his fairy-soul's name. It belonged to the stinging particles of dust in his chest.

His eyes shot open, and he inhaled sharply. The droplets fell from the air, buffeting the water at his feet.

"Fergus?" Pip whispered, edging away.

"What's happening to me?"

He clutched his head. His lungs were on fire. Each breath forced the shards in deeper. They were invading him, smothering him. He didn't know how he could stand it.

"It'll be okay," Pip said, but his eyes were wide and frightened, and Fergus doubted anything was or would be fine.

Three pushed away from the wall, pulling her hair back from her puffy face and blinking blood from her eyes.

"What's going on?"

"Don't come any closer," Pip hissed, keeping his eyes trained on Fergus.

Fergus looked past them to Jun Hyo, who still smelled like Terry. He shoved Pip aside, shuffling through the water towards the buckled figure of the man who'd haunted Pip and Three for Fergus didn't even know how long.

"What are you doing?" Three asked in a small, uncertain voice.

"Finding Terry."

"No, Fergus! Don't go near him!"

He ignored her, halting before Jun Hyo. He stared down at the would-be assassin. "Where is Terry?" he asked, nudging the man's leg. Jun Hyo moaned softly, but didn't respond. Fergus knelt down and shook his shoulder. "Where is he?"

Jun Hyo's hand was so swift, Fergus didn't even catch the light glinting off the blade. Three grabbed him from behind, saving his eye as the knife skimmed his cheekbone. Jun Hyo rolled to his feet, his breathing labored, but now with knives in both hands. He sneered at Fergus and spat at his feet.

"Where is Terry? What did you do to him?" Fergus shouted, springing at him, but Three grabbed him around the chest, pulling him back.

And then the temperature dropped. Lines of ice like veins spread over the water until the surface was covered in a brittle shell. The air throbbed with magic, and Fergus could hear something large and canine breathing close behind him.

"Pip, no," Three said softly, shaking her head.

Every hair on the back of his neck stood on end. He knew the enormous wolf spirit could only be a yard or two away at most, but he kept his eyes on Jun Hyo.

"I'm sorry. I wanted to settle things more personally, but this has to be done," Pip said, his voice thick with regret. "Fergus, stand down. If Terry's alive, we'll find him some other way. If you don't . . . " He let the threat linger for a moment. "I'm sorry."

"Pip!" Three yelled, abandoning Fergus for the boy and his wolf.

Fergus slowly lifted his foot, stepping back. The ice groaned and snapped beneath him. Jun Hyo's black eyes flicked from Fergus's face to his shoulder. He didn't seem afraid of the creature crouching behind Fergus, but he didn't seem quite so cocky anymore either. For a moment, he looked from Fergus to the wolf, and then he burst into motion. Fergus felt a searing pain as the blade pierced through muscle and hit bone.

He doubled over, clutching his shoulder, and Jun Hyo leapt into the air. Fergus yelped as the man's toes found his injured shoulder, using it as a springboard to vault to the window above. He watched Jun Hyo's foot disappear and, with a sinking feeling, realized he was going to get away.

Cold air cut through his clothing. Tiny pieces of ice pelted the back of his neck. Then a rush of thick, hot blood poured over him. Without straightening, Fergus turned his head to the side, blinking as blood dripped onto his temple and slid into his eye. Three was shouting at Pip, but Fergus couldn't hear his reply. Jun Hyo cursed furiously, stabbing at the beast's face, but it did nothing more than loose a few icy locks of hair.

The spirit stood with its front paws against the wall and Jun Hyo in its massive jaws. Fergus very slowly got to his hands and knees and crawled out from under it. The wolf released Jun Hyo, and he fell with the heavy grace of an inanimate object.

"I'm sorry," Pip said. "Just with Fergus acting *crazy*, and you hurt, I couldn't take the risk."

Fergus cautiously straightened. The spirit wolf turned its head to watch him, and he swallowed thickly. He looked down at the blood spreading into the thin layer of water at his feet and shuffled backwards. Jun Hyo gazed up at him, his breaths issuing in rattling gasps.

"Return," Pip commanded, and the wolf turned away, loping towards him, and leapt into the air, disappearing in a flash of blue light.

Three let out a sigh, dropping to her knees.

Pip scurried over to her. "I'm sorry. I didn't want to."

She shook her head. "I know. You did what you had to. Is *he* still alive?"

Fergus turned from them to Jun Hyo. Blood dripped from his lips and nose, but he'd managed to pull himself into a sitting position. He regarded

Fergus with bold, unwavering eyes. Only now his expression struck Fergus as shock rather than defiance.

Fergus rubbed his arm and averted his eyes. "He is."

He heard Three trying to get up, and Pip trying to keep her down. Very cautiously, he edged closer to the wounded man, crouching just out of reach. The fresh, coppery smell of Jun Hyo's blood drowned out all other scents.

"Where is Terry?"

But Jun Hyo just stared at him silently, taking shuddering, uneven breaths that grew increasingly weaker and shallower until he stopped moving at all.

Fergus cursed, putting his head in his hands.

Chapter Seventeen.

"Yes, he is acting weird, but there's bound to be a reason."

"And until we figure out what that is, what are you suggesting we do? Tie him up and stow him in the attic? We don't have enough people to babysit him."

"But it's Fergus! We have to help him."

"He's more of a danger to us than we are to him! We have to deal with the city's situation before we can sort him out, even if he is Ainslee's son."

Fergus groaned and pinched the bridge of his nose. His head was throbbing so hard, he felt compelled to check his nose for blood, but his fingers came away clear. He was lying on a couch in an empty room. The couch, like all the other pieces of furniture around him, was covered in white sheets and dust. He wrinkled his nose, stifling a sneeze. Closing his eyes again, he pressed his face against the cushions and tried to drown out the sounds of the argument outside.

He felt nauseous, and his mouth was unpleasantly dry. The last thing he remembered was Three grabbing him by the arm and hauling him to his feet. The rest was a blur.

"Maybe he'll snap out of it, Three. We just need to keep him out of the way until then." Pip's voice.

"Someone needs to watch him, though. We can't leave Fergus with *him*," Three said, and he was surprised to hear resentment in her voice.

"What are you implying?" The Count. Definitely the Count.

"You turned him over to Harriet." And that was Rosslyn.

"And then you lot locked me up like a criminal! *In my own house!*"

"Well . . . " Rosslyn drawled.

"You never complained about any of it before. Not until it was 'Ainslee's Son.' What's so special about him?"

"You're going to wake him up." A new voice: Deirdre.

Fergus rolled onto his side and swallowed back acid. His shoulder, hands, and chest were bandaged. It felt like Pip had worked some of his magic, because when he prodded the wounds, they didn't hurt. That was a plus, or at least it was one less grievance. He returned to rubbing his temples, trying to figure out why they were arguing over him. What had he done? Why were they talking about locking him up? What was wrong with him? He tried to remember what had happened before he woke up in the penthouse, but his memories were a dizzying blur.

He shivered, putting them aside, and sat up.

"They're still sweeping the city. If he's going to stay in my home, I want him to be locked up and out of the way. I don't want to end up on that rock along with him!"

"We know, Evan," Rosslyn said, sounding more put out than usual. "But there's nowhere else we can take him. If we bring him to Beathag's, we'll have to fight our way through them. More importantly, it might inspire them to set the shop on fire, and if they burn down Beathag's, the runes go with it. The city is going to come down on our heads. Boom. The end. Do you get that?"

"What about Orson's place?" Three asked.

"They torched it," Deirdre replied. "They must have worked out we'd been staying there, and they made sure we couldn't return. Probably they also decided it was an easy way to force him out without having to risk searching inside and running into one of us."

"That's my point! Who's to say they won't do the same to my house?" the Count said, sounding shrill and insistent.

"If they're going to, they'll do it whether he's here or not," Rosslyn replied.

There was a moment of silence.

"I'll check on him," Deirdre finally said.

Fergus quickly lay back down, closing his eyes and trying to breathe evenly. He heard the door open and quietly shut again. Her feet were silent over the floorboards. He felt rather than heard her draw up to him.

"Awake, are you?"

He cracked open an eye. "Depends."

She crouched beside him, putting her hand on his cheek, but rather than soothe, she pulled the skin back, forcing his eye open.

"Hey!"

"Gold. It doesn't suit you. But I wonder how you managed that. Kelpies don't have golden eyes." She released him, tilting her head. "What happened between you and Jane Murray?"

"What? How did you know?"

"She's cut ties." She frowned at his puzzled expression. "She went turncoat. You must have scared her quite a bit. Our sources say she went straight to Harriet, begging for shelter in exchange for information about you. So they've redoubled their efforts and are searching for you across every level. It's lucky Three and her weird little friend found you."

"She went to Harriet? But she wanted to kill him," he said, rubbing his eye.

"Whatever you did, she now wants you dead even more than she wants to kill him."

"I—" he started and abruptly stopped, shaking his head. He looked away, but he could see her suspicious glare out of the corner of his eye. "Her house got trashed," he amended, choosing a different truth. "Probably because of me."

"Hmm," Deirdre said.

"Well, that's what happened."

"You seem lucid now, but I don't think any of us can trust you until you look normal again."

"What? How do I not look normal?"

"Didn't I just say? Your eyes are golden," she replied waspishly. "And you still haven't said how they got that way."

"I don't really know. She was using magic, and things just got out of hand."

He rolled onto his side, staring at the back of the couch. There was an oily stain on the sheet directly in front of his face. He tried not to think about its origin.

"Fine. If that's the case, are you willing to let us keep you in this room, or are you going to cause us problems? Because we can lock you in, or we can chain you down."

He turned sharply, teeth bared.

"So be it," she said.

Before he could get up, before he could even move an arm to defend himself, her hand moved, connecting with his head. His vision went a painful white and then black again.

•　　•　　•

He awoke to the smell of bread. His head still ached, and he could taste bile at the back of his throat, but even so, his stomach growled and his mouth watered at the promise of food. He risked opening his eyes. A single low-burning candle lit the room. It sat beside a plate of bread and a couple of slices of ham. He swallowed, sitting up, and the world spun before his eyes.

Letting out a groan, he put his head between his knees and suddenly realized he was bound at the wrists by a thin red string leading to the leg of an oak armoire. He tugged at his bonds, but the thread had the weight and strength of iron shackles. He cursed furiously, feeling betrayed and panicky. How he supposed to get out of this one? What should he do?

His stomach answered: food first, anger later.

The meal wasn't enough to quell his hunger or his temper, and he polished off the entire plate in only a couple of minutes. At least they'd been kind enough to leave him with a little wine to wash it down with, though it tasted under-ripe and sour. He drank it anyway and then returned to the issue of his shackles. The thread was obviously operating under someone's magic, so he didn't think he could snap it by force.

He considered the candle, though it seemed too simple an option. Still, better to rule it out now than find it was the answer all along later. He held his wrists over the flame and instantly felt the heat of the fire on his skin. Hissing in pain, he jerked away from the candle. The thread hadn't even blackened. He rubbed his smarting skin against his leg, frowning as he looked around the room.

There was the sofa he was sitting on, an armchair, the coffee table, armoire, and a small window looking out onto the square. He stood. The string wasn't long enough for him to go to the door, but he could reach the window. He pressed his forehead to the glass and saw a slender figure with short, black hair slipping through the square away from the penthouse.

Deirdre.

Well, at least, she was out of the way, so if it came down to it, he only had to deal with Three and Pip. He shook his head. No, that was even worse. He would be hard-pressed to take either of them on in a one-on-one situation, so there was no way he could deal with them together. He'd just have to find a way to sneak out.

He frowned at his reflection, noticing that his eyes did seem inordinately yellow. A strange name popped into his head. He thought the combination of letters sounded like nonsense, and yet something resonated in him – an intrinsic understanding that it was a name. It must have been a fairy's name. Perhaps Fand's true name? Had he absorbed her powers?

He closed his eyes, remembering the explosion of golden dust, the way it assaulted his throat and chest. The relationship between the gold dust and the color of his eyes couldn't be a coincidence. He tried to remember what had happened since he'd escaped the remaining members of Niamh, but all he could recall was terror and shadows and water, as vague as though it'd only been a nightmare.

In his mind's eye, he saw mountains falling away into water and heard the shrill, dying cries of something not quite human. What was this? He certainly had never experienced anything like it. Was he seeing Fand's life? He shook his head, opening his eyes and moving away from the window. Even the slightest brush with those memories threatened to loose the viscous, churning shadows on him again.

Maybe he *was* a danger to himself and others. He didn't like the idea of being treated like he was deranged, but he couldn't say he felt particularly sound either. A chill ran down his spine, and he reached for the back of his neck to rub it and maybe dispel some of his lingering anxiety, but the thread cut into his wrist. Sighing, he walked back over to the couch. Perhaps he *should* wait until Fand's magic stopped messing with him. They'd let him go then, wouldn't they?

But he felt angry about being confined in the first place. When he was a child, his mother sometimes told him stories about kelpies. Early in the evening, sometimes late at night, they'd climb out of their lakes and rivers and go hunting. The kelpie would appear as a splendid horse, all flowing mane and limpid eyes. Any unsuspecting human who happened across it would be bewitched by its apparent beauty and obedience. Amazed by such good luck, the human would reach out to the creature, to climb onto its back or harness it. That's when the fairy would drag them into the water, to drown and then devour the unfortunate soul.

She told him once that some kelpies wore bridles, and if a human should steal the bridle, the kelpie would have to become his slave. Some humans were wicked and clever and purposefully set out to steal the bridle. After all, a single kelpie was as strong as a team of horses. The kelpie would be forced to submit to the human's will until it could recapture its bridle.

He snorted. Maybe it was instinctive for him to hate the feeling of being bound. Bitterness alone wouldn't free him, though.

Fergus stepped away from the couch and went over to inspect the armoire more closely. The binding spell had to have been written on it somewhere. Maybe they thought he was too stupid to find it. No, they probably thought he was too crazy to even think about it, much less figure out how to dismantle it. He frowned. Well, if they were underestimating his sanity, all the better for him.

He pulled the sheet from the armoire, letting it pool on the floor at his feet. There was nothing written on the sides, so he tried pulling the cupboard away from the wall. Its legs groaned loudly, and he paused, holding his breath, but no one came running.

He waited a moment longer, and then he dragged it out a little further, so that he could see behind it. There was nothing there either. He stepped back, sighing, and went around to the front. There was a lock on the door. The spell had to be written inside. He pulled at the handle, but it was small, and as he grew frustrated and started yanking on it, it broke off in his hand. He cursed and kicked the door. It was too well-made to splinter, and the effort just made his foot ache, so he went to sit on the couch again and scowled at the remains of the candle, now more liquid than wax.

The door behind him opened, and he turned to glare at his visitor, but stopped short when he saw Guillory. He blinked, momentarily doubting his eyes. It felt like it'd been weeks since he saw the former captain. Guillory had looked so angry that morning that Fergus had thought he might have written him off entirely, but now his face was calm and composed, though a little surprised.

"Sorry, I just followed the sound of kicking," Guillory said, looking around. "No one answered the door, so I let myself in."

Fergus snorted and slumped deeper into the couch. "Top-notch security they've got here."

Guillory came over, leaning against the back of the sofa. "I was hoping I could borrow you." He smiled a little, something eager and hopeful crossing his face. "Ashton has agreed to meet with us in private. We finally might be able to talk to him properly."

"You know he's combing the city for me, right?" Fergus replied, craning his head back to give Guillory his best deadpan stare.

"But this is alone – just the three of us."

Fergus was silent for a moment. "What makes you think he really wants to hear what we've got to say?"

"I'm sure he doesn't, but at least he's giving us a chance to say it."

"Well, too bad. I can't go, because I can't leave this room."

"What? Why not?"

He held up his wrists, revealing the string.

"That? That's all that's keeping you?"

Fergus shook his head. "There's magic involved. They've written something in that armoire, but it's locked, so I can't get into it to break the spell."

Guillory chuckled, walking over to inspect the door. "I might be able to lend a hand," he said, running his fingers down the panel. "You broke the handle, but I can pick the lock."

He pulled something from his back pocket and began to fiddle with the keyhole.

"What're you doing?"

"Picking it. Almost always carry a few hairpins on me. Souvenirs, you see. That should do it."

Fergus got to his feet and came over to watch. Guillory picked up the broken handle from the floor and slipped it back into the hole. The door swung open to reveal an empty space with a circle of characters written in ink on the baseboard.

"Do you know how to break that?" Guillory asked.

"I can try."

Fergus went over to the candle, licking his fingers before squeezing out the flame. He snapped off the wick, rubbing it between his finger and thumb until both were coated in soot.

"I'm useless at magic." Or was, but he wasn't sure he wanted to share that right now. "I've read some theory, though. I think you just have to break up the design, and the spell will fail," he said, crouching down and running his finger over one side of the runes and his thumb over the other. He closed his eyes and yanked his hands apart. The thread popped easily. He rubbed his wrists, snorting. "Looks like those books were good for something after all."

"Will you come with me?" Guillory asked as he stood.

Fergus looked down at the toes of his worn-out sneakers and sighed. He was certain it was a trap, but at the same time, Harriet had helped Fergus free Guillory, and Guillory held him in high regard. Maybe there was a slim chance that he actually wanted to listen to them.

"I'll come with you," he said at last, meeting Guillory's eye. "But you go first. Suss it out, and then I'll follow. There's stuff going on that's way more complicated than you realize."

"I don't doubt it, but I also believe in him. I want to give him a chance. If we can resolve this diplomatically, everyone will profit, and we don't have much time left," Guillory said as the windows began to rattle and the door of the armoire swayed back and forth. "Maybe we can still save this city, but if we can't, we need to make sure everyone is evacuated."

"Or at least get him to leave us alone while we evacuate all the hybrids from that colony."

Guillory's lips thinned, but he nodded. "Or that. Come on," he said, putting a hand on Fergus's shoulder. "Let's go."

•　　•　　•

They decided to split up. Guillory gave him directions to a warehouse in the center of the slums. Fergus wasn't especially familiar with the area, though once upon a time, he and Terry had gone to a concert there that had ended in a fight with the Knights of Evalach, a fire that had burned down a huge chunk of the slums, and the two of them fleeing to the countryside. In short, it was not a spot that held good memories.

That said, he thought it was kind of funny that he was headed back to that place. In a way, it felt like his journey had started that night behind the warehouse with Evalach and the fire.

Perhaps it would end there, too.

He approached from the west, Guillory from the south. There were still some hollowed out, ash-blackened buildings around: warehouses that were too resilient to burn all the way. They made for okay cover. If nothing else, it meant that it'd be just as hard for others to hide.

Fergus managed to find a spot behind a building that was really no more than two broken walls and rubble. Slipping under the remains of an upper floor, he found a crack in the wall from which he could see Harriet. Guillory hadn't arrived yet, but Harriet didn't seem too worried. His calm made Fergus even more apprehensive, but he sat back and waited for the sound of Guillory's voice, not wanting to give Harriet the impression he was being watched. He didn't have to wait too long.

"Thank you for meeting me," Guillory said as he drew up to Harriet.

"Where's Irvine?"

"He'll be along shortly."

Fergus peeked through the hole. He could only see Guillory now, but he thought that was good enough. Guillory was looking around, trying to seem nonchalant as he surveyed the area.

"It's rare to see you alone these days," Guillory said.

"I didn't know you'd been watching."

"I've had an eye on you since you were covered in spots and squeakier than a mouse."

He heard Harriet snort softly. "You sound like an old man."

Guillory shrugged. "Ashton, I know we don't agree, but I hope you will at least hear me out. It's obvious that this city cannot survive without her hybrid citizens. Staying here is suicidal, and there's no way to salvage the situation unless you bring them back from the colony immediately."

Harriet sighed. "I'm aware, but Mother . . . "

"Can you not convince her of the danger? This city was built on magic, and now that magic is all but gone."

"She won't hear of it. She won't listen to anything that could possibly redeem them."

"But you disagree."

There was a pause, and then Harriet asked again, "Where is Irvine?"

"He'll be along soon," Guillory said, looking over his shoulder, which Fergus thought might be a signal for him to show himself, but then Guillory abruptly returned to the subject. "If you won't let the hybrids return to the city, then you must evacuate everyone who's still here. And if you can't bear to do it yourself, let me use a single airship, and I will evacuate the colony myself."

"I can't let you do that."

"Leaving them trapped on that rock is cruel. I know. I know what happened back then, but that was one man. Any man – human or hybrid – might do evil, but you must not let yourself become evil because of those actions. You must evacuate the city *and* the colony."

"Mother would never allow it," Harriet said, his voice just above a whisper. "I can't betray her."

"You will be betraying yourself if you leave them to die when this city falls."

"You don't understand!"

"I understand who you are, Ashton: who you *really* are. You have it in you to see what's correct and to do it. You proved that at the prison when you let Fergus rescue me."

"Where is Irvine?" Harriet demanded.

"I'm right here," Fergus said, coming out of the building and into view.

Harriet turned to him, eyes flashing, brow furrowing. His entire face was awash with loathing.

"So why do you want Guillory *and* me here?" Fergus asked, glaring right back at him.

Harriet turned from Fergus, the anger melting away. There was shame in his face, apology in his eyes. He stared at his feet, unable to look Guillory in the face, and then he turned back to Fergus and smiled mirthlessly.

"I didn't want the Captain to be here, but it was the only way I could think of to find you. Seize him."

Chapter Eighteen.

It sounded for a moment as though an entire army was coming. Their boots echoed in a hundred angry rounds, coming from the surrounding streets. But he'd known this would happen. He'd known it was a distinct possibility, and still he'd come. As Harriet's men assembled, Fergus allowed himself a moment to puzzle over that decision. Why *had* he come here, knowing it was a trap, knowing Harriet wouldn't listen?

He eyed the men cautiously surrounding him. There were fewer than the echoes would have led him to believe. He could fight his way free. Probably he and Guillory would both end up hurt, but it was possible. Water was already coalescing in the air around him. He could use that, too.

He could take them.

But he closed his eyes and shook his head, surprising even himself. Pressing his palm to his forehead, he continued to shake his head, finding himself overrun with laughter. He heard one man gulp, another cock his gun. Other clicks followed, and Fergus stopped laughing. He dropped his arms to his sides and wearily turned to Harriet.

"You're really predictable. Guess I must be, too, or else we wouldn't be here. So, are you supposed to shoot me on sight? Cut off my head and bring it back to Jane? Or are you handing it to Mommy instead?"

Harriet frowned at him silently.

"C'mon. Get it over with."

"My orders are for your capture," Harriet replied, his lips quirking into the ghost of a sneer.

He had expected Harriet to look triumphant, but the Captain was strained and pale. Fergus shrugged, stepping closer to him and Guillory, and cast a brief, uncertain glance over his shoulder at the awaiting grunts.

Lowering his voice, he said, "I could take your men on. They might get lucky and kill me, but I could do a lot of damage first."

"Is that a threat?"

"I don't really see why I should come quietly, *Captain*." He paused. "But I could."

Harriet raised an eyebrow, but said nothing. His fingers rubbed the butt of his pistol.

"I could make it easy for you, if I had a reason to."

"*You*," Harriet scoffed, "would make it easy for *me*? I could just shoot you in the knee."

"But a kelpie has four legs. Do you wanna see what I can do with only three? Sure you could run fast enough?"

"And what might incentivize you?"

Fergus bit back a smile. "Evacuate the hybrids. The ones still in New Peiling and the ones in the colony."

"Preposterous," Harriet said, shaking his head. "Even if I wanted to, we don't have the manpower to rescue all of them and arrange to evacuate the remaining human population."

"Then let Guillory have just one ship. I know he can do it, even if he has to do it alone," Fergus said, glancing sideways at the former captain.

Harriet's eyes narrowed, and he stepped between Fergus and Guillory.

"He'll take them far away. You looked the other way once."

Harriet lowered his eyes, grimacing. "It's my duty to avoid doing so again."

"You can waste time splitting hairs about *us*, or you can turn a blind eye to Guillory and get the people you care about to safety." Fergus paused, taking a deep breath. "And if you have to throw someone on the fire to make the rest get going, I . . . I'll volunteer."

"Fergus, no!" Guillory said, stepping forward, but Harriet held him back.

"And you will come quietly?"

Fergus squeezed his eyes shut, nodding.

"This is ridiculous! What do you think you will achieve dead?"

Fergus opened his eyes, meeting Harriet's. He nodded, and Harriet smiled humorlessly before striking Guillory with the butt of his pistol. Guillory's eyes rolled back, and he fell to the ground.

Fergus sighed softly, looking down at the back of Guillory's tawny head. "So we have a deal?"

"We have a deal," Harriet said. He turned to his men. "I'll take it from here. Return to headquarters immediately. You are dismissed!"

Fergus listened to the receding din of their boots. He shook his head, running a hand over his face.

"We should go before he comes to, cuz he's gonna wake up mad."

"You know, it really is just the two of us now," Harriet said, staring at Fergus inscrutably. "You could do your fairy magic and escape. I imagine Captain Guillory has enough supporters that he could find a vessel for the . . . offshore citizens with or without me. So why? Why aren't you running? Why isn't he just taking a ship and doing what he wants?"

Fergus shrugged. "He thinks you deserve to be reasoned with, not tricked. He doesn't want to fight you. He just wants to save lives. And me? Guess I'm just an idiot, but I believe in him, so I'm just gonna have to hope that what he says about you is right and that you'll keep your word." He smiled thinly. "Anyway, I'm one person compared to hundreds."

"Funny. I always thought I'd relish this moment. You, the monster, in iron. Put in your place at last. Me, victorious." He trailed off, eyes distant, and then shook his head. "Let's go."

•   •   •

Fergus could see the sky from his jail cell. It reminded him of being on the *Wyrd*, except that the persistent vibration of the tremors had replaced the hum of an engine. He supposed he wouldn't have to worry about those much longer. He wouldn't have to worry about anything. Worry seemed like a luxury from where he lay. After all, worrying was for someone with a future. It was a depressing thought.

He watched the clouds drift past the window and morbidly considered how he'd never find Terry's body, never find out if Ursula came out okay, never apologize to Three and Pip for meddling with Jun Hyo. Deirdre would never scold him again, he'd never puzzle over whether Rosslyn's scowl was affectionate or angry, and Guillory would never again lecture him about truth and justice. He wouldn't even have a chance to meet the people Flynn and Terry's souls had attached to – or would. He was going to be completely erased.

It wouldn't be a quiet affair. He was sure there'd be some sort of broadcast defaming him as whatever was needed to get people to pack up and go. But all traces of Fergus Irvine would be gone. He wondered what they would do with his body afterward. Would they just leave him there while they escaped? Let him be swallowed up with the plates when New Peiling fell? Or would they just throw him straight over the edge? Maybe they'd burn him.

He rubbed his arms, closing his eyes tightly. He really didn't want to die. He really, really didn't want to be exorcised. But he couldn't think of a single thing he could do to change what was happening, and the most important thing was getting everyone away from the city. It was ridiculous that this was the only way to get the stupid humans to go, but he'd learned a lot about people in the last year, including the fact that they were rarely able to move on without having something to prove they'd stood by their principles for as long as they could.

Pride was his real executioner, and it left a bitter taste in his mouth.

He stood, going to lean against the window. He couldn't even hear through the glass. Maybe he should try to escape . . . escape and rejoin his friends, and they'd fight their way through Evalach and everyone else. They'd do it for him. He knew they would. But he couldn't ask them to. He had Harriet's word that Guillory would have an airship, that he would go unmolested while he rescued the others.

Even if Fergus could escape from a heavily manned tower in the center of Evalach territory, he'd just be provoking Paige Harriet. She'd resume her witch-hunt, until they'd hunted down every last hybrid. Not that long ago, Ashton would've done so with zeal, but he hadn't seemed all that eager since Fergus had turned himself in. Maybe he was also tired of the incessant fighting. Maybe he was sick of every aspect of his life adhering to the status quo. Fergus wasn't sure how thinking of all these maybes could help, but he had nothing else to occupy him.

The door opened, and Harriet stepped into the room with a tray of weak chicken broth and some bread. He nodded to the guard, who shut the door behind them, before walking over and unceremoniously holding it out to Fergus. Fergus looked at the soup, which had some onions and carrots and a little rice in it, and tried not to feel annoyed about the fact that he was going to be living on chicken water and gruel until they exorcised him. He sat up, setting the tray in his lap, and dunked a stale slice of bread into the broth.

"How come you're bringing me food?" he asked, swallowing. "This is the third time, you know. You should just put a slat in the door."

Ashton shrugged, crossing his arms. "You won't hurt me."

"So you finally worked that out?" Fergus said, taking another bite. "You can go. I don't need company to eat this mush."

"I'm not keeping you company."

"Then why are you here?"

Harriet swallowed, looking away. His arms tightened over his chest. "I suppose," he started and then stopped, glancing at the door behind him restlessly.

Fergus said nothing, chewing slowly and waiting for him to finish the thought.

Ashton meandered to the other side of the room, inspecting a crack carved by the tremors. "I suppose I'm not so sure of myself anymore."

"Look," Fergus said, putting down the bread, "I'm willing to play nice, I'm willing to go quietly, but I'm not gonna absolve you of guilt while I'm at it. Gotta draw the line somewhere, you know."

"I don't want your forgiveness," Harriet hissed, turning on his heel.

"Good." Fergus returned to his bread and broth. He swallowed, making sure to take his time about it, before speaking. "So you want Guillory's, then."

Ashton shrugged, once again turning from Fergus. "I'm not saying that I think you're worth much more than dirt."

"Much more? Seems like I've gone up a peg or two," Fergus said, but was ignored.

"I've always respected everything Captain Guillory said to me, even when I didn't agree. Even when I thought he was foolish or ignorant or just . . . excruciatingly naive." He fingered the crack in the wall and sighed.

Fergus looked up, rubbing the corner of his mouth with his thumb. "But now you're thinking you're the one who was wrong?"

Ashton didn't reply.

"I'm not Guillory, so I can't speak for him. But it's nice that you're finally thinking about the stuff he's been trying to drill into your head."

Harriet remained silent, and Fergus sighed.

"I don't know what you want from me. How many times have you tried to kill me for no good reason? I mean, that's why we're here right now. I can only feel so sorry for you and this whole internal conflict you've got going on. If you really do want my opinion, and you're not just trying to fool yourself into thinking I can forgive you in Guillory's stead, I think the fact you're conflicted says everything. You should think about that."

"You're such a simpleton," Ashton muttered. "And you sound just like—"

He abruptly went quiet, eyes widening on the door. Fergus followed his gaze, eyebrow crooking as he turned to see what had Ashton spooked.

A woman stepped inside. She wore a stern expression on her otherwise pretty face. Her dark hair was pulled back into a bun, with just a few carefully selected strands loosely framing her cheeks. Her dark eyes were partially obscured by glasses, but they had the same feline slant as Ashton's. Though she had to be at least a foot shorter and looked about as dangerous as a lazy housecat, Ashton's face had gone as white as the scar cutting across it.

"Ashton, don't you think you've spent enough time playing with your prisoner?" she asked in a pert, no-nonsense tone.

"I'm not playing with him."

251

"Then what are you doing, my love?" Paige Harriet asked, her eyes narrowing.

Ashton was silent, his lips pressed together.

Fergus blinked, looking between the two of them, wondering if what he was seeing was real. The one and only Paige Harriet stood in his jail cell, reprimanding her son right in front of him. He would have laughed if it wasn't so absolutely absurd. Instead, he frowned at her, his eyes also narrowed. He turned back to Ashton, wondering if he would shut her down, but he just stood there looking sullen and ashamed. Something told Fergus that now might be a good time to blend in with the bed, but he couldn't resist gawking at her.

This power-hungry, vengeful little woman had wrecked so many lives, and yet she looked harmless, insignificant even, as she stood there scolding her son. He felt that was really uncomfortable unto itself.

In terms of messed up mothers, Fergus was pretty sure his was at least in the top ten. He'd seen her wear a lot of ugly faces during her brushes with madness. He'd seen her hungry, savage, and belligerent more times than he wanted to recount. Yet she'd never patronized him. For all the other horrible ways she'd looked at him, she'd never looked down on him.

He wished Ashton would say something to defend himself, but he just pushed away from the wall, chin lifted in a parody of defiance.

"Interrogations, Mother. You understand," he said, walking past her into the hall.

Paige Harriet remained in the doorway, regarding Fergus for the first time as though looking upon a giant, festering boil. He raised an eyebrow, waiting for her to say something and telling himself that he wouldn't react, no matter how infuriating it was, but she just sneered and stepped outside.

The door swung shut with a *bang*.

"Wow," Fergus muttered, rubbing his eyes.

He leaned over to put his empty bowl onto the floor and then lay back on the bed once more, crossing his arms behind his head. Though he knew it was unkind of him, he couldn't help but wonder what Ashton Harriet would have been like if his mother had been eaten instead of his father.

•   •   •

He smelled wet fur, pungent and tangy as loam. The dog's spine curved into his stomach. Rainwater bled from its sodden coat into his shirt. Its scent permeated his skin. He felt around for the dog's head, scratching its ear, and it groaned happily.

Its body was so cold. He wrapped himself tightly around it, listening to its soft mumbles of content.

"I'm glad you're here," he said.

The dog wagged its tail.

"But you're very cold."

The dog didn't seem troubled by this, but kept lazily smacking Fergus's leg with its tail. He sighed and stopped petting it, letting his hand rest on its shoulder. He could feel its body rise and fall with every breath, each one growing slower and deeper as it lapsed into sleep.

"It's good we can at least say good-bye. I think that would have been my only regret."

"I would never have wanted you to go this way." Terry's voice filled the air, coming from every direction at once.

"I know."

"You aren't really going through with this, are you?"

"I have to."

"You don't."

"I do."

The dog whimpered and curled into a ball, shivering.

"I do," he repeated softly. "You won't remember me anyway."

The sun slanted through the window, painting the cell walls a dreadful, blistering white. Fergus groaned and closed his eyes again. He'd spent most of his life waking up in shadow and gloom. He used to think it'd be nice to wake up to sunlight, but it turned out having the sun searing through his window every morning was more annoying than romantic. Yawning, he forced himself to sit up and began combing his hair with his fingers.

He could smell bacon.

His eyes popped open, and his attention snapped to the door. He heard the lock turn, and then Jane stepped inside. Fergus frowned, moving towards the end of the bed.

"You don't look happy to see me," she said, pouting as she set down a tray full of eggs and bacon on the floor in front of the bed.

His eyes followed the path of the food, even as it disappeared beyond the mattress. He swallowed and forced himself to look away, trying to affect disinterest. His stomach growled treacherously, and he pursed his lips.

"Why are *you* here, Jane?" he asked, ignoring his stomach's complaints.

She looked put together for once. She wore a black gown tightly laced over a grey blouse and black gloves. It made her skin look very white – unflatteringly so – but her hair was vibrant, blazing against the dark fabric. She smiled, arranging her skirt, and sat on the edge of the bed with her hands on her knees.

"I'm here to see you off, because Ashton is forbidden to see you."

"Oh?"

"His mother doesn't like that he was hanging around here," Jane said with a shrug.

"I'm surprised she's happy to see him with *you*."

"She doesn't know what I am," she replied in a lilting tone.

"And what about Gavin?" Fergus asked.

"He's keeping his head down, but he's fine. No thanks to you. You flooded my house."

"You tried to steal my soul."

"And now you're giving it away. You're a curious man, Fergus Irvine," she said, pulling one glove free with her teeth. "I imagine you could escape from here if you really wanted to. I suppose you won't. I can't say I'm not pleased. You never avenged Flynn, and you killed Fand."

"Flynn didn't need avenging, and also: *she tried to steal my soul*."

"So you ate her."

"I didn't eat her."

"You might as well have. Ashton said your eyes were golden, though they seem blue now." She paused and then sulkily added, "I loved Fand."

"She didn't love you."

"She did," Jane insisted. "She really did. I know she was a real fairy, but she still loved me."

Fergus sighed, running his hands over his face. "If you say so. Can I eat my last meal in peace? Oh, and do I get to bathe before I'm axed?"

Jane bent over to pick up the tray and set it on the covers. "I don't really know. I've never been to an execution before."

"And yet you have the outfit for it."

"I have been to a lot of funerals."

"If you could act a little less happy about the fact I'm gonna bite it in a few hours, it'd be nice."

"No, I fully intend to enjoy every second of this."

"You're making me miss Harriet." Fergus sighed, taking the tray. The metal burned through his trousers, but he ignored it, digging in. "No chance he's gonna poison me?" he asked, swallowing. "The way his men were gonna do Guillory?"

"I'm sure I have no idea what you're talking about, but don't worry, it's fine. I saw the cook's assistant test it myself. Governor Harriet definitely wants you alive." She tilted her head, scooting closer to stare into his face. "I didn't know you had struck up such a rapport with Ashton."

"I wouldn't say it was a 'rapport.'"

"Still, he's never tolerated a hybrid before. Well, besides me."

"I'm irresistible," Fergus replied between bites, ignoring her proximity.

He hadn't had anything this savory in ages, and he tried very hard to eat it slowly and appreciate it. But he felt half-starved, and it was so good . . . He gave up and gobbled it down, sighing sadly when he wiped up the last trace of bacon grease with his toast. He made sure to lick his fingers, just in case he'd missed any.

Jane giggled, pulling her glove back on. "It's hard to completely hate you, though I definitely do."

"Your willpower is admirable," Fergus said, still caught up in licking his fingers.

"I could have forgiven you for not killing that Deirdre woman, even though it's her fault Flynn died," Jane said.

"Your fault, you mean."

Jane ignored him. "I really could have. But I loved Fand. She was everything to me. After my parents died, she was all I had. She kept my secrets. She taught me everything. I can't ignore the fact that you killed her."

"And I can't forget that you killed Flynn."

"Except I didn't."

"Then who told the Count to go ahead with it?"

She fell into a perplexed silence, staring into space.

"I'll see if you can take a bath before they bring you to the exorcism table," she finally said.

"Thanks," Fergus replied, suppressing a sigh.

"Oh, and Ashton asked me to tell you something."

Fergus turned to her, blinking. "He did?"

She nodded. "'He has the weird.' Don't ask me what that means."

"The weir— *The Wyrd*?!" Fergus turned to the window, eyes widening.

Ashton Harriet had let Guillory get his hands on the flagship of the Air Guard? The fastest ship in the fleet? It probably wouldn't be big enough to fit all the hybrids and Guillory's supporters, but it was large enough that it almost could, provided the Count threw in a vessel or two. This could happen.

She shrugged. "Well, I've done what he asked me to. Good-bye, Fergus."

"Yeah," he mumbled, still looking out the window.

This could really happen.

He smiled.

Chapter Nineteen.

For once, the top level of the city was not just warm, but sweltering. Fergus quietly shuffled behind his escort, feeling an uncomfortable pinch in his shoulders and a chafe at his wrists where they were bound. A breeze sifted through the streets, teasing his hair and tugging at his prisoner's garb. He breathed it in, smelled grass and trees, and closed his eyes. It would have been nice to stretch in the sunlight one last time. One of the guards shoved him with the butt of his rifle, and Fergus glared over his shoulder.

As they made their way from the prison to the square with the so-called "exorcism table," Fergus noticed that all around, the once pristine skyscrapers were riddled with broken windows and cracks webbing their walls, and many buildings were boarded up. Fergus wondered who was even left to attend his execution. Probably only the stupidest and most stubborn of the Governor's supporters. It was funny to think that Jane and Ashton might be the friendliest faces in the crowd. His estrangement from everything and everyone he cared about settled over him, an asphyxiating layer of would-haves and should-haves, and for a moment, he considered making a break for it.

But as they trudged along, the city quaked. The buildings around them rippled as they were never meant to. Glass broke from the few unscathed windows, and several of the guards jumped, letting out cries of alarm as they dodged the shattered panes.

The glass hit the ground, smashing into infinite fragments. Fergus flinched; he couldn't even cover his head. It would probably be better to be killed by falling glass, but he couldn't imagine it would be pleasant. Besides, it might not immediately kill him, and then he'd just be horribly wounded as he was strapped down and exorcised. Not a happy thought. Giving himself a shake, he allowed the guards to move him along at a faster pace.

They arrived upon the square. He'd never seen the exorcism table before, but he'd heard that it stood like a monument, never moved or touched except by children, thrilled by the allure of the ghastly. Statues of bygone luminaries framed the space. The square was larger than he had expected, filled with people in festive attire: women in yellow and red bonnets, men wearing green and tan suits. It felt weird to see them dressed in such lively colors. Then it sank in that the humans had come to see a *spectacle*. He could taste the morning's bacon at the back of his throat.

Yet as the ground trembled and the buildings swayed, very few looked cheerful. He took some comfort in that.

Out of the corner of his eye, he saw someone with red hair dart through the crowd. He jerked to attention. He was certain he'd just seen Guillory's first mate, Orson, but whoever it was had disappeared beyond the wall of bodies opening up to suck him in. His eyes skirted the surrounding faces. Some of the assembled booed and jeered as he passed through, but most stood back, looking quietly dignified and expectant. He caught a glimpse of Jane, wearing a white dress with matching daisies in her hair. She smiled at him, but he barely spared her a second's glance before continuing his search for the redhead.

Was he fooling himself? Did he really see Orson? Had his friends arranged a last minute rescue? And could he stop them?

Did he really want to?

Perhaps it had been a panic-induced hallucination. No, it had to be, because he couldn't find anyone he knew among the pitiless faces surrounding him.

His entourage stopped, and he stumbled to keep from running into the guards ahead of him. Up ahead stood the exorcism table. It wasn't a gruesome torture device, covered in old blood and crammed with hooks and gears and lengths of chain. It was just a simple block of dark polished wood with anchors at each corner, connected to manacles. Seeing it was different from imagining it, and though it looked very harmless, Fergus's heart pounded in his chest and a dull ringing filled his ears. He swallowed thickly.

Sunlight glinted off the droplets of water forming around him. The crowd blurred, obscured behind the blanket of light and water. He could use this. He

261

could draw the beads together, pool them into a wave. He could wash away all these horrible humans who had assembled to see him disappear. There was a lot of water in the air. He'd easily have enough for a life-saving deluge.

He could do this. He didn't have to die like this. He could sweep them off the plate entirely and flee. He couldn't help but feel they deserved it.

But what good would it do? He wasn't sure that the sum of their lives *was* equivalent to his own, and yet he knew he could not live with the idea of killing so many to save himself. Plus, if he used Fand's powers, he might live, but his friends would be doomed, crushed under a falling city, their skeletons buried deep under the waves for all time.

No, despite the fear and rage he felt for these people, he couldn't do it. The mist slipped away, the air cleared, and the guards behind him pushed him to the front of the retinue.

He tried not to look at the humans. He tried not to look at the exorcism table. Instead, he locked eyes on Ashton, standing just behind it with a stack of papers. His hands were shaking, though when he spoke his voice was clear and commanding.

"I, Ashton Harriet, Captain of the Air Guard, will now read out the list of offenses committed by the accused, so that he will know why he is being put to death."

Fergus watched Harriet's Adam's apple bob in his throat and his dark eyes roam the page, as though he had lost his place. He took a deep breath before continuing.

"The man before this assembly is one Fergus Irvine, accused of the following crimes: the murder of Senator Trevor Fennis, the arson of the lower city, and treason and conspiracy against this city and its people. For these heavy and terrible crimes, I – as acting defender of this fair city and by order of Governor Paige Harriet – sentence the accused to exorcism." He looked up, meeting Fergus's eyes, and then squeezed his shut. "Bring him forward."

Two guards grabbed Fergus by the elbows, dragging him along. He struggled to get his feet underneath him as he was pulled to the table. It seemed as though they had teleported through space, for as suddenly as he felt the jerk on his elbows, he found himself blinking down at the surface of the table. It was deeply engraved with all manner of runes. He wondered how many hapless young men and women had been chained to it, struggling to keep their souls intact against forces beyond their control.

He licked his lower lip, feeling the breaks in each section, and looked up at Ashton. The Captain of the Air Guard regarded him coolly, though his mouth was set in a firm line that spoke of an exaggerated effort at apathy. His mother stood just to his right with the rest of the remaining delegates. She had a distastefully triumphant look about her as she sized him up. Fergus turned back to Ashton, staring at him blankly as the guards maneuvered him onto the block. They cut his hands free, quickly seizing upon his wrists.

He considered escape once again. He could get away if he wanted to. They might shoot him, and he might be left to die, stranded in a falling city, but his soul would continue to exist. Then he imagined Guillory landing outside the colony, throwing open the gates, and all the prisoners rushing into the sanctuary of the *Wyrd*. He couldn't risk letting the

Governor's eye stray in that direction. Not when the others were so close to safety.

He took a deep breath and closed his eyes, as the iron shackles closed around his wrists and ankles. He opened them again to the rich blue sky. It wasn't as lovely as before. Somehow, it seemed paler and more distant.

His view of the clouds was abruptly replaced by a vision of a charcoal grey sky. He smelled surf, heard it smashing against stone, and found himself sitting on the edge of a cliff, high above water-blackened rocks that jutted up through the ocean like fingers. The earth trembled beneath him, and he tightened his hands in the thin beach grass, waiting for the ground to still. Lightning crossed the skies, brushing the surface of the ocean. Many miles to the right, another bolt sang in chorus. Fergus could just make out a storm cell forming on the edge of the horizon.

A woman sat beside him. She had dark hair and pale blue eyes with a dash of freckles lining her cheeks. Her hair curled around her face and under her ears, but for her impish appearance, Fergus knew she was human. She reached out and put her hand over his.

A groaning sound came from below as the ferocity of the water forced one of the rock-fingers to come loose and fall, clattering under the waves. Still they continued to sit at the edge of the drop-off, their legs dangling over certain doom. He couldn't understand why the woman's hand over his, now much smaller and finer than he knew his actual hand to be, made him feel so comfortable.

They sat at the edge of the world, watching what might be the end of all things. But the woman was singing very softly, her voice muffled by the wind and the waves.

"The crows will cry tomorrow, the sun will warm their wings, but oh, oh, the little changeling will never see such things. Under the dying mulberry, he spoke his very last: 'Thank you, of you I was blessed.'"

It was a song his mother used to sing to him when the weather was poor, when the rain lashed the outskirts of the city so viciously that they could feel the storm in their little apartment. It was a song about a changeling baby raised by crows, but doomed to die. The song was a very sad one, and yet the woman's voice was soothing, and he closed his eyes, lifting his face to the wind. There was a kind of magic in the way it beat against his face and tore at his hair.

Not his hair, *Fand's*. This must have been one of her memories.

"I don't mind dying here with you," the woman said as the song ended.

"But what happens to a fairy if she dies?" Fand replied.

"It doesn't matter. We'll find a way to be together," the woman said, her smile full of adoration.

The ledge gave way, and they plummeted towards the hateful rocks. The woman kept smiling at Fand. She reached for her lover, but their fingertips never came so close as to brush. A primal fear overcame Fand, and she changed. She turned into a blackbird, flying up and away from the debris. She didn't look back – she couldn't – at the love she had abandoned.

She flew high into the air, above the clouds, above the ruined earth, and felt a flicker of surprise at how easy it was to cut through them. She soared ever upwards, her heart as capricious as the forces rending land and ocean below.

Fergus's eyes snapped open, and he screamed.

The ceremony had begun.

The sky blurred before his eyes, hot tears pooling at the corners. He gulped raggedly, trying to catch his breath, to prepare himself for the oncoming torment, but there was no preparing for this. It was worse than when Declan and Darya tried to steal his soul, worse than Fand and Jane's attempt. He screamed again, straining at his bonds.

For a moment, there was nothing but pain and animal instinct, and every ideal that had brought him to this place slipped away into the unseen, unheard background along with the droning of Ashton Harriet's voice.

Stop! Stop! Please stop!

The words jumbled somewhere between his head and his lips, coming out as sound without form. His teeth closed on his tongue, and he tasted blood. He tried rolling from side to side, but the iron manacles held fast. He had to escape, but he couldn't focus to use his newfound magic or to transform. He tried to imagine orange fish and rain and smoke, but all he could think of was the searing white pain jolting through his nervous system.

"You're gonna give up just like that?"

For a moment, he thought he'd heard Terry's voice. But it couldn't have been Terry, because if it had been, then Terry would be right there, punching Paige Harriet in the face and tearing up Ashton's invocation. Instead, there was the crowd, jostling each other to get a better look, the spring greens and crisp yellows of their outfits swirling together. He wished they'd go away. He wanted nothing more than to hide from their fascinated eyes, but there was nowhere to run.

He wished that Terry was here. Maybe if Terry was leaning over him, telling him it was all right, he'd feel a little better. Terry wouldn't tell him this was all right, though. He'd probably yell.

He hoped Terry had experienced a gentler death. Maybe he'd had a heart attack during the fall, or missed the rocks and hit the water. Drowning was supposed to be one of the more peaceful ways to die.

Terry would never forgive him for this, but maybe he would never realize. Probably his fairy-soul would only remember Fergus if he came into contact with him, and that was never going to happen again.

They'd come so far since that rainy day by the docks: Terry hinting at the dangers posed by the Knights, Bandersnatch, and Niamh; Flynn's death a thousand-pound weight in Fergus's stomach. Fergus had known so little. He'd thought he could change things. If he knew this was all he'd be able to achieve by returning, would he have turned down the chance to go to Tír na nÓg? He could still recall the pucker of Terry's brow as he begged Fergus to go through. If he had, maybe they both would've been okay.

Ashton must have faltered. For a second, the pain ebbed. Fergus panted, blinking erratically. Sweat and tears seeped down his cheeks, and the coppery flavor of blood was on his tongue. He gagged. His vision flickered and blurred, and he realized that he had once again summoned the water in the air to him.

Should he? There was still time. He could make use of that magic. He could feel it. Without even lifting a hand, he could use it. He knew that it would do whatever he wanted it to. He didn't deserve this.

Out of the corner of his eye, he could see Paige Harriet moving closer to Ashton. Her handsome face was lined with irritation. Ashton looked pale and confused.

He could escape.

He could wash away all the hateful bigotry, all the ugly sadism that surrounded him. They would die, and he would live, because he had done nothing worse than grow up differently. *He was innocent.*

The crowd was cruel. They were sacrificing him for an evil principle. He couldn't imagine that anyone who'd stayed to see this was a decent person. But if he killed them, he'd be just as evil. He was a fairy – a big, scary one at that. But Fergus had never been a monster. He couldn't do it. He closed his eyes, biting his cheeks.

Salvation was right there, and he willed it away.

Maybe he'd changed Harriet's view of things. If he'd managed to plant that seed of doubt, maybe someone like Guillory could help it to grow to fruition. Humans listened to Ashton Harriet. If Guillory could finally win him over, then maybe they could find a way to change things. He could feel satisfied being the catalyst for that. His friends would be safe, and Ashton Harriet might, through their acquaintanceship, become a better man – the sort of man who saved instead of condemned.

A memory of Terry sprang to mind. He stood on the deck of the *Returner*, the wind sweeping his red-brown hair from his face. His cheeks were pink with excitement, his grey eyes bright with the sheer pleasure of flight. Because of him, Terry had lost all of that. His choices had brought them to this end, and knowing that, Fergus was once more filled with doubt.

Who was *he* to make that call? Who was he to have decided the course of their lives? Where had he gone so wrong?

Another memory broke through his self-recriminations. It was the day he'd discovered his mother was gone. It'd been an unusually warm winter day. Not quite warm enough to divest his coat – two inches too short since he'd put it on the year before – but still warmer than he would have expected. When he'd come inside, he'd thrown his books down by the couch and gone into the kitchen for a drink of milk. There was glass on the floor. She'd had a fit the night before. Fergus had just gone into his bedroom and shut the door until she went quiet. He wondered why she hadn't cleaned it up.

The room was warm, like she'd been cooking, but the oven door was cool to the touch. He eyed the broken glass, sipping his milk. It was almost off. He took his drink into the living room and sat down on the couch to read comics, comics that he now knew had been hand-me-downs from Terry. Time slipped by. He finished one and started another. He'd read them all before, but it was better than idly waiting for his mother to come home and make dinner.

His stomach was growling. He got up and looked in the cupboard, finding some old bread and a little butter in the icebox, but it wasn't much of a meal. He hoped his mom was out buying food. It would explain why she was so late. He took a piece of bread, buttered it, and ate it at the counter, straining his ears for her footsteps on the stairs.

But they never came.

He went back into the living room and put on some music. At some point, he fell asleep, but when he awoke the next morning, she was still gone. He had a notion then that she wasn't coming back. Still, he went through all the motions, taking a shower and getting dressed for school. He had forgotten to do his homework, and he was starving, but he made it through the day.

And again, she wasn't home. She would never be home again, and it would be years before he knew exactly why.

She had run away.

Rather than confide in anyone, rather than try to get help, she decided to remove the danger. She removed herself. She'd run away, and his life became a long series of hunger and cold and unease.

She ran away, but he wasn't going to run, and he wasn't going to feel bad for having walked this road, because this was the only path that didn't involve saving his own skin and leaving everyone else to figure it out on their own. Facing life alone was hard. He hadn't made it this far by himself. He wouldn't have been able to. And now he was doing this for everyone who had sustained him and followed him and cared for him, whether he was the leader they deserved or not.

He thought his voice must be gone. Sound had slipped into another place. His vision, too, was fading. The pain was still there, but it seemed to be growing dimmer, or else he was enjoying the numbing relief of shock. He was aware that his chest was heaving and that it was hard to breathe. He was aware that he was half-choked on his own blood. But it was easier to let his mind drift.

270

His chest rose and fell, the muscles pulling with each inhalation. The air burned in his raw throat. It filled his lungs impotently, simply ballooning inside them and escaping again.

Not long now, he thought, and it was a comforting thought.

His vision filled with little bursts of black and white. He turned his head. Ashton was more a smudge of shadow than any particular shape or color. He seemed to have paused again. For a moment, Fergus felt his lungs fill with air, and a little of the pain returned as feeling seeped back in. He saw another blur coming at Ashton, moving in angry, jarring movements, pushing him out of the way. And then his vision blinked white again.

This was it. This was the end.

A murmur of protest rumbled in the back of his throat, unbidden but unheeded. He turned to the sky. Even that was disappearing, dissolving into the vacuum. He closed his eyes, hoping to see the red-hot color of the sun burning through his lids. He wanted to see color once more before he disappeared – just one more time . . .

He was weightless. He was empty. He was so close to being free of this suffering. He wished his soul would just let it end. Yet he knew it would not. The kelpie inside of him, or rather, the kelpie he had become, was strong and resilient. It would never politely submit to annihilation. As peaceful as it would be to let consciousness slip away and to let his soul follow it into oblivion, the fairy in him struggled to exist against the odds.

It's okay. Just let go. It'll be okay.

He couldn't feel the sun on his skin or the wind ruffling his hair or the magic jumping and spiking over his body. He couldn't even feel the table beneath him. There was no sound. There was no smell. There was no taste, though his throat was full of blood. Just feeling without sensation and the dichotomy of light and shade. It was a nice feeling, this dullness that transcended even numbness. He tried to steady his breathing, to make himself comfortable, but he wasn't sure that he was uncomfortable anymore.

A shadow crossed the sky, blotting out the sun. Behind his closed lids, the light momentarily slipped away. He tried to connect the momentary loss of light to the idea of "cool," but his brain was unable to invent the sensation.

He wondered which breath would be his last. This one? Maybe that one? Yet they kept coming, and as they continued to come, other sensations began to trickle back in. He could feel the tips of his fingers and toes, tingling painfully. The sting from his outer digits worked its way up through his arms and legs. The discomfort seeped from his limbs into his body, and he thought he could feel each and every organ throbbing separately and yet with equal complaint all at once.

His vision began to clear. The blue of the sky and white of the clouds became distinct again. The swirl of pastel dresses and bright hats resolved, as well. People were running, pushing each other, tripping and stumbling. Then sound returned, and he realized that they were screaming, and over the clamor of human voices, he could hear gunshots and the gyrating roar of an airship engine.

Paige Harriet stood over him, holding a snub-nosed pistol with a pearl handle. Sunlight glinted off the barrel.

"It's too dangerous! Just go!"

Fergus turned his head and blinked wearily. Ashton struggled with his mother, trying to get her to lower the gun and run. She shook him off.

"I won't. I won't go anywhere while any of them are left in this city!"

"Do you hear yourself? That's insane!" Ashton shouted, managing to wheel her around to face him.

"Whose side are you on?" the Governor hissed.

"Yours! I've always been on yours, but—"

Ashton was interrupted as a particularly violent shockwave hit the plate. Fergus heard a loud grinding sound from not too far away. Then the air was filled with smoke and debris.

Chapter Twenty.

"*Fergus!*"

A man's silhouette formed from the grey-brown haze, still too muddied to recognize. Fergus opened his mouth and choked on the words. Turning his head, he spat out blood and saliva. His mouth remained uncooperative, and he didn't want to think about what he'd done to his tongue.

"Fergus!" the man called again, and as the dust began to clear, Fergus saw he had eyes like a lion and a wild mess of dirty blonde hair.

Guillory?

"Hold on!"

The Captain raced over to the table, pulling out a shiv, and began chipping away at the keyhole on one of the manacles. The exorcism table shook, and Fergus's teeth clacked together. Guillory made a soft sound of annoyance, struggling to keep his footing and avoid stabbing Fergus in the arm.

"Go," Fergus mumbled. "Just go."

But Guillory ignored him and continued to work away at the manacle. Fergus felt the metal give, releasing his wrist. The cool morning air stung his raw skin.

"No," he whispered, pushing at Guillory's chest. "Go."

Guillory grabbed his arm, pausing to look him hard in the face. "I'm not going without you."

"You have to," Fergus slurred. Blood bubbled over his lips and down his cheeks. "Go. Please go."

"You aren't going anywhere."

Paige Harriet staggered out of the chaos, her pistol aimed at Guillory's forehead.

"Mother!" Ashton shouted from behind her, staggering out of the smoke. He froze as she drew back the hammer, his expression horrified.

Guillory stared at the Governor, ignoring the gun between them, his eyes defiant and fearless.

She sneered, disregarding his silent opposition. "This is convenient: two traitors for the price of one. And look how easy it was to catch Mr. Guillory. Funny how you failed so many times, Ashton."

"No, Mother, please . . . please don't," Ashton said softly, his brow pinched. "Let's just go. We'll say they all died. No one will ever know. Let's just leave them and go while we can."

"No," she replied, turning her attention briefly from Guillory to her son. "No, we will not just go. We will finish this. I didn't raise you to be so sloppy, so . . . cowardly."

Ashton flinched, stepping back.

"You're gonna . . . let her?" Fergus whispered, trying to catch Ashton's eye, but the Captain steadfastly looked away.

"It's okay, Ashton," Guillory said. "Everything will be fine."

His golden-brown eyes were trained on his protégé, and though Ashton was able to look away from Fergus, he couldn't deny his hero's gaze. There was an unspoken favor there, though Fergus's mind was too foggy to work out what Guillory wanted. Ashton shook his head, his expression pleading. Guillory, however, continued to regard him calmly, eyes proud yet beseeching.

"It's going to be okay," he repeated quietly.

"Don't talk to him!"

The Governor's fingers flexed, and Fergus lashed out, striking her in the wrist as the gun went off. Guillory let out a soft sound of pain, dropping his tool. He clasped his shoulder, leaning onto the table with his eyes squeezed shut.

"*No!*" he and Ashton shouted in unison.

Blood welled between his fingers. His knees gave, and he slumped over Fergus.

The Governor was already preparing for another round, pressing the gun directly to the crown of Guillory's head.

"No!" Ashton shouted again, this time grabbing her around her waist and hauling her away from the table.

Fergus heard Paige snarl as she grappled with her son, their hands frantically lobbying for the gun, but his focus was on the man crumpled on top of him.

"Guillory? Guillory?" he called, reaching out to shake his shoulder. "C'mon. Please don't. Guillory?"

Gravity called, and Guillory slipped free of Fergus's grasp, folding to the ground and out of sight. Fergus tried sitting up, but the remaining shackles protested, and he was too weak to resist their hold.

"*Guillory!*"

The Harriets' struggle gravitated closer to the table, and he was forced to turn his attention to them. Jane was standing a few yards behind them. Her red hair blazed in the shroud of debris. She seemed more intent on watching than aiding either mother or son, cocking her head and looking past them at Fergus curiously. Fire blossomed in the shadows around her.

"Get out of here! Run!"

The statue behind her collapsed, knocking her off balance, but she righted herself and turned to continue watching Ashton, who at that moment pinned his mother against the exorcism table.

"What are you doing, Ashton? I demand you stop at once!" the Governor shrieked.

She contorted and squirmed, and Fergus grunted as her elbow caught him in the chest, but Ashton held tight – one hand seizing her wrist, the other gripping the barrel of the gun.

"This has to stop," he said, the muscles of his jaw working as she continued to struggle. "Mother, this has to stop now. We have to let this go. We have to go."

"Think of what you're saying! Think of what they did to your father. You saw him, so why?"

"Because—" he said, grabbing the barrel with both hands. "Because I believe in William Guillory!"

Fergus winced as the gun went off. The bullet went astray, cutting through the air between Harriet and his mother, and both hesitated. Jane squealed in alarm, knuckles going to her mouth. Her head whipped from side to side, and she squinted into the dust, searching for something or someone unseen. She turned, lurching away from mother and son.

"Gavin? Gavin?!"

"Jane, wait!" Ashton cried.

His distraction lasted only a moment, but it was enough. The Governor ripped the gun away, stumbling backwards. Ashton looked between Jane, climbing over the rubble and calling for Gavin, and Paige, who was breathing heavily, regarding him with suspicion.

He *tsked*, cheek twitching. "Jane!" he shouted again, not daring to look away from his mother.

Jane paused, her back to them, and cocked her head. There was a terrible groan as another sculpture gave. She turned her head as the great metal man plummeted towards her, her mouth forming a little "O" of surprise.

"*Jane!*"

Gavin appeared out of nowhere, sprinting across the square and tackling her. He hauled her out of the way just as the stone horse struck the spot she'd been standing, cracking into two, and they tumbled out of sight.

"This is crazy," Ashton said, his voice barely audible.

Fergus turned back to the Harriets. Paige held the gun in both hands. With her son before her, she at least had the good grace to keep it pointed at the ground. Ashton raised both hands above his head, edging closer. His features were pinched, brow deeply puckered. She swallowed, lifting the revolver knee-height.

"Mother, this is madness," he whispered.

"Yes," she replied. "Yes, it is. And you have lost your mind. I'm sorry, Ashton." There was another explosion of gunfire, and Ashton yelped, hands going to his thigh as he fell. "Now," she said, her voice eerily serene, "I will finish what we came here to do."

Turning to Fergus, she smiled, taking off her dust-clouded glasses and tucking them into her pocket. She pressed the gun to his eyebrow. The metal seared his skin, and he cringed, turning away.

"Not today, Governor."

Fergus's eyes widened. His heart gave a mighty leap, rebounding off his ribcage. Slowly, he turned his head. There, just behind Paige Harriet, stood a tall man with reddish hair, pale skin, and a glass eye. Terry pulled off the black and silver Air Guard jacket, letting it fall to his feet. His good eye remained pinned on Paige Harriet, his face resolute.

Before she could fully turn to him, he grabbed her by her bun and wrenched her head back. She squealed in pain, clawing at his hand, but he yanked her hair again, throwing her off balance.

"I'll shoot him!" she screamed.

"No, you will not."

He grabbed her wrist, squeezing until she cried out and dropped the gun. Weapon out of the way, he took her by the back of the neck and thrust her aside. She shrieked, tumbling to the ground next to her bleeding son. Ashton looked up, watching Terry warily.

Terry coldly stared back. "If you want Guillory to live, you better get your ass in gear."

"My mother . . ." Ashton started, glancing at Paige. She looked up at Terry with round, frightened eyes.

"As long as she stays down, she won't be hurt."

279

Ashton's eyes flicked from his mother to Terry. He nodded, pulling a handkerchief from his jacket pocket and tying it tightly around his leg. He limped to the other side of the table.

"Captain, can you hear me?" he asked, crouching out of sight.

Fergus turned back to Terry, smiling and blinking sluggishly. "Hey."

Terry's face softened, a smirk teasing the corner of his mouth. "You get into more trouble than anyone I've ever known, *including me*."

He reached over Fergus, retrieving Guillory's pick, and ignoring the churning of the city all around them, began to work at the manacle binding Fergus's other wrist.

"But how? How did you . . .?" Fergus asked, gingerly propping himself up on his elbow. His stomach rebelled, and he squeezed his eyes shut.

"We didn't hit the water. That guy pulled out some kinda hook, and I grabbed him. We were swinging around like crazy, and then we hit the fence. Line snapped, and I grabbed the bars, but he grabbed me. Clipped a few layers before I could get ahold of another. He fell past the plate."

There was a creak, and then the shackle snapped open, and Fergus tentatively took his wrist in hand. Terry moved to his legs.

"I couldn't move for a while. Came pretty close to dying. Good thing it's harder to kill a gytrash than a human."

"I'm just . . . You're just . . . " Fergus mumbled. His eyes burned, but his mouth refused to stop smiling.

"Save it. I am so freaking pissed off at you right now."

Fergus opened his mouth and shut it again, brow knitting. "Why?"

"How about, because you're the stupidest person I know? You let yourself be arrested. You were about to be *exorcised*. You are a serious freaking jackass, and I kinda wanna punch you into tomorrow."

"Sorry," Fergus said as his left foot came free.

"Not sorry enough. I almost . . . I would've never seen you again." Terry's voice broke. He shook his head sharply. "We are gonna have a long, long, *long* talk about this, but later. The city's about to go."

"Ursula?"

"Alive, but her magic's too weak."

"The others?"

"Already rescued 'em."

"And the colony?"

Terry nodded. "Them, too."

The final bond popped free, and Fergus drew his legs up. They tingled and cramped, and he wasn't sure they'd support him. He rubbed them, looking up at Terry.

"You can be mad, but I'm really happy," he said, smiling softly.

Terry tried to hang on to his angry façade, but failed and smiled back, putting a hand on Fergus's knee.

"I'm afraid the reunion ends here."

Fergus turned, his heart sinking.

Paige Harriet climbed to her feet, gun in hand. Her hair was askew, her face smeared with ash, but her eyes held a terrible determination. She raised the pistol, patting her hair back in place, and aimed it at Terry's chest.

"I believe you are Terry Bridges? Badb Catha, if I am correct. I may not be able to exorcise either of you, but I *will* make sure neither of you leave here."

She drew back the hammer, and Fergus knew she wouldn't hesitate. Terry realized it, too. His head jerked to the side, his eyes fixed on Fergus. A small, apologetic smile lifted the corner of his mouth. Fergus shook his head, struggling to make his limbs work, but he was too slow.

The smell of gun smoke burned his nose. Terry turned from him, his expression grim as he attempted to twist out of the way. The bullet grazed his shoulder, tearing a hole in his sleeve, but the wound wasn't fatal. Fergus let out a sigh of relief, turning from Terry to Ashton. He held one of Guillory's pistols, the barrel still smoking. Fergus followed the line of Ashton's arm to Paige Harriet. She swayed in place, her hand clasping her arm. Blood welled between her fingers.

"Ashton," she said, her face twisted in pain. "Why?" The gun slipped from her fingers. She faltered, but remained on her feet.

"I said 'enough,'" Ashton quietly replied. "And I meant it."

Her eyes widened, her body going perfectly still. Ashton looked back at her with a complicated expression. Fergus thought he looked sad, but maybe triumphant, too. There was strength there, and it cowed his mother. She dropped to her knees, teeth gritting, and clasped her wound. Wisps of hair fell over her face, and she stared down at the ground.

"Is he okay?" Fergus asked, dragging himself to the side of the table and looking down at Guillory. His eyes were closed, his face unnervingly white.

The bloody circle now encompassed his entire shoulder.

"Maybe," Harriet said, tucking the gun away. "If he gets help fast, maybe."

"Then what are we waiting for?" Fergus said, sliding from the table.

He immediately regretted it. His vision flashed white, and his legs gave. Ashton grabbed his arm, steadying him.

"Thanks," he muttered, blinking away the static.

Terry pushed between them, giving Ashton a withering glare. He put Fergus's arms over his shoulders and hoisted him onto his back. Fergus did his best to help, wrapping his arms around Terry's neck. Harriet attempted to balance Guillory across his shoulders, though with much less grace. The handkerchief around his leg was already soaked in blood.

"You gonna manage?" Fergus asked.

"Yes," Ashton said, schooling his features as he maneuvered Guillory into position.

"And what about her?"

He paused, turning to his mother. "Come with us," he said gently.

She shook her head.

"*Please.*"

But she shook her head again. "I don't want to see you ever again, Ashton."

Fergus looked away, not wanting to see the injury in Ashton's eyes.

"Mother—"

"Go!" she shrieked, head jerking up. Angry tears streaked her sooty face, leaving pink trails in the grime. "I said I never want to see you again!"

"C'mon," Terry said. "He'll die if you don't. The airship's close."

"I—I can't. I can't leave her." Ashton lowered his face and shifted under Guillory's weight, favoring his wounded leg. "She's my mother. Even if she says she hates me, I can't leave her to die."

Paige lowered her head, remaining silent.

"We only have four arms between us," Terry snapped. "I don't give a damn about her or Guillory or you, so if you want to die with them, fine by me."

Harriet's hands tightened around Guillory's arm and leg, and he glanced at his mother, indecisive and miserable.

"Looks like you could use a hand!"

"Three!" Fergus all but crowed as he turned to see her and Pip scale the debris, trotting over to them.

"We'll take him! You grab her," she instructed Ashton.

Ashton nodded, carefully turning Guillory over and limping to his mother's side.

"I said I don't want to go with you," she said, staring up at him balefully.

"You don't have a choice," he replied.

"I do."

She reached into the pocket of her jacket, pulling out a slim knife.

"Are you going to stab me?"

"If I must."

"Then do it."

Her hands shook as she looked up at him, rage creasing her features.

"I *will*."

"Do it!"

Her eyes filled with tears, her hands shaking so badly she nearly dropped the blade. Ashton leaned down, taking her by the wrist and gently slipping the weapon from her fingers. She dropped her head, choking back a sob.

"You betrayed me. How could you? *How could you?*"

"I'm sorry," he said, pulling her to her feet.

"This is his fault," she snarled, turning to Guillory.

Pip stood beside Three, his hands pressed to Guillory's wound. He chanted softly, his fingers glowing green. Guillory's eyes were closed, his face grey and slack.

"No," Ashton said, shaking his head. "I'm tired. I can't stand what happened to father. I can't stand the idea of anyone else going through that. But I'm tired of this. I'm tired of the hunting and the executions. I'm tired of being used. I'm just tired."

"Enough with the damn speeches. The airship's gonna leave without us!" Terry said, turning and jogging towards Erstwyre Park. Fergus whimpered, features crumpling and fingers digging into Terry's chest.

"Hold in there," Terry murmured, slowing just enough.

Out of the corner of his eye, Fergus saw Pip say something to Three, but didn't catch the words. Her head bobbed, and the two of them propped Guillory on her back, hurrying as best they could after Terry and Fergus. Behind them came Ashton, dragging his mother by the wrist.

Terry led them through the crumbling buildings and rubble, zigzagging to avoid falling concrete and brick. Whole avenues were blocked off, filled with wreckage. Nevertheless, Terry managed to find a way, leading them to a long avenue of government buildings. Most were still standing, but the increasing shockwaves were eliciting foreboding groans of steel and brick. Pebbles bounced across the walk underfoot.

"Watch out!" Three shouted.

A spire came crashing down from a church across the way. Fergus vaguely recognized it as the church where he'd once stood and listened to one of Paige Harriet's followers calling for the complete removal of hybrids from the city. He recalled it as a moment of awakening: the moment he'd realized just how bad the rift really was between humans and hybrids in the city, and the moment he'd understood just how real the threat behind Paige Harriet's campaign was.

He winced as the spire struck the walk in front of them, Terry barely pulling up in time. The red and yellow glass from the church's central window scattered across the street. It cracked and snapped under Terry's sneakers as he climbed over the ruins. The buildings all around them were coming apart now. A statue of a lion guarding a nearby library tumbled over, breaking into pieces. One of the steeples from the church followed, knocking over a maple tree in its path.

"Not good," Terry muttered, struggling to stay upright. Fergus tightened his grip. "This plate's gonna cave any minute now."

"Let me down. I can run."

"I don't think you can. Just hold on."

Terry put on an extra burst of speed, making for the courthouse square. The fountain had split, and water was gushing every which way. They rushed past it, slipping and sliding on the water-slick marble. Fergus risked a glance over his shoulder. Three and Pip were back by the fallen spire. Ashton was attempting to help them as best he could, but his limp had grown more pronounced.

"Wait. We have to wait for them."

Terry slowed, coming to a stop. He eagerly looked towards the park, where a large ship with bronze accents and purple sails hovered – one of the Count's by the look of it. Ahead of the Count's airship, already moving away from the city, was the magnificent flagship of the Air Guard, the *Wyrd*, and its departure was not a moment too soon. Approaching from the east came the black airships of the Air Guard fleet, bearing down on the city with frightening speed.

"They won't be able to wait. The Guard will shoot them down," Terry said, looking over his shoulder at the others.

"We can't leave them behind," Fergus said, pressing his face to Terry's shoulder.

Terry cursed under his breath, turning to watch the others struggle to close the distance. They were closer, but Ashton's face was drawn, and Three labored under Guillory's weight.

"I can run," Fergus said. "I promise I'll be okay. You help with Guillory."

"Fine," Terry said, letting him down and running over to the others. "Give him to me."

"Keep running!" Fergus shouted as Terry heaved Guillory onto his back and sprinted for the park.

Fergus turned and hobbled after him as quickly as he could. They ran past the lines of apple trees and beyond the empty duck pond to a clearing. The air vibrated with the hum of the airship's engine.

They were too late.

As they arrived at the clearing, the Air Guard ships began to fire. The first volley missed, blasting great clumps of dirt and grass into the air. The Count's airship rose into the sky.

"Wait!" Terry shouted, waving one arm. "We're right here!"

But the Air Guard continued to fire, rocking the air with each boom of the cannons, and the little airship sped away.

Chapter Twenty-One.

"Son of a—" Terry growled, kicking the ground. Guillory's head bobbed on his shoulder, and Fergus cringed.

"Maybe they'll come back around," he said, hobbling closer to Terry's side.

"If they aren't shot down. If the city is still standing." Terry wheeled around. "This is your fault," he said pointing at Ashton. "Now we're all gonna die."

"I'm sorry," Ashton said, dark eyes vacillating between anger and regret.

"Wait," Fergus said, pointing to the sky.

The black ships were already in hot pursuit of the purple-sailed airship, but a small ship with red streamers and fin-like sails trailed in their wake.

"Hey . . .!" Fergus waved his arms. Black dots erupted in his eyes, and he stumbled, but he felt the flat of Terry's hand between his shoulders, steadying him. He cast a brief, grateful smile Terry's way and continued to wave with all his might.

"Hey! Down here! Help us!" he called.

The airship drew closer, reducing speed. The pilot seemed to see Fergus, for it began to descend.

"It's Jane," Ashton said, mouth parting in surprise, and then he released his mother to join Fergus in shouting and waving.

The airship came to a stop, hovering over them. Gavin appeared on the deck, dumping a rope ladder over the side and beckoning for them to hurry aboard. They scrambled up and over the railing, closely followed by the others, and carefully lowered Guillory to the deck.

"He's in bad shape," Ashton said, leaning over and checking his pulse.

"I can help," Pip said, clinging to the railing as the ship chugged back to life.

Fergus glanced over the railing and saw the top layer abruptly drop several feet. Great fissures cut across the grass. Several white buildings shrank from the sky, tumbling over the edge of the plate. He hugged himself, shuddering, as he watched the city collapse in on itself and begin its heavy and laborious cascade into the ocean.

Gavin spoke, snapping him out of his horrified trance. "We can take him to the cabin. Follow me."

"Wait, we have to stop them!" Fergus said, turning to the Air Guard.

Paige Harriet smiled with an ugly kind of satisfaction, but her son frowned at the swarm of black ships bearing down on the little purple one.

"Please," Fergus said, grabbing his arm.

"How fast can this ship go?" Ashton asked.

"Faster than you'd think," Gavin said.

"Get him below, and show me the control room."

Gavin nodded, opening the cabin door and leading them down to a narrow hallway. There were three doors: two on the left and one on the right. Fergus could see the gleam of brass controls to the right.

"Bring him in here," Gavin said, opening one of the left side doors to reveal a simple room with a cot and desk. "The control room's that way," he added, nodding to the room on the right.

Ashton dashed to the door, Fergus just behind him. Inside, Jane stood at the wheel. She turned, blinking at Fergus in surprise, and immediately scowled.

"Oh. You're still alive."

"Funny thing, that," Fergus said.

"You probably can't be convinced to throw yourself overboard, can you?"

"Not really."

"You're a real thorn in my side, Fergus Irvine. You're lucky I'm busy, or I'd have Gavin throw you out."

"Move," Ashton said, shouldering her out of the way and commandeering the controls. "We have to catch up."

"How rude!" She scowled.

Cannon fire thundered, even louder than the rattling of the ship and the roar of its engines. She turned her attention to the chase ahead, taking out a telescope and holding it to her eye. Her lips thinned, and she shook her head.

"This is a small ship. If they shoot us, we're done for."

"I know," Ashton said, pushing and pulling levers all over the place.

The airship rocketed forward, making a beeline towards the others. The fleet had the Count's ship surrounded. The smaller airship was more agile, but they had more engine power, and though it dodged and weaved, it wasn't able to put any space between them.

"We'll never make it," Jane said, gripping the doorframe as the airship gained momentum, surging through the sky and closing the gap.

"You're talking to one of the best pilots in the world. We *will* make it."

Fergus pressed against the wall opposite Jane. The rattling of the airship was near deafening, and his stomach was rolling in a very unpromising fashion, but he could see that the airships ahead had lost speed thanks to the Count's evasive maneuvers. He briefly wondered who was on board. Ursula? Rosslyn? Deirdre? Orson? The Count himself? He hoped some of them were safely on the *Wyrd*. He hoped Orson was piloting the Count's vessel. Though he was sure the Count knew how to fly his own airships, Orson might be able to save them if Ashton couldn't catch up.

"This is foolish. Stop at once, Ashton. They're doing their duty," Paige Harriet said, appearing in the doorway.

Ashton *tsked*, glancing over his shoulder at her.

"I command you to cease this ridiculous esca—"

Terry cut her off, stepping up from behind and grabbing her mouth.

Ashton pursed his lips, but managed a grumbled, "Thank you."

Fergus grinned at Terry, who rolled his good eye.

"This is it," Ashton said, his attention trained on the airships growing larger in the window. "I hope your radio isn't one of those secondhand jobs, or we may be shot down right behind them."

"My equipment is top of the line. You better not let your trigger-happy friends blow up my airship."

The fleet was close enough now that Fergus could see the silver insignias of New Peiling – two great falcons framing a laurel wreath – gleaming against the black hulls. The shaking of the airship grew more violent, the vibration of the blasts adding to the strain. Fergus's fingers tightened against the doorframe, and he withdrew his lip from between his teeth, just in case.

He looked over his shoulder at Terry, who was watching the battle from over the Governor's head. He swallowed roughly, Adam's apple bobbing. Paige Harriet mumbled furiously against his hand, struggling, but unable to slip his grasp. Fergus turned to Jane, who looked oddly pleased. Her eyes were trained on Ashton's shoulders, and for all her fussing about being shot down, she was smiling.

Ashton reached up, pressing the button on the intercom. "This is Captain Ashton Harriet. Do you read me?"

There was a grumble of static.

"This is your Captain speaking. Do you read me?"

"Yes, sir! We read you, Captain! This is Lieutenant Bramson." There was a brief pause before the deep voice added, "You're alive!"

"Yes, I am. Lieutenant, I want all Air Guard vessels to cease fire immediately."

"Um, pardon, sir. I don't follow."

"Cease fire immediately, Lieutenant. That is an order."

"But, sir, our orders came from the Governor herself!"

Ashton's shoulders tensed. He glanced around at his furious mother, still trying to bury her elbow in Terry's ribs. His mouth thinned, and he closed his eyes tightly. He took a deep breath and turned back to the intercom.

"The Governor is no longer with us. Crushed by a falling building."

Paige stilled, eyes widening, and Terry towed her away from the door and out of sight.

There was a pause on the other end of the line, and then Bramson replied, "I'm sorry for your loss, sir."

"I believe that in this case, my orders take precedence. Therefore, I command you and all Air Guard vessels to cease fire. Do you understand? Cease fire immediately!"

"Y-yes, sir!"

The intercom went silent. Fergus held his breath, eyes glued to the window. Several final shots were fired, and then the black airships began to fall back.

"Told you so," Jane said with a sniff.

"But how do we get the others to stop?" Fergus asked.

"Oh, that's easy. I know his private line."

She leaned over Ashton to push a button on the side of the intercom box. A small numeric pad detached, and she began punching in numbers before pressing the intercom button.

"Who the hell is this, and how did you get this line!" the Count barked.

"You're leaning on the controls!" Orson shouted in the background.

"That's mean, Evan."

"*Jane?*"

"We called off the Guard, so we'd be grateful if you would turn around and come back. I have a little horsie I'd like you to take off my hands."

"Like hell we will!"

"Terry's also on board, and Guillory, too," Fergus said, raising his voice over the rattling of the controls. "We promise that the Air Guard won't attack you anymore."

"But I *can* always arrange for them to start firing again," Jane said, glowering up at the intercom with a hand on her hip.

"You wouldn't."

She giggled.

"You crazy cow. If this is a trick, I'll make you pay *three* times over."

The line abruptly went silent. Fergus watched as the vessel hesitantly changed course, turning back to them.

"Well, there you go. You owe me a biiiiig favor now, Fergus." Jane returned to her spot by the door, combing her hair with her fingers.

Fergus started to open his mouth, but shut it, shaking his head. "Now what? Where do we go?"

"I haven't the slightest clue where you should go from here, but Gavin and I were thinking of starting over somewhere new. Somewhere far away." She smiled contritely at Ashton. "You understand, don't you?"

Ashton's reflection was too blurred to read his expression, but his shoulders were tense, and Fergus thought he must have been disappointed.

"Well, you could come with us." Jane paused and, gesturing to the fleet ahead, amended, "Or rather, *you* can come with us, but not your men. They're not part of the contingency plan."

"Contingency plan?" Fergus asked.

"I thought I'd see how things progressed. I *have* put a lot of time and effort into New Peiling's politics. But then the city fell down. So it looks like we have no choice but to start over. Gavin has always been there for me. He doesn't care about *what* I am." She looked to Ashton. "*And* he trusts me," she added, wrinkling her nose at Fergus.

Fergus bit his tongue on the remark that what she happened to be was *completely insane*, and that Flynn shouldn't have trusted her to begin with. He forced himself to smile and nod instead.

"That doesn't answer the question about what the rest of us should do," he said.

"I'll go where the Captain goes," Ashton said. "I'm sure he must be planning to build a new city. I want to live in his city, whatever that may mean for me. But I do have one favor to ask: Jane, please take my mother with you."

"What?" Fergus said, eyes narrowing. "After everything she did? What about justice?"

"She'll be executed," Ashton replied softly. "I know what she's done, but she's my mother, and I did just save your friends. Isn't exile punishment enough?" he asked, turning to look Fergus in the eye. "Please . . . Fergus."

Fergus stared at him, a million things going through his head at once. Paige Harriet practically paved the way to New Peiling's fall – single-handedly at that. She'd incarcerated and executed people just for being hybrids. She'd obviously been controlling the Knights of Evalach from the shadows all along. Because of her, Flynn was dead – Flynn and Audrey. Because of her, Evelyn and Raja might never be the same again. She had indirectly caused so many tragedies in the lives of the people around him – in his own life.

Yet he understood.

It was the very same reason he hadn't wanted to hurt Deirdre, despite everyone telling him that she'd killed Flynn. It was why he had done everything in his power not to harm her, but to help her. It was why he had forgiven Ursula and Terry for all their lies and manipulations, and why he had felt misgivings about tossing Declan and Darya into Tír na nÓg to fend for themselves against the fairies despite their repeated attempts to murder him.

Many times, the people Fergus cared about had done things he could never agree with. Yet those people were still important. He still loved them. Reconciling love and principle was never simple. All he could say was that standing here today, love had served him greatest, and he didn't regret having made his choices out of love.

He nodded. "Will you take her?"

Jane frowned, twirling her hair around her finger, and stared into the space just above Ashton's head. "She'll hate being with us. I can only do so much, and I can't be held responsible for her actions. But yes, we can take her with us. Though now you both owe me."

"Whenever you want to collect, I'm sure you'll find me," Ashton replied, stepping away from the controls.

The Count's airship had stopped just ahead of them, as had the Air Guard fleet. They all waited for the next move, caught up in an uneasy moment of suspension. Jane returned to the helm, and Gavin came to stand behind her, resting a hand on her shoulder. He had a happy little smile on his face, and he hardly even looked at them, as Fergus and Ashton stepped out of the control room and into the hall.

"What about you? You know all the hybrids are gonna hate you, and Guillory will want them to come, too, if he founds a new city," Fergus said.

"I know. I will accept whatever punishment Captain Guillory thinks appropriate. All I can do now is try to help him in his work."

"That's it? You're not gonna think for yourself? Isn't that how things came to this in the first place?"

Harriet smiled wryly. "For now, all I want is to see his vision realized."

Fergus shook his head, snorting, but smiled a little. "Let's see how he is," he said, leading the way into the cabin.

Paige Harriet was sitting tied to the cot and gagged. She glared at Fergus ferociously, but refused to look at her son. Ashton likewise avoided her eyes. Guillory was stretched out on the floor. A little color had returned to his face, but he was not yet conscious. Pip sat next to him, sponging the sweat from his face with the tails of his shirt. Three and Terry lingered at the back of the room. They looked up when Fergus and Ashton entered.

"We're gonna join the others. Jane and Gavin are going their own way. They're taking her," he added, nodding at the Governor. Her face turned red, and she let out a muffled shriek. Terry's eye narrowed, but before he could speak, Fergus added, "She won't be able to hurt anyone again. That's good enough."

Terry closed his mouth and shrugged, pushing away from the wall. "Guess we should get going, then. Can he be moved?"

Pip frowned down at Guillory. "He should rest, but if he has to move, he'll live."

"Get him up. We've got an airship to catch."

"He'll come with me, with the Guard," Ashton said. "If we're together, the men won't question us."

Terry glowered. "And why should we trust you?"

"I stopped them in the first place, didn't I? I don't know what else I can do to prove that I have no intention of harming you."

"He's right. I trust him, Terry. We need someone to keep the Guard in line, just like they'll need us to keep the Count and Ursula from doing anything crazy. So Guillory goes with him, and the rest of us will join Orson and the Count. We'll figure out where to go from there."

Terry's mouth quirked. "We're letting the humans follow us? And you're not worried that I wanna do something crazy, too?"

"Do you trust me?" Fergus asked.

Terry paused, the smirk faltering. The corners of his mouth twitched, words forming and withdrawing. He sighed, running a hand through his hair. "Yeah, I do. Of course I do."

Fergus smiled. "Then I guess you're just gonna have to follow my lead. You *did* promise, remember?"

Terry stared at him a moment and then shook his head. "A city built by Fergus Irvine and William Guillory. This I have to see." He snorted, sauntering past Fergus up the steps to the deck.

"Don't you need to heal that?" Pip asked, pointing at the bloody handkerchief wrapped around Ashton's thigh.

"It missed the bone. There are medics with the fleet. One of them can patch it up. Can you help me with him?"

Pip nodded, motioning for Three to come over. Fergus left them to it.

Jane's ship was a lot wobblier than the *Returner*, but Fergus managed to skirt the railing to the fore. Terry stood there, his hair whipping in the wind, gripping the rail. As Fergus drew up to him, he saw that Terry's eyes were closed, his mouth curved upwards as he inhaled the rushing air. Fergus smiled, feeling something warm fluttering in his chest, spreading through his stomach and into his head. He stopped beside Terry, bumping him with his shoulder, and Terry opened his eyes, regarding him quietly for a long moment.

"I honestly can't believe that anyone got through to Ashton Harriet, and yet it's hard to be surprised it was you."

Fergus shrugged. "He's not all bad."

Terry made a face.

"Not as cool as you, though."

"I did come back from the dead to rescue you."

Fergus smiled, blinking away the burn of the wind.

"I've got an idea. Wanna hear it? Someday, you and me, we're gonna find a middle ground. I mean, we both nearly died for some pretty crazy, ridiculous reasons. We've been stubborn and stupid. By all rights, we should never have made it this far. So maybe it's fate. We're still alive. I think we could change. I think we can find a way to be okay. Together, you know?"

"Maybe so. Then again, maybe I don't want you to change," Terry replied, reaching out to ruffle his hair. He paused, fingers buried deep in Fergus's dark locks, and his face sobered. "Just, you know, no more heroics. Stay alive, okay? Because I think we could be okay . . . together."

The airship came to a stop. Across the gap of sky, he saw Ursula and Rosslyn emerge, along with Raja. They came over to the railing, and Raja waved. Fergus gaped, rubbing his eyes. Terry laughed and waved back. Beside Raja, Ursula stood with her arms crossed over her chest and her lips pursed, but Fergus thought she might be trying to hide a tiny smile. She offered the faintest wave of her fingers in salute and quickly looked away.

Fergus laughed, shaking his head, and Terry slipped an arm around his back. Surprised, he looked up. Terry kept looking ahead, but his mouth was crooked, holding back a grin. A slow smile spread across Fergus's face, and he rested his head on Terry's shoulder.

"Hey, Terry? Scrap 'okay.' For the first time, I think things might actually be *great*."

GLOSSARY

Banshee: A female fairy that foretells death with her cry. Example: Lady Gemini.

Boobrie: A fairy that appears as a large bird with a large hooked beak and webbed and taloned feet. Often steals farm animals to feed on. Example: Rosslyn.

Buggane: A large, ogre-like fairy covered in dark hair.

Cait Sìth: A cat fairy with a white marking on its chest. Example: Ursula.

Gancanagh: A male fairy that seduces human women, causing them to die of love for him. Example: The Count.

Ghillie Dhu: A tree guardian, which appears as a dark haired man dressed in leaves and moss. Example: Raja.

Gytrash: A large black dog fairy with glowing eyes. Sometimes considered a harbinger of death, at other times a guide. Example: Terry.

Kelpie: A fairy that appears as a black horse, luring travelers onto its back and dragging them into the water to eat them. Examples: Fergus and Ainslee.

Púca: A shape-shifting fairy that often appears as a black horse. It sports a fondness for taking drunkards on wild rides across the countryside. Example: Evelyn.

Selkie: A fairy that appears as a seal, which can shed its skin to become a beautiful woman. If a man steals its skin, he can force the selkie to marry him. Example: Jane.

Sidhe: "The Good Folk." Fairies known for their beauty and terribleness. Example: Fand.

Tarbh Uisge: A gentle water fairy that appears as a black bull with no ears. Example: Flynn.

ABOUT THE AUTHOR

Addison Lane was born and raised between a small town in the Deep South and the Big City. Though wanderlust ever calls, she presently resides on the East Coast, where she's a mild-mannered web designer by day and literary crime fighter by night.